WATER MUSIC

WATER MUSIC

Melanie Kershaw

Avocet Press Inc   New York

Published by
Avocet Press Inc
19 Paul Court, Pearl River, NY 10965
http://www.avocetpress.com
books@avocetpress.com

AVOCET PRESS

This novel is a work of fiction and each character in it is fictional. No reference to any living person is intended or should be inferred.

Library of Congress Cataloging-in-Publication Data

Printed in the USA
First Edition

水
音樂

for
mad Margaret, crazy Meg
and
Jill, whose mother left her

I used to wish you'd died. I'd tell people 'my mother's dead' so they wouldn't ask questions. You hear all the time about mothers fighting to see their children, to visit them, to have custody. Where were you? Why didn't you ask what we wanted?

I've waited so long to hear from you, but you've never even sent us birthday cards. Did you think it wouldn't matter?

Now that I'm older, I don't think that I still hate you. How can you hate someone you don't even know?

I'll be in New York at Kennedy Airport BA Flight 183 on April 2nd. I hope that you'll be there to meet me but even if you're not, I'm coming.

Your daughter,
Caroline

Fanny had been dreading the letter for twenty years, and now it lay unfolded on the kitchen table in front of her. The handwriting reminded Fanny of her own, rounded and tidy. She never wrote by hand now, always used the word processor. She found herself wondering if handwriting is genetic.

She sat alone in the kitchen. Wind blew the last snowflakes of a late winter storm around the leafless maples. It had been a long, white, cold winter. She could hear Sarah upstairs giggling into the phone to one of her friends. Nigel's SEGA game whizzed and dinged. The kids had been cooped up all winter. Too long.

Nigel and Sarah didn't know about her former life, that they had a sister and two brothers. She had shielded them from the terrible things she'd done.

She thought she'd protected herself too, but still deep within her like a block of ice, frozen and carefully preserved, her past remained. She'd have to force herself to let it melt.

Here was the letter written on heavy blue paper, and the oddest thing about Fanny's reaction was her overwhelming need to return to Hong Kong. It wasn't avoiding Caroline, but more like facing it head-on. Yesterday she never would have dreamed that she'd want to go back. Now she had to. It was all she could think about. Rider would have some theoretical explanation about why she felt compelled to return. But it wasn't logical. She had an urgent, nearly primitive need to go back and face the people and the situation that had propelled her away from her other life.

Over the years, her perception of the events that led up to leaving her children had clouded. The cliché about time healing wasn't true. The pain hadn't gone away, but the rawness had. She'd become used to it. It was a part of her.

Fanny sighed. Here she was, the owner of a small design studio, living in a comfortable old house in the suburbs and she had no choice but to risk it all. At fifty-two, she felt too old to be facing this sort of emotional slide. The tea she'd made half an hour ago had gone cold. Rider had to be told tonight. In a moment Sarah would be downstairs demanding dinner or Nigel help with his homework. She stood up, reached for the telephone and dialed.

Rider, a psychiatrist, specialized in addictions. That was how she'd met him—not that she'd ever been addicted to anything stronger than gin.

Zelda answered, "He's with a client. I'll have him call you when he's through."

"It's important." Fanny always bought Zelda something extravagant at Christmas time in return for these small favors. Last year she'd forked out for a black leather bomber jacket. Probably too yuppy for Zelda's taste.

Then Fanny called several babysitters before she was able to find one who would walk over through the snow and watch the children.

When Rider returned her call, Fanny heard Sarah answer. Fanny picked up the receiver, "Thanks Sarah, you can hang up now." She heard the click.

"What's up?" Rider sounded distracted.

"Have you seen the snow?" Her voice was higher than usual.

"What's wrong?"

"I've got problems. We need to talk. Let's go to dinner."

Arm in arm, Fanny and Rider crunched through the drifting snow from the car to the wrought-iron doors of their favorite Mexican restaurant. Just inside they waited for a table though the place was almost deserted. A fountain sent shimmering bursts of water into the air. Colored lights played with the reflections, a stark contrast to the white storm outside.

Fanny knew what she wanted to order. Comfort food, Chiles Rellenos. She hoped they'd be hot. And a beer, a Corona.

When the tortilla chips and salsa were in front of them and the glasses had been filled, Fanny handed Rider the letter.

Her limbs were heavy. The letter was real now that she'd shared it with someone.

His face turned pale. "My God," he said looking up at last. "You all right?"

"No, but it was bound to happen."

They looked at each other. She was trying to read his thoughts and she knew he was trying to read hers.

"How long has it been?" he asked.

"Twenty years." She took a deep breath. "I have to go back to Hong Kong before I meet her. I'll go balmy if I have to see her without straightening it out in my head first."

"But she's going to be here in a couple of weeks."

"I'll write to her. Tell her to put it off. Tell her I'll be away."

"It's going to be hard for us to come with you...."

"No." She spoke a little too loudly and avoided meeting his eyes. She didn't want him to go with her. She certainly didn't want Sarah and Nigel there. This was her own mess and she needed to face it without distractions. She knew he was thinking about her instability and depression. What if it hit and she was alone? "I can go by myself," she said. "It doesn't happen to me like that any more." She wondered who she was trying to convince.

Dinner arrived. She put two fingers on the burning hot plate. Reality hurt. "I have a plan. I'll hole up in a hotel. I'll call the people I used to know. There's been enough water under the bridge. I have the courage to face them. I need to go see the house. If I'm going to make peace with my children, I have to understand first." She looked down and asked quietly, "How am I going to make amends?"

Rider was always kind. He didn't mention that she'd had twenty years to think about it. That he'd offered to take her back to Hong Kong over and over again. That he doubted that anyone who knew her there would speak to her. He ordered another beer.

"How long do you want to go for?" His voice was low and sober.

"Two weeks. Probably less. Can you handle it?"

"I handle it when you go on business trips—of course I can. But you've never left the studio for more than a few days before. Weren't you working on getting the Neil & Greer account? Didn't you tell me last week that it would put you on the map?"

Fanny wondered how it could have seemed so important at the time. "We can still get it. We've got some good ideas cooking." She sat still watching him.

"The children will miss you…."

She forced herself to say nothing even though she knew this was the crux of the matter. She'd left the other children. She might leave these. She might not come back. But she'd changed. There was no reason for her to leave this small comfortable family or the business she'd started that had become profitable against all odds.

He shrugged. "All right. Go to Hong Kong if you are sure you can handle it. Make sure Caroline knows first. It would make matters worse if she showed up and you weren't here." He reached out and took her hand.

That night, when they were lying in bed close together, Fanny said, "I wonder what she looks like now."

"She looks just like you. Always did. She was a good kid, even if she did hate me." Rider corrected himself, "Does hate me."

Fanny knew how Rider knew what Caroline looked like. Fanny's mother sent a Christmas card every year which contained a snapshot and a letter filled with anger and blame. After the first couple of years Fanny refused to open the envelope and Rider took it away. Rider was in closer contact with her mother than he admitted. Fanny suspected that Rider sent her parents money despite the fact that she'd told him it wouldn't help them like him better.

She pulled the flannel sheet closer around herself. "You'd better give me the pictures. I'll take them with me on my trip." She didn't tell him that she'd already booked. That this time next week she'd be on the plane to Hong Kong.

During the next few days Fanny organized herself and her family with unusual vigor. She rang clients, apologized and recommended alternatives. She made hasty decisions. She gave the Bresso account to Clara, her inexperienced assistant, and gave her directions on how to follow up on Neil & Greer. She lied that she had to go overseas to see her parents.

At home she made piles of clothes for herself and the children on the spare bed. She postponed dentist appointments, made camp decisions for summer, made lists of the things that the children would need when she wasn't there.

She also wrote to Caroline. She wrote at least eight versions before she settled on what to say. In the end, she decided that formality was necessary after all this time.

> *Dear Caroline,*
> *I would be delighted to see you. I have, however already arranged a trip to Hong Kong, which unfortunately falls exactly when you were intending to visit. I cannot change my plans. I'll contact you when I return and we can arrange a mutually convenient time for a meeting.*
> *Your mother*
> *P.S. I'm glad you wrote*

As though that would make up for anything. She knew the letter was awful. She debated with herself a long time about whether to sign it with love. Caroline hadn't, so she didn't, even though she worried that it was up to her to take the initiative. She mailed it anyway.

Sarah and Nigel each reacted differently to their mother leaving so suddenly. Although she had been away on short business trips many times, they sensed this was different. They knew that she'd lived in Hong Kong, but Rider or Fanny hadn't told them about Fanny's other children. Instinctively, they felt insecure. How do children know when something is being kept from them, Fanny thought, and why can't I tell them? She knew that if she told them, they'd ask all kinds of questions, which she wasn't yet ready to answer. She was afraid she'd make them more insecure and confused. Or maybe that was an excuse, too.

Sarah developed a scratchy cough that couldn't be suppressed no matter what inhalers, vaporizers, humidifiers or cough drops were administered. Fanny spent a long, precious afternoon in the hospital, when she should have been at work, watching Sarah get x-rayed and inspected. The doctors wanted to prescribe steroids, but Fanny refused them, brought Sarah home and listened to the coughing all night.

Nigel became uncooperative and clingy. He insisted that Fanny watch him do his homework. He wanted her to dress him in the morning even though she hadn't dressed him for years. He tricked her into playing board games with him. He asked her to make things for him to eat that he hadn't wanted since he was small. Cream of Wheat. Shepherd's pie. Alphabet soup.

Rider remained calm until the night before Fanny was due to leave. Then he lost his patience at the dinner table. "Sit up properly, Nigel. Use your fork. Sarah, for Christ's sake, stop coughing. How much money are you taking?"

It was unusual for him to ask, because they never fought or spoke about money in front of the children. Fanny knew this was important, a test. Too little would mean she had been unrealistic and therefore unfit to travel such a great distance alone. Too much would mean she was either being too generous with herself or planning on staying away longer than she had said. Although tempted to tell him to mind his own business, she didn't. "I've got five-hundred in traveler's checks, I'm taking my bank card, because I'm told there are ATM machines on every street corner, and the hotel is pre-paid. I'm also taking my American Express and VISA. Stop worrying everyone. I'm coming back. I wish you were coming with me."

She stood up too suddenly and started to clear the dirty dinner dishes from the table. She had lied. She didn't want them going with her under any circumstances.

She tried again. "Some day I'm going to take you all."

Very tired, Fanny put the children to bed. She had a raging headache brought on by either fear or guilt, she wasn't sure which. She knelt down beside the bed where her suitcase lay open on the floor. Her blouses and dresses nestled against zip-plastic bags of shampoo, shoes and deodorant. She could hardly concentrate on what to take. Everything around her took on a new importance. The old mirror they had bought at auction in the Catskills, the lamp by the bed with its stained glass shade that cast cerulean blue and scarlet streaks up on the ceiling.

Rider sat down on her side of the bed and smoothed his hair, the way he always did when embroiled in a situation he couldn't control. He handed her a small plastic bottle of Valium. "Not enough to do any harm. Just so you have them. In case."

She took the bottle without answering and slipped it in next to the hiking boots and T-shirts. She stood up and kissed the crown of his head, just where his hair had thinned.

That night in the dark, when the kids were asleep and Rider snored beside her, she changed her mind over and over again. She thought about going to England to meet Caroline on her own turf. Then again, she hadn't been back to Hong Kong since 1974. She felt a need to visit the old house, feel what she had felt then, and better understand the despair and treachery. Maybe then she could explain everything to Caroline—even the worst, the most unsayable. Then she changed her mind back again. She couldn't leave work when she was just about to land the Neil & Greer account. Maybe she just ought to stay home, a sitting duck waiting for Caroline to fire potshots.

Rider and the kids drove Fanny to the airport. Sarah didn't say a word. She had brought her Walkman, plugged the head-phones in and stared out of the window at the piles of gray snow on the littered concrete Cross Bronx Expressway. Nigel talked and talked. He told jokes. He was going through a scato-logical phase.

Just before she left them, Rider handed her a large thick brown manila envelope. "Only open it if you're feeling strong. Your mother's Christmas letters are in there. I recommend that you throw them in the garbage before you're tempted to read them, but I feel obligated to give them to you. Don't drink on the plane. With dehydration its effects are lethal and if you're reading that stuff...." He pointed to the envelope, "Don't touch it. Promise me."

Fanny smiled to herself. She hadn't had more than an occasional glass of wine for fifteen years. She complained about his drinking, not he hers.

But he was remembering.

She stuffed the envelope into her carry-on bag. "I prom-ise. Don't be so protective. I'm okay."

She bent down to Nigel. He hugged and kissed her. Unusual for him. Usually he welcomed only the barest of af-fection. Normally it was all on her side.

Sarah turned away. Fanny put a hand on Sarah's shoulder and whispered in her ear, "I'll be home before you know it. I'll send you a postcard every day, and bring you back something good. Thanks for letting me go."

Sarah nodded slightly and then burst into a coughing fit. "I can't believe you'll be gone for Easter."

Fanny felt tears swelling. What if Sarah were really ill? She picked up her carry-on and turned towards passport control. "Less than two weeks, guys, and I'll be home. Be good." Her voice wavered.

She felt heavy and sad as a tall man with a silver bracelet and dreadlocks checked her bag for weapons. Then unexpectedly, as she sat, waiting for the plane, a wave of euphoria and freedom struck. It hit her suddenly. Absolute freedom for nearly two weeks. She couldn't think of any other time in her life when she'd had that long all to herself with no one else to think about except the time she'd been hospitalized.

She settled into her seat and fastened the seatbelt, relieved to see no one was sitting next to her. The United flight was taking her to San Francisco. She tuned out the video of orange straps, whistles and oxygen masks and forced herself to think, for the first time in many years, of things she had trained herself to forget. It didn't work. The children she had just left behind in New York kept blending into the children that she had left behind so long ago in Hong Kong. Not their faces exactly, but the size of them and who they were.

She decided that there would be plenty of time to confront these things. She dug out a mystery novel that she'd bought at the airport, carefully avoiding the envelope that Rider had given her.

She put the book down. Concentration was impossible. Her thoughts kept returning to the one face that kept emerging from that time. Peter Ardel-Rhys, her husband before Rider. She wondered if she had the courage to see him. He was still supposed to be in Hong Kong. His name appeared in the papers sometimes. He had become important, just as she always knew he would. He had been a key negotiator for Britain in the Chinese takeover talks, spending a lot of time in Beijing. Fanny smiled. She doubted that he had changed at all.

She remembered Peter, as she had first known him. They had met when she was eighteen and in art college. He was going out with her best friend, Glenda. She had been impressed with his brilliance, wit and strength.

Funny. She remembered his legs. So different from Rider's legs. Rider had long, white, skinny legs with bony knees. Intellectual legs. Peter's legs were athletic. His thighs were large and powerful and covered with long dark hairs. He was a tennis champion. How could she not have known from his legs that they weren't suited at all?

Because Peter was so bright. He recommended books. They were young and they talked Jean Paul Sartre and Kierkegaard deep into the night. They drank whiskey rather than beer because Peter was rich and aristocratic. He could hold his booze. His control of everything was legendary. Fanny always knew that Peter would change the shape of the world and she'd wanted to be there when he did it.

Peter loved her in his own way, but he had been too spoiled and self-absorbed to love her enough. She should have known right off. He'd had been going out with beautiful, dark Glenda, while he had pursued Fanny. He had come on so strong. She should have known then and there that if he would be unfaithful to Glenda, he would be unfaithful to her. She fell for his charm.

She played at being the kind of woman that Peter wanted. Physically she fit the bill. As luck had it, she was naturally languid in a 60's sort of way. Her hair hung long and straight.

She wore mini-skirts with wide belts or chain belts, always with boots. She'd always had an extraordinary color sense. At that time she wore pinks and pale colors. She hated pale colors now.

What did he see in her? There was no doubt that he was attracted to her looks, but also that she seemed to him different from the public school girls he'd gone out with before. Fanny had gone to grammar school and spoke with twinges of a Lancashire accent. He found her exotic and interesting. Lancashire had become suddenly fashionable. After all, where had Georgie Best, the Beatles, and Herman's Hermits come from?

She insisted to herself that Peter had needed her, too. She was a much better judge of character than he. When she met a person and had spoken to them, she knew instinctively whether she trusted them, what made them tick, what she liked and didn't like. It took Peter longer to form an opinion. After parties, she would give him her impressions of people and he would admit later that she'd been right.

She could remind herself of the logical, cerebral things, but really it boiled down to the attraction. They'd merely locked eyes and nothing else had mattered. The intensity and depth of their passion for each other was something she'd never felt before or since. There were days that they couldn't break apart, they were so hungry for each other. Fanny's flat mates joked about it. During a short separation she would yearn for him and when they met again, it would be a wordless need. He'd felt it too, there was no doubt about it.

Why had it all fallen apart?

Then she listed what she had blamed: Peter's infidelity, the haunting, and the strain of the twins as babies. She could say all that, even out loud. She could blame the situation, but it wasn't that. It was her. Her madness had led to disaster.

She wasn't really the person he thought he'd married. She'd deceived him. She couldn't maintain the pastel, compliant façade.

The plane droned her to sleep. The last few weeks had taken their toll.

A long way over the Pacific she started thinking about it again. About why Peter had married her rather than any of the other more eligible young women who were equally keen on him.

She'd often thought that marrying her was his first and only rebellion against his family. They'd hardly heard of the gloomy, industrial Northern town she'd grown up in. Peter always lived a little dangerously. He took chances. It paid off for him in sports. He'd always reach for the outside ball. He'd often risk injury to score that extra goal. It was one of the things that later distinguished him from the other young civil servants and one of the things that had brought him success. She'd always thought he'd proposed to her on impulse, because of Hendrick and the prize.

Although Lancashire born and bred, for her entire adolescence Fanny had been consumed with the idea that she had to escape what she saw as her parents' dull fate. When she received a scholarship to the art school in London, she had been afraid her parents wouldn't let her go so far away. Her father, too wise to restrain her, surprised her when he said, "Right you are, then. Go down to London. See if you have the stuff to be an artist. Make us proud, love."

So she did. At first she pined for home, but this was the London of Mary Quant and the Rolling Stones and anything was possible. Never before or since had Fanny been so inspired and never had she had so much fun. She lived in a small dark flat behind Heals, with four other girls from the college. There were parties most nights. She'd worked at losing her Northern accent. Fanny painted vigorously and figuratively. Huge bright canvases and small dark ones. She drew little smudgy drawings and long lean romantic stuff. She designed jewelry and made all her own clothes.

One afternoon in May of 1962 Fanny was called into John Hendrick's study. The art school was housed in a huge, drafty early-Victorian building. Fanny wore the lime-green, lemon-yellow, op-art mini-dress she'd made. John Hendrick, a famous sculptor married to a wealthy titled woman had been Fanny's teacher for two years. He was so famous that even her parents had heard of him. He'd walk around the room while his students painted and he'd ramble on about all manner of things: how life came to be, Harold Wilson, symphonic theory, the nature of beauty and the benefits of fasting. He was a success, a hero. Running up the worn stone steps to his office that afternoon, Fanny had a premonition of change.

Hendrick stood when she entered and asked her to sit down. His study was large with high ceilings, but dark. Strips and globes of black and rusting metal littered the floor. Fanny had never been there before. She sat on the edge of a hard wooden bench. He offered her a cigarette, which she refused. He asked her if it was still raining or if the sun had come out. Massive, tall wooden towers of flat drawers for holding drawings blocked all but the top windowpanes, which were so dirty it hardly mattered that there was no sun to shine in. Fanny realized he was still talking to her. She forced herself to listen. He told her he'd recommended her for the art college prize. If she won it would mean a thousand pounds and an exhibition of her work. It would be the beginning of a serious career and the opportunity of a lifetime. As he spoke he walked around the room absentmindedly juggling rusty lumps of metal.

Fanny was more astounded than excited. She hadn't

known he thought she was any good at all. He'd never spoken to her directly before and she knew she wasn't the best in the group. He said that although her art wasn't perhaps the most original or certainly not the most flamboyant, he thought she had great potential and staying power.

Then just when she was starting to believe him, John Hendrick paused beside her, and, as though he had suddenly realized she was in the room, stretched out his hand, pushed a strand of hair back from her face and told her he desired her. Fanny stared at him aghast. She saw his white hair grown eccentrically long below the collar, the creases around his eyes, his thin face, his bony fingers and he appeared to her cadaverous. And old. She kicked back the bench, which fell over, and ran out the room, down the stairs, out the heavy oak doors and stood in the drizzle of a warm afternoon, washing the insult away.

Hendrick never said another word to her about the prize and she assumed that it and the future it promised was lost to her.

Fanny wasn't even at college when they announced the winner one Friday afternoon. Peter had driven them to Norfolk for a weekend visit with his grandmother. He was his grandmother's favorite. She lived in an eerie Victorian house as big as the houses of Fanny's parents, grandparents, uncles and aunts combined.

They'd been expected in the drawing room at six and only just made it. While they stood talking, glasses of sherry in hand, the telephone rang and Peter answered it. Fanny learned several days later that Glenda had telephoned all over trying to find her. She finally reached Peter and told him that Fanny had won the prize. Peter hadn't mentioned it to anyone, just said a few words into the phone and dismissed the call as unimportant when his grandmother questioned him about it.

That very night after dinner, Peter took Fanny into the garden. The sun still shone with late-afternoon early-summer metallic brilliance. There past the lavender and delphiniums in the yellow rose garden with buzzing bumblebees and stone birdbath, he proposed marriage and adventure. He gave her an old gold and pearl ring that had been in the family for years. Fanny accepted immediately.

He planned a gigantic expensive wedding in Norfolk, far more extravagant than her parents could possibly afford. His grandmother paid for it. His sister had scoffed when Fanny had designed and made her own wedding dress; a sleeveless brocade sheath on which she had embroidered a band of multicolored flowers around the hem but it was exhibited afterwards at the art school.

At the time, the game was to get the fella who would achieve the most in life and hold on to him. Who knew that the rules would change? The problem was that she changed before the rules did. It all seems so women's lib, Fanny thought, to have run off and left him. But it wasn't that at all. She hadn't thought about buying her freedom in that way. She had been frightened and alone while married. A million girls would have killed to be in her shoes, and she'd wanted to kick them off and start again.

She tried to concentrate and remember his face. She couldn't be sure. Tanned, narrow and long with a Roman nose and glittering eyes slightly farther apart than they ought to be. What color? Pale brown, she thought, amber. She knew they weren't blue. She had liked his sun-bleached eyebrows that got bushier over time.

She wondered why she hadn't after all this time confronted the terrible things she'd done. At first she'd told herself, that in time she'd deal with it, but she never had.

She resented that Rider hadn't worked it through with her. After all, he was a professional. It was his job to know how to cure these things. When she'd asked, he'd said that it would hurt their relationship and be unethical to shrink one's wife. She surmised that he wouldn't want to entrust her to his friends or colleagues, because then they'd know too much about him. So her fragile mental state remained her own business. He treated the symptoms, and ignored the source. He was afraid to hear how much she'd loved Peter, she thought.

She conjured up times after she'd left that memories had crowded in about Caroline and the twins. The time she walked out of the subway on a summery day and two little boys had run up to her talking and laughing. She'd responded quite naturally and taken their hands as though they were hers. Another time, she had been buying towels and a family of girls was picking out colors. She knew what color Caroline would pick—yellow, of course. Caroline had been such a sunny little thing. Each time speculation drifted through her mind about Caroline and the twins, she had tried to suppress it.

Rider had wanted to have children. She wouldn't have had more; she'd decided to put all her energies into opening the studio and making it work. In those days she didn't think she was fit to be a mother, in fact she knew she wasn't. "You'll see," he said. "You'll love them more than anything." Fanny remembered him saying those exact words because she silently corrected him—more than the others.

She wondered if she had really borne Nigel and Sarah in order to drive away thoughts of Caroline and the twins. If so, it hadn't worked. Thinking about her first family was like a bad habit. Giving it up worked for a day or maybe two, but then her thoughts settled back on them no matter how hard she tried to think about her latest design, hiring someone, grocery shopping, or new sneakers for Nigel.

It was as though the other life had been a movie she'd seen a hundred times. She knew all the scenes, especially the unsatisfactory ending. Why pick it up now and live the sequel? It was too disturbing.

She tried to sleep as the plane hummed around her. This journey seemed too short a time to prepare. The enforced inactivity was a good thing. She couldn't call anyone, or back out. She only had to sit with her eyes closed and wait for time to pass.

Fanny unzipped her sweatshirt trying to ignore the waves of exhaustion rippling over her. She stood on the pavement just outside Door 5. Just beyond this pickup point she could see cars, taxis, bicycles, buses buzzing past, an loud assault on her senses. It wouldn't be so hard just to walk over and take a taxi to the hotel, but someone named Imelda from the Double Sunshine Travel Service was supposed to meet her, and it seemed so much easier just to wait than make any decisions.

It was going to be hotter and more humid than she'd thought. She remembered that at Easter time the azaleas would be out, and the pink, waxy peach blossoms and miniature orange trees from Chinese New Year gone.

She clutched her travel documents and feared that she might have made a dreadful mistake coming alone. She tried to decide if it was self-doubt or self-pity that made her feel so helpless. If she hadn't been so tired she would have gone right up to book the next plane home. Here she smelled only jet fuel and car exhaust. Inside Kaitak airport, it had smelled of the East, jasmine and Tiger Balm.

A large group of Taiwanese grouped themselves next to

her. The heat didn't seem to be bothering them. They pushed and jabbered. The familiarity of their guttural tones comforted Fanny, but she only recognized a few words of Cantonese. She stared at them trying to focus and then forced her eyes away. It must be the jet lag, she thought; she'd been traveling for twenty-six hours.

She let the continual flow of traffic mesmerize her. She'd forgotten that the taxis were silver and red. Surely the double-decker buses weren't painted with advertisements when she lived here. She remembered them as red, but maybe that was England. A bus went by that looked like a Rousseau fantasy, a jungle of color. Fanny thought she would enjoy decorating a bus for one of her clients.

She scanned the faces of the people coming and going. None of them looked likely to be Imelda. Eventually she noticed a broad-shouldered Chinese girl watching for passengers at another entrance some way down. The girl held a small card in her hand, too small to read from where Fanny stood. She fixed her stare on the girl, but the girl didn't notice.

Fanny had no idea how long she watched the girl, willing her to turn and look in her direction. Fanny had no intention of carrying her suitcase any farther than she had to and she couldn't leave it unattended. She'd had experience with pickpockets at Kaitak. Eventually she persuaded a strolling policeman with a Union Jack on his lapel to point the girl in her direction.

Imelda sauntered over and introduced herself. "The Hyatt. Nathan Road. Kowloon side. Is this your first time here?"

Fanny wondered whether to lie and decided against it. "No. I lived here." Imelda would probably have given her a lesson in geography and she didn't want to be told. She wanted to dredge it out of her memory. Kowloon side. Fanny had chosen to stay on the Kowloon side of the harbor because it was familiar to her and she thought it had probably changed less. "Hong Kong side" meant Hong Kong Island, across the harbor reachable only by ferry in the old days, but now by subway and tunnel. Hong Kong Island had the most prestigious addresses, the most expensive hotels and the tallest, most pretentious buildings.

Imelda punched some numbers on a little telephone she carried. Everyone carried telephones. As far as Fanny could see, she was the only one waiting without one. A small, white van pulled up in front of them and Imelda, then Fanny, climbed in. She sat down right under an air-conditioning vent and luxuriated in its chill. The vehicle hurtled towards the hotel. Her exhaustion subsided and she tingled with excitement. It looked the same. She recognized no streets, no landmarks, just a swath of red and gold, bold Chinese characters, dense traffic, whining music, the street life. The rushing frantic colorful world was still there. Home again.

"How did you get the name Imelda?" Fanny asked.

"I choose it when I took this job. Westerners can't pronounce my Chinese name. I liked it. Makes me feel successful. I am your travel consultant in Hong Kong. If there's anything you need, please contact me."

Once settled into her silent, cool room at the Hyatt, Fanny took stock of the situation. She had chosen the hotel because of its location and lack of distractions. No pool. No view. No tropical oasis. American, she had thought. Impersonal. Clean. A room to lock the world out just above the central, hot, crowded, busy thoroughfare of Nathan Road. If she ever left the room she'd be right where the action was.

That was the point.

If she ever left the room.

The room smelt faintly of sandalwood and jasmine. The

walls were covered with tawny grass paper on which hung scrolled Chinese landscapes. A rice-paper blind covered the one window. Fanny pulled it up. The serenity of the hotel room undone by the city of rooftops littered with a jumble of clotheslines, potted plants, construction scaffolding, peeling paint and old furniture. She watched an old woman water plants, two men exercising in their white cotton vests, and a group of children riding around on plastic tricycles. It brought a sense of the real world into her room. Fanny quickly pulled the blind back down and drew the heavy, teal, silk curtains over them.

She undressed, took a long shower, and collapsed into bed.

At 2 a.m., she awoke disoriented and lonely. Years of time zone change experience taught her not to allow herself to wake up completely, so she didn't turn on the light. She lay in the room, a cell with purified cold air, listening to the airconditioner hum. She wished that Rider were there. She wanted Sarah and Nigel asleep in the next room. She felt stripped of their protection. She drifted back to sleep feeling sorry for herself.

The telephone woke her at 7 a.m.

"How was the flight? Do you miss us yet?" Rider hadn't forgotten her.

"Okay. You woke me up. How's everyone?"

"We've just come back from McDonald's. Kids were hungry. Have you called anyone yet?"

"Not yet. Ask me tomorrow. I'm going to grit my teeth and ring today. How's Sarah's cough?"

And so it went. The inquiries into health and the beginning of baseball, and how's the weather? Reminders about Easter Eggs for the kids and brushing teeth. Fanny went through motions, missing them, regretting that she had come on the trip, reassuring Rider that all was well.

It wasn't.

The office would be closed so Fanny rang Clara at home. Clara needed consoling because she'd forgotten to send Louie from Bresso a comp he'd requested. Clara asked Fanny about her parents. Fanny almost forgot and said, "Who?", but remembered in time and made something up. Fanny asked about Neil & Greer. Clara said that they were dickering around and someone ought to go visit. Really only Fanny could.

Mildly distressed from the calls, she dressed and went for breakfast. She filled a bowl from the buffet with pink-orange diced papaya, cantaloupe and lichees. The tastes triggered memories of eating these fruits years ago, slicing into them, making fruit salad.

After breakfast, she returned to the room. It had been magically restored to order. She fantasized how it would be to have armies of invisible servants in their New York house. She sat on the bed and started to worry. She knew she had to get going. Make decisions. Make phone calls. Make a plan. There were no excuses. She worried that if she didn't do something now, she'd fall between the cracks. The real danger she knew was that she would sit in the hotel for her stay in Hong Kong and not leave it. Perhaps drop into a catatonic state and need to be rescued. She had to prove that she had progressed beyond that. That Rider's shaky faith in her was not misplaced. She'd had a reason to come back and she needed to get on with it.

She found a notepad and wrote LIST on top. Then, out of habit and procrastination, she started to sketch the room. She had completed the mirror and lamp when the phone rang again. She picked up the receiver.

The voice sounded familiar, but she couldn't place it. "Mrs. Rider, please." The voice sounded so British and proper.

"Speaking."

"Fanny, is that you, really?" It sounded like the Queen.

"Yes. Who's this?"

"It's Jean. Jean Meade. I understood you were going to be in Hong Kong. I wonder if you have a free evening to come have dinner with us."

"How did you know I was here?" She could picture herself with Jean sitting on the sand on Gordon Hard Beach years ago. The newborn twins lay in a carry-cot under the beach umbrella. Jean, older and wiser, had taken Fanny under her wing and helped her with Caroline and the babies and finding amahs and furniture. Jean would be nearly seventy by now. Fanny wondered about Jean's children.

"Rider rang me. He asked me to rouse you from your pit, so to speak. I hope you don't mind."

Fanny did mind. Jean was her friend, not Rider's. How dare he call her without telling? She said, "Of course not. I'm glad you rang." It was clear that Rider had no confidence in her at all. How did he know how to get in touch with the Meades? She, Fanny, hadn't known they were still here in Hong Kong. She hadn't communicated with Jean since she'd sent her a wedding invitation in 1977. Jean hadn't responded. "I'd love to come. When?"

"Alan will pick you up Hong Kong side Star Ferry tomorrow night at six. It's been so long. We'll dig the dirt when I see you, chum."

Fanny asked something she knew she shouldn't have. "Are you still friendly with Peter?"

"Oh, he's always in and out. He's in Beijing now, actually. Ann's gone with him. I think Ann said that they'd be back at the end of the week." She paused a moment too long. "Did you want to see him?"

Fanny felt her throat dry out. The room almost spun in

front of her. "Not particularly."

"Anyone at all you want to see. I'll fix it up. Everyone will be so anxious to see you after all this time. Tomorrow it'll be just us, though."

"Thanks."

"See you then. Toodaloo."

She wanted to meet Jean, and then again she didn't. Jean knew everyone. Jean would want to gossip to her and about her. Fanny understood immediately that Jean had called her first, because Jean wanted an exclusive on her visit. Wanted to know. Wanted control. On the other hand, Rider was right. She had to start somewhere and Jean was a good place to begin.

But Rider had no business interfering.

Now was the time to look into the brown envelope he had given to her at the airport.

Fanny opened her suitcase and pulled the envelope out. She put it on the bed and then walked over to the mini-fridge under the television. She opened it and wavered between a can of Diet Coke and a Gordon's Gin with Schweppes Tonic. She picked up the gin. "Clear and poison," she said out loud. Then said, "The first sign of madness, talking to yourself." The sound of her voice annoyed her. She got a glass from the bathroom and poured gin into it.

She sat on the bed and shook the contents out of the envelope. A pile of rectangular envelopes came flapping down onto the bed. She picked one up and then another. Rider had opened and dated each one. She put them in order. 1974 to 1993. Nothing this year. Christmas hadn't come yet.

They weren't all in the same handwriting. She remembered a large square envelope addressed in her older brother John's scrawl. He'd announced the cancer death of their father, including the local paper's obituary, which predictably exaggerated his achievements. She'd loved her father and after reading he'd died, she'd wallowed in a deep, black place for months.

Some of the envelopes were addressed in children's writing. Her children had written to her and Rider hadn't given her the letters. He was right not to. She hadn't wanted to see them. Occasionally he'd asked. "Do you want to get into contact with the children, or is it too soon?" He'd always give her the option of saying no and she always took it.

She thought about what Caroline had said about not having sent birthday cards. Of course she hadn't! She had forced herself to make the break as clean and complete as possible— for the children, not for her. She knew she'd never be back. If she'd had her way she would have phoned them, written to them and hung on to them desperately. The hardest thing of all had been not to leave, but to ignore her own need for their need. She had ached for their smiles and comfort for years. She wanted to hug them and reassure them that no matter what, she loved them and she hadn't left because of them. She thought of their tiny hands and their anxious faces. The napes of their necks were vulnerable and perfectly formed, the ridges and valleys, the soft fuzz of the fine hair growing there.

She'd wanted to send birthday presents. One year she had even bought, but never sent them. She felt guilty every time she bought Nigel or Sarah a present. She wasn't a bad mother. How many times did she have to tell herself that to believe it? She'd never believe it, because even though almost no one knew the darkest truth, she couldn't forget.

She picked up the glass and smelled the gin. Then she picked up the tonic by the cap and wound it open. "Dose of quinine," she said out loud. She poured it into the glass and stirred it with her finger. She put her finger in her mouth.

Warm and sweet.

The familiarity of it frightened her. She remembered drinking gin all day and well into the night, the ice cubes and the straws. She had collected stirrers from restaurants. She wondered what had happened to them. She thought of the rows of colorful stirrers standing tall in a crystal glass on the rosewood sideboard at Water Music, the house she and Peter had moved to after he'd received his New Territories posting. He'd promised that they'd be there just for a year or two. A back-of-beyond posting was a testing ground for new administrators in training. Peter's jurisdiction went up towards the China border. He'd be visible to his superiors. He wanted to be Governor one day.

The first day she'd seen Water Music, Peter had to work. Gregory and Lydia Butterton had driven her there just after Caroline had been born. Why Peter had to work when Gregory didn't was a question she asked herself, because Gregory had taken the day off especially to take her there. She'd been amazed at how large and grand it was.

A circular, gravel driveway led to the house on a promontory just beyond the village of Ting Kau. Surrounded by the sea on two sides, a rock cliff to the north, and bordered on the west by the road, it was naturally isolated from its neighbors. Whitewashed colonial with wide porches, high ceilings, and a grand central staircase, the old house seemed much too large for them, and remote. The servants' quarters alone had eleven rooms. Mary Butterton had insisted that they'd have servants enough and parties to fill the house. She'd been right.

The flagpole in the garden on the spit of land facing out to sea worried Fanny. That flagpole seemed to demand a pomp and circumstance that she had no idea how to deliver: bugles playing "God Save the Queen" every morning, or something. That first day, Fanny had wandered from room to room.

A few furnishings left by previous tenants stood forlorn and dusty. The teak dining room table had been left because it would have been too large for any but the longest dining hall, but the chairs had all been taken. A carved, Chinese, four poster bed, swamped in mildewed, pebble-gray silk draperies, waited in the corner of a bedroom. She loved the house, the light, the breeze, and the sea.

No one had to ask why the house was named. Even on a still summer day, water sounds could be heard from every room in the house. On the front and along one side the South China Sea crashed in on the rocks below, and on the other side, a stream cascaded down a man-made waterfall from the cliff. The stream had been diverted so that it wound through the garden from one end to the other. It ran through a pool that later Fanny and Peter converted to accommodate feathery goldfish. Standing on the farthest point of the headland, the water made so much noise that it could drown out the sound of an approaching car or someone calling.

She'd especially liked the narrow steps, sculpted of concrete and rock that twisted down the almost vertical escarpment. A tiny beach protected by huge, jagged boulders, just big enough for two or three people, hid at the bottom of the steps. She imagined it a place for a sampan to land and smugglers to negotiate.

When she thought back, she tried to remember who had let them into the house. Did the Buttertons have a key? Did she? She remembered asking Lydia why the house had to be that big. Lydia's answer had stuck with her through the years, "It is imperative that an overlord have an imposing residence. And this, my dear, is yours."

Fanny didn't see herself as the wife of an overlord but Peter certainly could see himself in the role. She tried to ignore that tendency in him.

As she sat on the bed in the hotel, holding her gin and tonic, Fanny realized that she needed to get back to Water Music as soon as she could. She placed her drink on the bedside table, picked up the phone and dialed the number of the Double Sunshine Travel Service and asked for Imelda. The woman on the end of the phone understood enough to promise that Imelda would ring back.

She tasted the gin. She recognized the liking of it, the seductive sweetness. She jumped up, poured the gin down the bathroom sink and rinsed out the glass. She picked up the unopened envelopes, thrust them into their envelope, and stuffed it in a drawer. She picked up her handbag, took the key out of a holder that turned off all the lights, and hurried to the elevator.

As Fanny walked into the street, a blanket of heat ambushed and smothered the sliver of energy that she had mustered. She had to force herself to walk towards the Star Ferry. She remembered Imelda telling her about a tourist information office there.

After she bought maps and received bus schedules, she paid her dollar twenty and took the ferry across the dirty green harbor to the Hong Kong side, just for fun. She didn't want her first time on the ferry to be the next evening. She'd be too worried about seeing the Meades to take in the changes and the view. The ferry was named the Southern Star just as it had been twenty years ago. She wondered if it was the same boat.

The harbor seemed smaller. It was smaller. Even as she sat on the ferry and watched, barges dumped piles of cloudy dirt into the water, reducing the harbor still further.

The view of the island, seemed larger. The buildings were taller, equal to many in New York, both in architectural obtrusiveness and grandeur. She'd only seen the new Pei Bank of China in photographs but she recognized the gleaming geometric tower immediately, triangle upon triangle, gleaming in the afternoon sun. The skyline had been transformed since she'd left. Buildings she'd admired had disappeared only to be replaced with a taller dazzle of shimmering glass and metal. She was glad to see that towards the top of Victoria Peak, the background for all this, a forest of trees still surrounded the mansions and expensive apartment blocks there.

When the ferry reached the Hong Kong side she walked around the terminal, paid her fare again, and took the Meridian Star back to Kowloon. Even that landscape had changed beyond recognition. The old colonial railway tower remained but the station below it had gone. A huge dome blocked the view of the grand old Peninsula Hotel, and massive new hotels had been positioned to overlook the view of the harbor and island.

Fanny walked back to the hotel by way of the Cultural Center complex. It was an immense improvement over the railroad lines that had marred the harbor side years ago. A two-tiered walkway had been constructed, and as she walked along it, a sense of well-being and contentment suffused her. She'd missed the frantic, noisy energy and the smell of food everywhere. She thought, looking around, we are all a product of our pasts; everyone here is from somewhere else.

She was glad she hadn't tippled the gin, but her tiredness couldn't be ignored. She sat on a bench and stared out at the harbor for a long time. She recited as many names of city districts she could bring to mind, as though to confirm that she was really here: Hung Hom, Causeway Bay, Kwun Tong, Kowloon Peak, Shau Kee Wan, North Point, Sai Kung, Aberdeen.

It occurred to her how lonely she was. She had thought that being alone would be enjoyable, but, in fact, she wanted to share her adventures with Rider, Sarah and Nigel. Tell them

about these places and what they meant to her.
     She asked a blonde-bearded, pony-tailed European for
directions to a bookshop. He sent her back through the
crowded streets to Swindons, on the street next to the hotel.
She browsed there among overpriced medical and economics
textbooks and finally bought a Hong Kong directory. Focus,
Fanny, she thought. Why did you come here? Make a list.
What do you want to accomplish?
     She walked around the block. Every other shop sold tacky
gold jewelry or silk shirts and postcards. She bought some
postcards to send to Nigel and Sarah and a blue fiber-tipped
pen from a bored, chunky, mini-skirted girl at Chun Kee Sta-
tionery. It made her laugh. She wanted to tell Nigel. Chun
Kee—chunky—get it? She missed Sarah and Nigel. She
wondered what they were doing. Sleeping probably.
     When she got back to her room, she made a list.
     Go to Water Music
     Meades/Yuens/Hudsons
     See Peter—from a distance if possible
     So that's the real reason, she told herself. The house
may be important to me, Hong Kong may bring back old
memories, good and bad, but mostly, I want to see Peter.
     She needed to know who was at fault. She'd have to see
him and talk with him. She wondered if she'd be able to and
most of all whether he would remember her for what happened at the end, or the happy times at the beginning. After
Fanny had left him, he'd married Ann Graham, a climber if
ever there was one. She'd been the children's babysitter. Fanny
hadn't thought she was sophisticated enough to interest Peter.
Well, Fanny thought, Ann Graham had got what she'd deserved and no doubt knew it by now.
     The red-lit digital numbers on the hotel's clock flashed
17:00. The whole day had gone and in this city that moved

faster than a waterfall, she'd done nothing. Fanny knew she ought to eat, she'd had nothing but fruit for breakfast, but she just felt tired. She lay on the bed and stared at the ceiling.

They'd had a good time when they first got to Hong Kong. Fanny still flush with her art school success. The sixties were a heady time for an art student in London. Marrying Peter, she'd anticipated a lifetime of adventure. She'd been glad to escape the dark, rainy, impoverished northern town she'd grown up in. Hong Kong, by contrast, was bright and prosperous, fueled partially by China's need to funnel out its vast resources, the American troops who came from Vietnam on R&R, and the Chinese desire to make money.

When they'd lived in a small midlevels flat, before Caroline was born, she'd had good friends who laughed with her at her mother-in-law's machinations. She and Peter fell in with a fast-living social set that regularly went to Macau to gamble and drive in the Grand Prix, had launch parties every weekend and lived recklessly for the moment. Peter and his sister had lived in Hong Kong before they'd been sent away to school in the U.K. He knew so many people. She remembered him teaching her to use chopsticks.

She took tennis lessons to please Peter but she hated them. Her uncoordinated limbs and wandering mind betrayed her good intentions over and over again. She'd humiliated herself. She took Cantonese conversation lessons every week, even though Peter told her it wasn't necessary.

She'd been mildly surprised when she'd become pregnant. She hadn't thought much about children and she hadn't considered that they would change her life. After all, that was what amahs were for. The best thing about being pregnant was giving up tennis.

Fanny's mother, Marjorie, had flown out from the U.K. to be there for the birth. Peter was in London when the baby was born, but he sent a congratulatory telegram and two-dozen yellow roses. Men weren't present at a birth in those days— probably just as well.

Fanny knew he'd wanted a boy and was probably disappointed, but she didn't let it dampen her spirits. It's good it's a girl, she'd thought. Peter won't be interested.

Marjorie had taken over. She'd changed baby-amahs when the first one proved more interested in her boyfriend than the baby. Fanny lived through those weeks in a daze. On the one hand, she was grateful for her mother taking charge the way she did, but on the other, she wanted the baby to herself without all the interfering, advice-givers. Only at night, when everyone else was asleep, did she nurse the baby in privacy and contentment.

When Peter returned, it became clear that Marjorie had outstayed her welcome. Peter eventually lost his temper with her. She'd told him he was spoiling Caroline by picking her up when she cried. He said he'd do as he damn well pleased in his house with his child, and if she didn't like it, to get out. Marjorie said that she damn well would if he was so ungrateful for all she'd done to help when he was where he shouldn't have been. Fanny wanted everyone to be happy. Every time they fought, she picked up the baby and left the room.

Marjorie left and, not long afterwards, they moved to Water Music. Although Fanny missed her mother, she only had to share Caroline with the amah.

The move had gone relatively smoothly. They hadn't yet had time to accumulate much furniture: a few Ming vases, silk carpets, painted scrolls, but what they had was packed up by an army of wiry men in gray shorts and white socks, who arrived at the flat with wooden packing cases and straw, and did the whole job in an afternoon. She had hardly unpacked her wedding presents because they gave her a suspicion she wasn't up to the job. She'd wanted modern things. Peter's mother, Penelope, had called her gauche and chosen traditional china, silver and crystal patterns. As it was Penelope's family buying most of the wedding presents, Fanny hadn't had the nerve to protest. At her first important dinner party, Fanny had set it out knowing that it all far out sparkled her taste but looked right in the dining room of Water Music. The cook boy, hired by Penelope, had chosen the menu, had reset the table, folding the napkins into lotus flowers, and moved the plates and cutlery around. From then on, Fanny treated those things as though they weren't hers. She thought of them as trappings belonging to some foreign establishment run by Peter and Penelope.

Although Fanny tried to take an interest in Peter's work, he didn't encourage her as she hoped he would. Sometimes, at the beginning, she visited his district offices. Once she went to the Fanling District Office. She and Peter were meeting the Buttertons at the golf club afterwards for dinner. While she waited for Peter in one of the outer offices, a graceful young woman in her late teens entered with a black lacquer tray and offered Fanny a glass of tea. Fanny accepted, looking her over curiously. She had heard something from Peter about this girl, who must be Lingling. She had sparkling eyes, full of fun, and a bounce to her walk. Peter had told Fanny that Lingling, the daughter of a prosperous farmer, had begged her father to let her work in an office, rather than help on the farm. She had pestered her father to such an extent that he asked Peter if he would take her on and watch out for her. Peter, with some misgivings, offered her the job of tea-girl, predicting that she would be back on the farm within a month. It wasn't the first time he was to be wrong about Lingling. She thrived in the office. She taught herself to speak, read and write in English. Peter recounted how she had charmed an older clerk into helping her and how diligently she worked.

That day, after giving Fanny tea, Lingling hesitated for a moment then said in a clear confident voice, "Need-ee name. Inglish-ee name. Help-ee?" Then she grinned.

Fanny nodded and sipped her tea. She scrutinized Lingling for inspiration. Her face was round and serious. One name came to mind and it seemed absolutely right. "Julia," she said, "Julia."

Ling-ling tried it, "JOO-LEE-AH." Then nodded and giggled.

They laughed together, not friends exactly, more like conspirators. From that moment no one except Lingling's family were allowed to call her anything but Julia.

Peter's first leave coincided with the last illness and death of his grandmother. Peter, Fanny, and Caroline stayed in his parents' two-bedroom leave-cottage for the three months they were in England. It was a tense time. Penelope flew back from Hong Kong to be with her dying mother and moved in with them. Elizabeth, Peter's sister, and her husband Paul came up from London for the weekends.

When Peter's grandmother finally died, she left a complicated will with detailed instructions. She left all her money to Peter's parents and the house and all its contents to Peter and his sister. Elizabeth wanted the jewelry, but Peter thought Fanny should have some. Penelope claimed to have sentimental attachment to an emerald necklace, bracelet and earrings. Elizabeth wanted her to pay for them. There was the question of death taxes, which Peter and Elizabeth would owe on the articles left, with no money to pay. All this talk of

possessions and what belonged to whom, gave Fanny a un-
yielding headache. She didn't care. She didn't want these things.
She imagined the red brick, tile-roofed Norfolk mansion right
out of a gloomy gothic romance. The heavy Victorian furniture oppressed her. She desperately looked forward to the
few weeks she could get away to stay with her parents up north.
She took a train with Caroline, Peter being far too busy to join
them.

Although Fanny had been looking forward to it for
months, the visit to her parents was not a success. Her old
bedroom had been turned into a study where her father, now
retired, built model ships. She and Caroline slept fitfully in her
brother's old room, which was small and airless, the bed too
narrow. She had become used to spending money freely and
her frugal, careful parents disapproved. Her clothes were too
bright and tropical, her accent too southern. She had defected
to Peter's world. Caroline was learning to walk and with her
antics gave some comic distraction, but they were all relieved
when she and Caroline climbed aboard the train to return
south.

Peter, Fanny, and Caroline returned to Hong Kong heavily
laden with plunder from his grandmother's estate. The Norfolk house had been put up for sale. Of all the possessions
they took, Fanny only liked the set of silver bone-handled
cutlery, delicately engraved with curlicues. She was mildly sorry
to leave a seventeenth-century painting of young sisters, but
the experts said that the climate in Hong Kong would damage
the painting and it was too valuable to risk.

Back at Water Music, Fanny found places for Peter's in-
heritances. She wondered when they would ever use such elaborate silver. Six months later, Fanny was surprised by a truck,
which arrived, loaded with packing crates containing grand
mahogany furniture. She hadn't remembered Peter telling her

about the shipment. Perhaps he'd told her about it when she hadn't been listening. There were several hall tables, a card table, a chess table and the many chairs that went with them. The only piece of furniture that Fanny liked was her gleaming black grand piano. Peter had bought it from a lawyer who was retiring back to England. He'd had it delivered to their flat on their first wedding anniversary as a surprise for Fanny. It needed maintenance: tuning every three months and a heater installed in among the frets to keep the humidity at bay. Fanny arranged these things with pleasure. The more she played, the better she became. The piano took up most of the main room in their first mid-levels flat, hinting to cramped visitors, "This is temporary. Soon we will have grander accommodation." Sure enough, after they moved, the piano fit comfortably, with room to spare, in a corner of the lounge. Little Caroline danced while Fanny played.

To Fanny's delight, Penelope showed very little interest in Caroline. When the twins came later, it was a different story. Penelope liked boys.

Fanny thought of herself as she was when they'd moved in. Twenty-three, married to Peter, with a baby, and living in a colonial mansion with all that gold-edged china and heavy silver cutlery. She'd been so unsure of what was right. She'd wanted to be perfect for Peter. She wanted him to love her completely.

They'd needed even more furniture. Fanny wanted to go to a rattan place on Carnarvon Road with Jean Meade and buy just what they needed, a glass topped table, perhaps, and some comfortable tropical chairs for reading on the terrace. She would have agreed to simple teak chairs, or European slung-leather chairs.

Penelope had officiated. She ordered twenty-six formal, rosewood, dining room chairs to go with the table that had

come with the house and overstuffed settees covered in cab-
bage roses. Penelope and Peter ordered expensive Tianjin
carpets from China, as the carpets made in Hong Kong weren't
knotted finely enough. At least they had enough sense to con-
sult Fanny on color. She'd enjoyed choosing unusually subtle
tints: pearl gray, earth reds and azure.

She couldn't imagine giving a dinner party for twenty-six
self-important people, but before long, she actually hostessed
just such a party: Peter, gregarious and in his element, the
cook-boy overpaid and demanding, the servants superior.
She'd dressed in a figure-fitting, mauve, shot-silk cocktail dress,
pinned up her hair, decorated her fingers, arms and neck in
Penelope's sapphires and smiled and laughed when she was
supposed to. She remembered her shoes being uncomfort-
ably narrow. Caroline slept upstairs, safe in the care of the
baby amah.

Fanny tried to remember who was at that first dinner
party. Jean and Alan Meade, the Buttertons, certainly. Ann
and Susan Graham must have been there with their parents.
Penelope and Alistair keeping score. The other people had
vanished from memory: a score of blank faces, the New Territories elite. A police commissioner with his wife, probably, a
magistrate and his wife, and a dreadful mustached army cap-
tain and his wife whom they all agreed was terribly common.

The house encouraged romance. After the dinner, when
the guests had gone, she and Peter, a little drunk (in her memories he was always drinking) stood out on the headland in their
formal clothes and listened to the waves lapping at the rocks
below. At night a whole community of boats emerged. Tiny
flickering lights and the bleating of fishing sampans and deep-
sea junks reminded them that they weren't alone under the
moon. They could hear the engines all through the night, yet
above and beyond, behind Tsing Ye Island, the sky glowed

orange-red, a halo of light reminding them that the bustling pounding city wasn't so far away.

Fanny conceived again. She remembered the pregnancy as a happy, trouble-free time. Her days were taken amusing Caroline, playing the piano, and shopping.

An invitation arrived. Fanny and Peter were the only Westerners invited to a wedding banquet for Jimmy Wo, Peter's number two clerk, and Julia, formerly Lingling. Jimmy was the second son of a large propertied New Territories family. Julia was not considered a good enough bride for him. A love match was considered foolish and modern, but horoscopes and the almanac were consulted anyway and an auspicious date for the marriage chosen. It was a huge rowdy affair with mahjong playing and serious drinking. Julia wore a white western-style wedding gown that contrasted sharply with the traditional red, embroidered, Chinese costume she changed into later. At the end of the evening she appeared in a tight gold evening gown. She served tea, and, together with Jimmy, graciously met all the guests. Peter made a toast. He told Fanny he knew they would be wonderfully happy together. That was the second time he had been wrong about Lingling.

Fanny got embarrassingly large, very fast. Twins were the only explanation. Early on she'd go to one of the beaches and sit, wearing a big blousy bathing costume, with the other wives. Jean Meade was the only real friend that she'd made among them. The friends that she'd made when she'd been childless and they'd lived on the Peak seemed worlds away now. Some had left Hong Kong for other places and some were still childless. Jean's children had just gone off to school in England and lonely without them, she welcomed Fanny's friendship. Later in her pregnancy, Fanny stayed home with her feet up, drawing, waiting.

The twins were born the summer of the riots. Just over

the border, a few miles from them, Mao's Cultural Revolution was causing havoc in China. Communists in Hong Kong agitated against British rule, and even usually compliant Chinese residents demanded reforms. Peter's days were filled with stress and worry. It was impossible for him to be everywhere at once. During this summer, without being recruited by him, Julia acted as Peter's spy. She would bring her husband, Jimmy, steamed dumplings for lunch and manage to speak to Peter. She told him where and when to expect trouble and, sometimes, even confirmed to him who the ringleaders were. She enabled Peter to "nip it in the bud." He received praise and even honors from his superiors as a result. It was her way of repaying the debt formed when Peter had agreed to take her off her father's hands and give her a job and help her learn English.

Of course, Chinese way, the situation was reversed and Peter was now in her debt.

The red message light on the telephone blinked on and off. A newspaper had been pushed under the door. Clothes littered the room. Disoriented, Fanny put the palm of her hand on top of her head. It was as though she had just woken up from her twenty-four year old self. She looked at her watch: 4:05 a.m. She calculated that she'd slept eleven hours.

Still floating in her dream world, she ruminated on how her life in Hong Kong could have ended in such disaster, how then a miracle had exchanged it for Rider and New York. How many people get a second chance at a new life? She stretched, forced herself out of bed and turned on the light and wandered into the bathroom to take a shower.

She let the hot water run longer than she allowed herself at home, savoring the warmth pulsing down her back. When she stepped out, she wrapped herself in a towel, sat on the bed, and rang for her messages: Imelda, Mrs. Meade, and a Mr. and Mrs. Maurier had rung. Rider had rung twice. They'd all phoned while she slept. Who were Mr. and Mrs. Maurier? She hadn't rung them. It came back to her slowly. Genevieve and Jacques. People she'd forgotten and didn't want to be reminded about.

Her anger built, block upon block, as she calculated the time in New York and dialed Rider at work. It would be quarter to five. He'd be worried that he hadn't heard from her and she didn't care. He'd phoned all these people without her knowledge. How else could they have known she'd come to Hong Kong?

Zelda Pinkus answered in her husky, nasal Brooklyn accent, "Dr. Rider's office." Fanny heard Zelda's bracelets clink against the phone receiver. She forced her voice to stay level and normal. "Hi Zelda! This is Francis. I'm ringing from Hong Kong."

"Oh sure, Mrs. Rider, he asked to be interrupted for you."

Zelda clicked her onto hold. Rider had chosen a Mendelssohn violin and piano concerto to calm his agitated patients but it wasn't calming Fanny this morning.

Rider answered the phone. "I've been waiting for your call. Have you been to sleep? Isn't it the middle of the night now? Did you take something?"

"No. I slept." She resented all his interference and concern. "How's it going?" She heard her voice high and brittle.

Rider gave a catalog of domestic events. Sarah still coughed; Nigel planned elaborate April Fools' tricks for the next morning. The children missed her. "And so what's your plan for the day?"

"Jean Meade rang me, thanks to you. I'm going there for dinner. Did you ring the Mauriers, too?"

"Sorry, just taking care of you. Looked up some old phone numbers."

She exploded. "I'm not one of your bloody patients! I can take care of myself! I was going to ring them. How does it look to them? It makes me look terrible. Are you going to call Peter too and have him invite me to dinner?"

"Of course not. I just thought you'd appreciate it if I

broke the ice. I wanted to make it easier for you."

"Well don't appreciate it. I didn't like Genevieve Maurier then and I won't like her now. Don't you ever call her again." She paused. "Don't worry about it. I'll ring you tomorrow."

She cut him off without saying goodbye or asking when would be a good time to speak with the children. Then she was sorry, worried that she was starting to separate herself from them. He didn't know about Genevieve Maurier. She'd have to remember to tell him. It would embarrass him to know she'd been one of Peter's lovers.

She looked at the clock again. Only 5:05. She lay back on the bed, letting her damp hair soak the pillow and the air-conditioning chill her thoroughly. She pulled the blanket back over her and reached out to turn out the light. It must be the jet lag, she thought, as she drifted back to sleep. The next time she looked at the clock it was 11:30 a.m, time for breakfast.

After she dressed, she rang Imelda. "I need a hire car. I need to go to the New Territories."

Imelda said rental cars were difficult to find and ferociously expensive, most of the roads were new, Fanny wouldn't know them, and driving in the city was a dangerous pastime that most certainly would lead to disaster and where would she park the car anyway? The travel agency could provide a car and driver for the equivalent of three hundred US dollars a day. However, she had a bargain. Her brother would be willing to drive Fanny anywhere she wanted to go on his day off if Fanny gave him five hundred Hong Kong. He was off Sunday and Tuesday. Fanny told Imelda she'd think about it and ring her back.

She rang Jean Meade, who answered at once, sounding like the person Fanny used to know, bright and energetic. "If you don't have any other plans for today, what would you think about knocking a few balls around the golf course at Deep Water Bay, just as we did in the old days?"

Fanny answered, "That would be lovely, but for one problem. I haven't played in years and I never did like it much. Don't be too upset if I pass, but thanks."

Jean wouldn't let her go that easily. "Francis, wait a minute. You asked about Peter yesterday."

"Yes?"

"Would you like to see him? I could arrange it, you know."

"I'm sure you could, but I don't know." She thought about it for a moment. "I don't think I really want to see him. We'll talk tonight."

Jean laughed. "You sound very American." She mimicked Fanny. "The way you say 'we'll talk' and 'really.' You're better as an American, you know. You've always been too forthright to be British. I've missed you. There's never been anyone to take your place. When you left I felt so deserted. I took it personally. I mean, you never even told *me* that you were going. There's no one left here anymore. I'm the survivor. There are people like Peter and Ann, but who the hell cares about them. When Rider rang the other day, you could have knocked me over with a feather."

Fanny felt Jean's energy infuse her. "I've missed you, too."

"Alan will meet you tonight at six o'clock sharp. We're having ham and asparagus...and you did like to play golf, you know."

Fanny couldn't face returning the Mauriers' call. She collected her maps, directory, money, and key. She took the lift downstairs for a belated breakfast in the hotel restaurant of congee, green tea, bacon and melon. All around her a crowd of black Americans wearing jogging suits, obviously with a package tour of Asia, excitedly discussed their plans for the

day and compared their jewelry purchases from the day before. Why is it, Fanny thought, that I am always an outsider
wherever I go?

Even as a teenager in grammar school she'd felt different. She read voraciously and every book she read added to
the possibility of other lives to be lived. She could travel to
India, to Africa, to South America. She watched her unhappy
mother and her disappointed father. Her father told her that
he had been adventurous before the war, but his years in the
Royal Navy facing torpedoes and gunfire, surviving battles
and sinkings, had cured him. He was happy pottering around
the garden. When Fanny's brother took a job with the local
council right out of school, and then married, Fanny made up
her mind to leave before anything quite so horrible happened
to her.

Now she was American. At least she'd become American enough to think that she needed a car to get anywhere.
How else could she see the streets and look for things she
recognized? It had begun to dawn on her that if she wanted
to be independent, she would have to use public transportation. She took out her maps and planned the journey.

The MTR ran efficiently. She took it to the end of the
line, Tsuen Wan. It was a full-fledged city now. It had been
little more than a small town with growing pains; textile factories had been overtaking farmland, and refugees from the
mainland had been forcing housing development.

Fanny used to drive to Tsuen Wan for fruits and vegetables, for pots and pans, for everyday supplies. They'd had
a post office box there and she'd used its Hong Kong and
Shanghai Bank. Tsuen Wan's frenetic humanity had always
restored her to sanity for a few hours. When she'd been sad
and afraid, she'd drive there and walk around and lose herself
in the crowds. The people there expected that she'd be differ-

ent, and, if she seemed more peculiar than other Westerners, it was only a matter of degree. The hustle helped her to detach herself from her isolated house and demanding children.

The MTR station loomed cavernous and gaudy. Orange-red tiles were a poor choice, Fanny thought, more like hell than a womb, but signified happiness and good luck to the Chinese.

When she emerged, she knew exactly where she was. Castle Peak Road still ran through the center of the town. At the tourist office she'd worked out a way to get to Water Music. The Number 53 bus passed right outside the station. She crossed the street using a pedestrian overpass. People jostled past her: a woman carrying striped bags of pomelos and melons, a couple of almost identical spike-haired youths dressed in black plastic motorcycle jackets with silver buckles. They carried portable telephones in one hand and tape decks in the other. A concrete staircase brought her almost to the bus stop. She waited with a stooped old man who stared at her with interest as he picked at his gold teeth.

The hillside facing her had sprung a forest of multi-storey buildings since she'd lived there. No trace of Tsuen Wan's agricultural beginnings remained. The smells hadn't changed though. The exhaust from large diesel delivery trucks occasionally overpowered the musty odors of dried fish and pungent meat being sauteed in rich sauces. The cacophony from competing transistor radios almost drowned out the roar of the traffic and the conversations around her.

Fanny didn't feel conspicuous being the only Westerner around. She felt as though she'd come home at last. She didn't care if the bus didn't arrive for an hour. Standing in the white, bright, morning light, she felt happier than she had since receiving Caroline's letter.

She tried to recognize the Chinese characters on the collage of signs hanging from the sides of every building but couldn't except for a few numbers. Bamboo poles strung with laundry were suspended from upper floors. She played an old game with herself. She tried to decide what was behind each window: a family, a small factory, or a makeshift temple of some kind.

The thing that Fanny liked best about traveling was watching people living their everyday lives, so different from hers. In every country, in every town, city and village, people going about their business wrapped up in their thoughts, with tragedies and love in their lives just as she had in hers. They dressed differently, spoke different languages and had different opinions perhaps, but, in general, they lived in human bodies and were subject to similar temptations and fears. Thinking about their everyday problems, food for dinner, wayward children, difficult families, low wages, trying to save money to emigrate, start a new business, put her frustrations into perspective. Maybe she really had been cured. She hadn't used to think that way.

When the bus came, it was a double-decker. She paid the driver and climbed up to the top. A thin man cracking watermelon seeds between his front teeth lounged across the left front seats. He'd placed a pile of bulging plastic bags on the right. She considered asking him to move the bags, but sat behind him.

She barely recognized the road. All along it were factories and blocks of flats that she'd never seen before, many still under construction. It all seemed dustier than she remembered, probably from all the building. She recognized the contours of the road. She'd driven along it thousands of times.

The bus turned a few corners. The time had come to stand up and climb down the stairs. She rang the bell, but sat almost mesmerized. The bus stopped. She became aware of people staring at her. She stood quickly and walked down the stairs and off the bus.

She was above the beach they used to call Middle Beach. She glanced down its two hundred concrete steps, two hundred and seven to be exact. The same steps. Caroline, younger than Sarah now, had a favorite orange bathing suit with turquoise angelfish printed all over it. Tired and sandy from a long day playing in the ocean, she'd stomp up the stairs demanding, in her high-pitched voice, a popsicle for each of them. The twins dawdled. The old man with his bicycle-powered ice-cream wagon had them ready: orange for Caroline, lime for Drew, and lemon for Will.

Fanny looked for the house. It should have been visible from where she stood through the trees, but she could see nothing now, just dense overgrowth and evergreens. The flagpole was gone.

She looked at her watch. One ten. She had plenty of time. She walked on the edge of the road. They'd always had to go in single file, she in the front, Caroline in the back.

She tried to see a sliver of the house through the trees. There was no pavement where she walked. She realized that in spite of the change from village to resort area, the road was much less busy than it used to be. She could see a motorway wind around the hillside high above a new pink concrete block of flats. They used to hike there. They had once met, on a rocky path, a large leopard cat with small ears and liquid amber eyes. The wild cats must have long since been driven away back into China.

The promontory seemed completely overgrown. She searched for the driveway, then failing that, an opening. Eventually after retracing her steps she pushed her way through bushes and found herself on rubble that must have once been the driveway. The house loomed ahead of her, almost obscured by foliage.

Unused.

Deserted.

A slice of cold knifed down her back. She shuddered. Never in her wildest dreams had she thought that she would find Water Music abandoned. Such a valuable piece of land, overlooking the ocean, could house a complex of flats, a small beach club or restaurants. Could the fengshui of the place be so bad that nothing could be ever built there? It was highly improbable. All kinds of tricks could be used to change the course of water, wind and fire, and thus change the luck of the place.

She stood still and tried to imagine what she had expected: a family living there, just as she, Peter, and the children had. A Chinese family perhaps, with servants and slick, expensive, silver cars. She had expected to walk around the house, to stand on the headland and look out at sea at Tsing Ye and Ma Wan and Lantau islands in the distance and feel home again, and at peace. She wanted to see that everything had gone on after she had left it and only she had changed.

Standing there, she had a suspicion that the house had fallen into disuse not long after she'd gone. She, Peter, and the children had been its last occupants. In a strange way, their failure had contributed to its downfall. She shook her head. She had no hand in its troubles. They had dealt with the haunting the best they knew how. She had been good to the house, had loved it even.

Fanny leaned forward and listened. She could hear the sea rushing up against the rocks. She listened more closely.

The stream had been silenced.

She kicked a rock with her sandal.

She'd worn an expensive cream Calvin Klein linen dress so that the present occupants of the house would believe, in spite of the fact that she'd arrived by bus, that she'd lived there once, and allow her access. The outfit was unsuited to clambering through underbrush. She might need the dress again; she hadn't packed many dressy clothes.

A distinct and unnatural movement in a pile of dead leaves reminded her that the grounds around Water Music harbored many species of snake: rat snakes, vipers, bamboo snakes, cobras. She recalled a particularly handsome, fat, coiled rock python the fawong had found one summer. He'd killed it by pouring boiling water on its gleaming lazy head as it sunned itself by the stream, having gorged itself on her most expensive fat goldfish.

Deserted, the garden would be a haven for any number of reptiles. Fanny looked down at her vulnerable legs and feet. No one in the world knew to find her here. She backed away and decided to return better attired for investigating the ruin.

As she walked back to the bus stop along the dusty, hot road she tried to make sense of her emotions.

Finding the house in such a condition had unnerved her. She'd prepared for changes, vulgar, flashy changes, but not dilapidation. She kept telling herself that you just can't leave and expect it all to be there waiting.

She peered through the trees towards the islands. To her amazement, the view had changed completely.

How could she not have noticed it before? The view must have been obscured when she walked towards the house.

One end of Tsing Ye, the high round hump of a barely inhabited island that lay directly opposite, had a whole quarter chopped off. Just like that. Gone. A wound of reddish soil marked the place where it had been amputated: a sheer cliff of bleeding sand. This was an island of reasonable size that had stood since the beginning of time. Huge new pylons stood out of the sea between Tsing Ye and Ma Wan islands.

A fury welled up in her. All was not right in a world where this could be possible. She knew that hills were regularly razed in Hong Kong in order to dump into the sea. Why would they have done this? What for? She thought about the new airport. Of course. They'd need dirt to build a runway. A road was planned to connect the new airport on Lantau Island with Kowloon. The new airport was a symbol of Hong Kong's optimism in the face of the Chinese takeover. But a road over Tsing Ye? As though it just wasn't important? What about ecology and environmentalism?

What had Peter been doing as leader and mover and shaker? She'd left in his competent, political hands, her children and the conservation of their world. He would have been involved in this, and certainly been in a position to put up opposition to it.

She waited for the bus in an emotional stupor. If an island as large as Tsing Ye could be made to disappear and her house abandoned, what other damage had been done?

The Meades lived in the same old ground-floor 1930's garden flat they'd moved to in 1970, out by Stanley. They had loved the garden where they could read quietly, cradled in deck chairs. Jean had placed potted nasturtiums and marigolds in the sunny areas. The wide-open living room with a terracotta floor, ceiling fans and bamboo roll-up curtains cooled even on the most humid, sweltering days. The view of the sea and outlying islands hadn't changed.

As she walked into the flat with Alan, Fanny relaxed. Ever since meeting him at the ferry, Fanny had worried about Jean. Alan had aged. He looked so small, withered and tired in his khaki trousers and safari shirt. She expected to see a similar transformation in Jean, but was surprised. Jean strode towards them, tall, thin and upright as a sapling after all these years. Her eyes glittered and creased in genuine warmth. She gave Fanny a hug that lasted long enough for Fanny to know how much she meant it. "My God, Fanny, you've gone to fat. Life is agreeing with you—at last."

Fanny laughed and pulled at the skirt of her dress. "Only a few pounds, is it that noticeable?"

Alan rushed to her defense, "I think she looks fabulous— better than ever, and she always was a looker."

Fanny blushed. Jean took a few steps back. Fanny looked Jean over as closely as she was herself being scrutinized. Jean's hair color had been allowed to take its natural course and shone pure white. It hung thickly and the cut was still short and blunt. It suited her. She wore white trousers, a loose, maroon silk shirt and gold strappy shoes. Her skin still glowed smooth and pale. It had none of the dusty, weathered texture of Alan's skin. Jean hadn't let herself be seduced into sunbathing in the old days and she was reaping the rewards now. Fanny had forgotten that Jean wore flashy shoes.

Alan clinked ice into tall glasses behind them and poured them generous gins. He disrupted their silence. "I'll leave you girls to your gossip. I'll be in the study. Don't forget to call me to dinner, I'm hungry." He handed them each a frosted glass topped with a twist of lemon and a sprig of mint.

As soon as they sat alone, Jean said, "Caroline's the absolute image of you. She has your smile, your hair. It's uncanny. Have you seen her yet? She's desperate to meet you."

Fanny looked away. "She's written to me. I had to come here first—to prepare myself." She forced herself to ask, "How well do you know her?"

"My dear girl, your children are like my own." Jean glanced at Fanny. "Forgive me for saying this, but they are more mine than yours. I used to think of it as taking care of them for you, but I realized that it's for myself that I love them. They were so little and alone." She paused and looked away. "There's a difference you know, between your own children and other people's. There's all sorts of nonsense between you and your own children, expectations, that sort of thing, but with Caroline, she makes no demands on me and I try not to make any on her. We love each other without recriminations. It's very pleasant."

Fanny felt herself sinking but struggled to stay calm. She took deep breaths. She wanted to know. She would keep asking and Jean would keep telling. It was as though they had never been away from each other. Sophisticated, well-bred, and in control of the situation, Jean hadn't asked the superficial questions, the social niceties. How's Rider, and so on.

Fanny asked, "When did you last see her?"

Jean looked way past Fanny out into the trees and the sea beyond. She took a sip of her gin. She didn't answer the question. "They used to come stay with us during school holidays. Alan and I would always go see them at school when we were in the U.K." She looked back at Fanny. "What's driven me mad is why you haven't made any effort to contact them. Why you didn't write to me."

Even though she knew that this is what everyone would ask, Fanny had no satisfactory explanation. Jean waited quietly, so Fanny blurted, "I wanted to. I couldn't, it's as simple as that. I don't mean that Rider wouldn't let me, or someone else was stopping me. I just had to *force* myself to let go." She shifted in her chair and caught Jean's eye. "I missed you. I loved them. But I wasn't well, Jean. I was sick, very sick. They think of it as an illness now, treatable."

"I know. That's the damned thing. You loved them. I've told them that a hundred times. Are you better? You look better."

Fanny answered slowly, "I think I'm better. Some times it's as though nothing was ever wrong. I can go along like that for months, and then I feel lethargy and tears taking over. I have to fight it. I can never forget it. It just sneaks up on me." Fanny needed Jean as an ally. Jean would be a more sympathetic interrogator than most, not merely curious, but kind, too. "I wasn't much of a mother." She heard herself plead, "Please forgive me, Jean."

Jean smiled at her, leaned over and patted her knee. It wasn't exactly forgiveness, more like comfort. "I hear you and Rider have two children."

"Sarah's twelve and Nigel's ten."

"Wasn't Sarah the name of your sister that died?"

"Yes. But tell me about Caroline, Andrew and William. What kind of people have they become? I can't make amends, but I can at least meet them on their terms."

Jean stood up. "I'd better check on dinner before we get into that. Damn Filipinos. The old Chinaman was a good cook. Do you remember Chow?"

Fanny nodded, "What happened to him?"

"He took his life savings and bought things: bicycles, radios, clothes, watches, blue-jeans. Heavily laden, he traveled deep into China by train to his sisters and brothers, his nieces and nephews. They stripped him of everything and didn't even say thank you. Broke his heart. He didn't live long after he got back. Dreadful, it was." She sighed. "We'd all told him not to do it, but turns out that's why he worked as a servant all these years, to buy things for that ungrateful lot. He was guilty about all the suffering in China. They weren't worth it, needless to say."

Fanny wanted to hear about her children, not some sad old cook. "Tell me about Caroline."

Jean sat down. "I don't know where to start. I feel disloyal telling you these things. I'm avoiding it, actually. In many ways, of course, it's high time this was all brought out in the open. I really do have to see to the dinner, dear. Get yourself another gin while you wait." She stood up again and walked into the flat.

For twenty minutes Fanny sat out on the terrace alone, clutching her empty gin glass, trying to resist her urge to refill it or leave. She shouldn't have had the gin. She mustn't have another. Jean was holding back, not ready to tell yet. She threw her ice cubes at a eucalyptus tree and forced herself to wait.

She thought about her mother, Marjorie, and Peter's mother, Penelope. She'd have to see them, too. They had taken on the shape of large black birds carrying her children away from her. They must be ancient now.

When she heard Jean call her from inside, she had collected herself. She had expected the gin to act like poison, but she seemed relatively undamaged by it.

She knew where the dining room was. It was the most formal room in the flat, spacious, yet windowless. Alan and Jean called it Our Vanity. Jean had covered the wall in royal blue silk and covered the seat cushions in the same. Jean's collection of ancient Chinese embroideries hung framed one on top of the other on three of the walls and the fourth, paneled in rosewood, opened into a wall-sized, electrically cooled wine refrigerator. Here Alan housed his collection of valuable burgundies and ports. Fanny hoped the room would look as it always had and she was not disappointed. Alan had chosen the wines for dinner and wiped the bottles with a large white napkin.

Jean introduced Fanny to the Filipina maid, Maria. The table had been set for three people and to Fanny's eye, at least six courses, complete with finger bowls. She knew that they ate this way every night, even when alone.

"Well, nothing's changed here," she said brightly. "Are we going to drink a fortune tonight?"

He laughed. "It's my only indulgence—humor me. A couple of 1970 Bordeaux." Alan showed her the bottles. "You never did approve of my hobby did you?"

"It's always made me feel special, drinking your wines." Jean winced. "Caroline says it exactly that way."

Alan shrugged. "Of course. The resemblance is there without question. Jean is upset about you coming back, but she's pleased, too. As you get old, change becomes more difficult. She may not show it, but she's been in a high state of excitement since Rider rang."

They worked their way through an asparagus course, a prawn course, a salad course, then baked smoked ham, a lemon sherbet and then an assortment of cheeses with their coffee. During the meal Fanny entertained them with Bresso stories. They in turn told Fanny about people they'd known, avoiding nostalgia. Jean said, "I think it marvelous the way you've turned into a businesswoman. You have now something you've always lacked—confidence. Being in Peter's shadow must have been the worst possible thing for you."

Alan roused himself slightly, "Yes, and, you know Francis, don't worry about Peter. Perhaps you did blot his copybook when you left, but he never really looked back. There was even speculation a couple of years ago that he'd be made the next governor." He sighed. "All he got was a bloody knighthood."

Fanny stared into her wineglass. She hadn't had this much to drink in years. Sir Peter. That was worth a giggle.

Jean offered more coffee. "And tell us about Water Music. You went there today? How did the old place look?"

Fanny described it.

Alan, who had consumed a great many glasses of wine,

laughed at her fury about the destruction of Tsing Ye. "My dear girl, what did you expect? They were carving out mountainsides in your day. It only stands to reason that a worthless chunk of rock should be put to use as a runway. Tsing Ye was never good for anything. It was only a matter of time. It wasn't arable land, not even grazing land, certainly it would have been too steep to build on. So why not?"

Fanny refused to be drawn into an argument over something so obvious. If he couldn't see the beauty in the island before, he wouldn't when she was finished. "I urge you to drive over and take a good look sometime, Alan. It isn't a pretty sight. It's a shame."

"I have seen it, quite a feat of mechanical engineering, actually. Progress has its price, my dear. The wheels turning and all that. Jean, pour her some coffee."

Fanny refused. She had relaxed. "I'm allergic to it."

Jean nodded, "Yes, I remember now. So are Andrew and William."

Fanny couldn't wait any longer. "Please tell me about them. It's difficult for me."

Jean said, "I've decided what my reluctance is. I need your reassurance. Are your intentions honorable?"

Before Fanny could answer, Alan stood up, flung his napkin to the table and said, "You're out of my depth. I'll leave you to it. I'll be in my study."

Jean stood too, and Fanny followed her outside. They settled back into the cushioned rattan chairs. Fanny thought quickly. Honorable intentions. She hadn't considered her intentions very carefully. Jean was asking about commitment. Would she desert again or was she back into the picture? The answer could only be that she was on the fence. Honorable, but on the fence. If Caroline wanted to inflict cruel and unmerciful mental anguish as punishment on her, she was going to retreat. No doubt about it. Everything depended. Fanny hoped that she could remain at least this strong. She wondered if she would excuse herself by telling the whole terrible story, but they would only think worse of her if she did.

She took the bull by the horns. "My intentions are honorable, but I'm not as tough as all that. I am still capable of collapse." She paused, " But I don't mean that to threaten you. It's just a fact. It just comes over me."

Jean relented. "I'm sorry, I didn't mean to frighten you. I just need to be sure that you aren't here just for curiosity and then won't disappear again for another twenty years. I want to know that you want to be in it up to your neck with your children again." She looked down. "It's also me. I want to know that I will see you again. I missed you, mate."

四

Fanny tucked her bare feet under her and concentrated on Jean's clear voice. "It's curious. I'm finding that the more I tell you, the less the children are mine. It's almost as though I'm giving them back to you." She smiled at Fanny. "The reason all this started is that Caroline's married and she's pregnant. You didn't know, did you?"

Fanny shook her head, but otherwise didn't outwardly react to the news. She didn't know why, but it didn't surprise her.

Jean continued. "Big wedding here in H. K., a couple of years ago. She debated a long time about whether to invite you. She was sure you'd refuse, but then again, what if you came? There would certainly be a scene. The marriage was her rebellion against Peter. Peter is being a bastard, as usual. That's why she's so desperate to see you. This is your chance.

"She's tough as old leather, Caroline, with a father like Peter and those two brothers. But being pregnant, she's feeling sentimental and broody. She wants her mother. As you know, Marjorie's not very good at times like these, and neither am I. I told her that it might be a mistake to write to you, but she's headstrong." She smiled at Fanny. "You don't know anyone like that, do you?"

Jean waited a moment, but Fanny didn't respond. She said, "Yes, dear, you're going to be a grandmother."

This was the last thing bothering Fanny. It hadn't even occurred to her. She laughed in a feeble attempt to cover her panic. She thought that this was the first time she'd ever been aware of her palms sweating. There was so much making up to do. She asked the first thing that came to mind. "How does Caroline feel about Rider?"

"Hates him, of course. It's natural. She thinks that he's what took you away."

"Is that what you think?"

"Of course not. If you hadn't have gone with him, you would have found some other way of escape. Are you happy at last, Fanny?"

Fanny thought about it. What does happy mean? On a day-to-day basis? She answered, "Put it this way. I'm busy and productive and it's been a long time since I've thought of suicide and murder. I guess you could say I'm happy."

Jean laughed. Her bracelets reflected silvery light from the house. Fanny noticed the bright sliver of moon. Clouds blew over it. She wrapped her sweater tightly around her. "You said Caroline's marriage was a rebellion against Peter? What's that all about?"

"Alan told you that Peter's been knighted? Sir Peter and Lady Ann, if you please. It's not gone to his head any more than any other honor that's been heaped upon it. But Ann— God save us all. Anyway, where was I? Oh yes, Tony's Chinese. You must know what Peter thinks of that. He's of good family, but his family feels the same way Peter does. These things never come to any good. She'll never fit in. Actually, he's charming. Educated in America, Harvard, I believe, traveled and well-read. He's a tall, aristocratic Chinese. He wears those little round spectacles like the last Emperor. His father owns factories here and in China. He's a delightful dinner companion, opinionated without being objectionable. I'm really quite taken with him."

Fanny smiled. Good for Caroline. She didn't turn into a prig after all. "Tell me about the twins. Is either of them married? How alike are they? Is either of them curious about me?"

Jean answered, "Andrew's been married. Still might be. It won't last, though. They're too much alike. They have a smash up, then kiss and make up. His wife, Helga, is blonde and rather beautiful. Danish, a model. God knows where he dug her up. He's needy. Of the three, he's the one most likely to have inherited your unpredictable side. Lives wildly on the edge and lets himself get depressed and angry. Won't fail. He's not going to forgive you easily, though neither of them talks about you. They wouldn't. They're men, and, in my experience, men don't like to talk about unpleasant things."

Fanny thought that wasn't true of Rider. Rider talked about most things. "Go on…. What about Will?"

"William's just like his Dad. Some girl or another is always trailing behind him, but he never seems overly interested in one in particular. He's a banker, wheels and deals, makes loads of money. They're gorgeous, the boys, and, of course, they garner even more attention being so much alike. Film star material, really. They look like their father did at their age. Good at school. Sports-minded, from discus throwing to tennis to cross country running." She glanced at Fanny as though to measure the amount of information she could accept before it overflowed. She went on, "Every time Caroline had a piano recital, I thought of you. She's become a good player. She's musical, like you."

Then her voice changed, "Peter spoiled the children though. They've had too much money thrown at them and not enough attention paid to their manners." She threw a quick look at Fanny who sat immobile and added, "It's my own opinion, of course. I wouldn't say it to anyone else."

"Peter was keen on sending the boys to separate boarding schools to toughen them up, but they overrode him and went together. Came away with all the prizes, that sort of thing.

"Caroline is another story. She never liked games and dreamed away her schooling. Always miles away, head in the clouds. Full of romantic notions, her head always in a book. You'd find her either reading swashbuckling adventures or soppy dog stories. She's not really changed. She did all right, but no one can say exactly how she got through with respectable results. Probably could have done a damn sight better. Does the right thing, does Caroline, but, under it all, one always suspects that the romantic side is bursting to escape. It doesn't surprise anyone that she's gone after you. She's wanted to go after you from the word go. She was furious with her dad for not chasing you—not fighting Rider in a duel or something. She accused him of not loving you enough. Incredible girl, Caroline. Stands up to him."

Fanny tried to organize her thoughts. She asked at last, "Who brought them up, really? Did Peter's mother participate in a big way?"

"She interfered as best she could. Died in a car crash not long after Alistair, two or three years ago. Everyone told her not to be such a damn fool speeding around in that flashy red Jag. What an old dragon—though it doesn't do to speak ill of the dead."

So, thought Fanny, a little guilty that she was so relieved, the old bigot finally got hers. She hadn't looked forward to seeing Penelope.

Jean asked, "Have you seen your mother?"

"Not since I left. I've not wanted to." She wondered whether Jean would believe her. She had missed her mother often.

Jean leaned her head back and closed her eyes.

Fanny's thoughts swung back. She remembered her mother's last visit. She'd gone over it thousands of times in her head. She thought of it as the turning point. No going back. If she'd done what Marjorie had wanted, things would have turned out quite differently.

Fanny's nervous breakdown had reflected badly on Marjorie and the rest of the family. On the one hand, Marjorie thought the breakdown self-indulgence on Fanny's part and unforgivable, but, on the other, she genuinely worried about her daughter and grandchildren. The breakdown had coincided with her own hysterectomy. She'd been forced to lie in bed and rest and couldn't come out to Hong Kong.

Then, just before Fanny left, Marjorie announced her visit. The servants had long since gone and Fanny couldn't meet her at the airport, so Ah Fong, Peter's driver, picked her up.

Fanny put the children to bed and waited nervously. She wore a blue, faded, cotton dress, which hung loosely after the weight she'd lost while in the hospital. She kept thinking she should check her hair and change into something that fit better, but it all seemed so much trouble.

When the car arrived, Ah Fong helped Marjorie with all her suitcases as far as the front step, then got back in the car and drove off. He hadn't been inside the house since the servants had left. As Fanny struggled in with the heaviest bag, Marjorie surveyed the front room with critical eye and questioning voice. "You're managing, I see?"

"Yes, Mum." Fanny saw the house as her mother saw it, not arranged as neatly as it might be, but within acceptable limits. She closed the front door behind her and looked her mother up and down. "You've recovered. Did you have a horrible time?"

"No worse than yours, darling." Marjorie was tired from the long flight. "I had to see with my own eyes that you are all right. I couldn't take Peter's word for it any longer. And in answer to your question, I'm quite all right. But the question remains…." She picked up a sweating ice-filled glass that had already marked the finish on the rosewood table, "…Are you?"

Looking away from Marjorie out to the sea, Fanny blurted it out. "I'm leaving, Mum. I'm leaving it all. I'm going away." Saying it out loud was final and real.

Just at that point, Andrew charged in crying that Will had taken his train and what was Mum going to do about it. Fanny hugged him, soothed him, savoring him, loving him, knowing that she wouldn't have him much longer. "I thought you lot were asleep. Let's have a cuddle before I put you back to bed."

Marjorie's exasperation surfaced. "Stop that, Francis. The world isn't coming to an end, you know."

Fanny wanted to scream: It is! It is!

Marjorie continued. "Get these children back to bed. No more talk about leaving, Fanny. You're going to have to pull yourself together and cope with life the way that the rest of us have to." She pulled Will away from Fanny. "Don't spoil him. Bedtimes are important." Then as if she could hold it in no longer, she said, "If you are thinking of going anywhere, come back to England with me. Your Dad and I would like you to stay with us for a few months. We'll get you back on your feet again."

Fanny considered this for half a second and rejected it. The only thing tempting about it was the desertion of Peter and the house, but Marjorie wanted Peter and Fanny's marriage to survive. She boasted of her ambitious and well-connected son-in-law to anyone who would listen and to many who wouldn't.

Fanny took the twins back to bed. Marjorie was hungry. She'd hardly eaten on the plane, so Fanny walked to the kitchen and prepared an omelet and salad for her dinner as though nothing was amiss. She forced herself to concentrate. She'd almost perfected her routine. I'm a good actress, she thought, and I'm getting better every day, as she beat the eggs at least five minutes too long. She washed each lettuce leaf in potassium permanganate to disinfect it. Cholera had hit Tsuen Wan not long before and they were careful. Her hands colored purple, but she liked them that way. Penelope told her to wear rubber gloves. In an effort to appear even more organized, she boiled drinking water while she worked. When the kettle cooled slightly she filled a waiting empty bottle with the water and put it in the refrigerator.

Marjorie ate dinner on the dark verandah. Then they sat together, drinking gin and listening to the ocean below. Marjorie's endless cigarettes, a slight breeze and mosquito coils repelled most of the biting insects. The waning moon that night reflected on the water, sending a path of shimmering sparkles towards the shore. I'm like the moon. Fanny thought, waning.

It was a relief to be with someone in the evening. She couldn't tell Marjorie her desperate terrible secret. She couldn't tell anyone. Marjorie hadn't mentioned it, so Fanny said, "Peter's out." She didn't want Marjorie to know the extent of her mortification or to know that this happened every night now.

Marjorie showed almost no sympathy. "You're going to have to make the best of the situation. You've made your bed, my girl. You're going to have to win him back, and it won't be by complaining. You haven't made much of a wife for him, you know."

The blood rushed to Fanny's face and her head went slightly dizzy. "You think it's all my fault?"

Marjorie ignored her. "I'm off to find another package of cigs."

They heard Peter finally banging through the front door. Marjorie motioned Fanny to stay where she was. She stood up stiffly and went to greet him.

Fanny heard their voices, low and conspiratorial. She didn't care. She didn't even try to hear what they were saying. She knew. They were talking about her. Marjorie was giving her evaluation of the situation, asking Peter permission to take Fanny and the children to stay with her. Of course, he'd agree. He didn't want her around anymore. She waited until they came out to join her, fresh drinks in hand.

Peter kissed her forehead and asked how she was feeling. Fanny jerked her head away. He never would have kissed her had he not had her mother as audience. "Don't worry. Things are under control. We missed you at dinner."

"Sorry about that. Johnson invited us. I know you can't stand Gabriella. I meant to ring you, but there wasn't a moment and then I completely forgot."

Fanny felt her voice rise far above her body. "Oh…and how is Gabriella? Who else was there?"

" Meades and Grahams. Jean asked for you. Your mother has kindly invited you and the children to go to England for a few months. It might do all of you a lot of good." He finished his drink and stood up to pour himself another.

All their friends had been there and Fanny hadn't even known about it. She wanted to act as though she didn't care, but she stood up abruptly, knocking over the chair she'd been sitting on. She knew she amazed them when she launched into the longest and most coherent speech she'd given in years. "You just want to get rid of me. I don't need a rest and I'm not tired. It's time you all stopped treating me like a child. I'm much better. I am working things out. The children and I have adjusted to each other and I'm actually quite happy at the moment. The least you could have done was tell me where you were. I couldn't have gone anyway. Are you ashamed of me, Peter? Your crazy lunatic wife? Do you think I'll embarrass you? Just you wait to see how I'll embarrass you."

Marjorie put her hand on Fanny's arm in a kind of warning. "Stop it, Francis. That's quite enough. You were busy this evening. He has to do these things." The timbre of her voice changed. "Come home with me, love, with the children. We'll find help for the children. You'll see all your old friends again." Her Lancashire lilt rose and fell in a singsong kind of way. The way she had comforted Fanny when she'd been a child having a tantrum.

Fanny took a deep breath. "I really am better. Just angry. Anyone would be. You don't know the half of it." She answered Marjorie in a calm, level voice. "I'd get disoriented again, if I went back to England...." She stared off into the distance, "...But I do have the right to change my mind."

"The offer is always open. You are very welcome, if ever you want to come." Marjorie walked over to the table where the bottles of whiskey and gin were lined up against the wall.

Fanny watched Marjorie and Peter exchange glances. She watched Marjorie shrug and Peter nod. Peter lurched to the door and leaned on it. He slurred, "So be it. I'm glad you feel better. I'm glad you both feel better. Now if you don't mind, I've to be up early tomorrow. I've got to pack it in. Hard day's night, so to speak," and he left.

Fanny held her tears back until Marjorie had gone up to a spare bedroom and Peter snored in bed. As she checked on the children, she couldn't help herself. They looked so sweet and soft. She exploded into wrenching but muffled sobs. They could always stay with her mother after she left, but until then she wanted to be with them every second. She burned them into her memory. Caroline no longer sucked her thumb and coiled her body into a circle, as perfect as a kitten's, under the sheet. Will with his ragged stuffed bear, and Drew, the one with the most imagination, covers on the floor, eyelids twitching in dream. She'd had nightmares at his age.

This thing she was about to do overwhelmed her. She didn't doubt her decision. It never even occurred to her that she had any choice. She either had to leave or she had to kill herself. Those were the only choices. She'd considered briefly killing Peter, but knew they'd lock her up for life for it. She kept asking herself over and over why life had to be so hard.

She stayed awake most of the night, taking in the sensations and sounds. The airconditioning wasn't on. She listened to consistent rhythms from the sea below, the heartbeats from the sampans and thought about how the ocean had sounded like that for thousands of years, and would for thousands more. People really didn't matter at all. The only thing that mattered was getting the most out of life and the living of it, but that was Dr. Greenwood talking. Towards dawn, the ocean lulled her into sleep.

The next morning, Marjorie stayed with the children while Fanny drove to her appointment with Dr. Greenwood. She left her freshly washed hair untied. The day was less humid than usual. In spite of her lack of sleep, she felt a burst of energy . It had been convenient, the hospital being so close. She drove past the building that had been turned into a shop to sell handicrafts made by patients: baskets, jewelry boxes, and lampshades. She'd never been involved in that. The man in uniform at the guardhouse outside the hospital knew her by now. He waved her on. She had privileges at the hospital that most patients wouldn't. She had her run of the place, except for the dangerous wards. She parked in the shade under a cassia tree, next to the old black Morris Minor that Bill Rider was using. Just parking next to him gave her a jolt of adrenaline.

Dr. Greenwood liked Fanny. He flirted with her. She'd completely won him over. Sometimes it annoyed her; sometimes it suited her purposes. She knew he didn't have many interesting or pretty patients. But of course, it wasn't Dr. Greenwood who had caused her recovery, and he was intelligent enough to know it.

She hoped that Rider would find an excuse to spend an hour with her.

She didn't have to wait long. Dr. Greenwood greeted her warmly and remarked that she looked tired. She told him that her mother had just arrived from England. She kept having the feeling that she was floating above her body, but had learned not to tell him these things. She knew how to handle him. She'd been able to fool him into releasing her from the hospital and she intended to keep up the facade. He thought of her as one of his successes.

It turned out that she did see Rider that morning. He came into Greenwood's office as though by accident and they spoke for a few minutes, then Rider invited her to have coffee with him. They sat in a visitor's sitting room letting their two white china cups filled with milky tea get cold.

With Rider, Fanny felt herself happy and maybe even interesting. Her heart beat like a teenager's in love. He was so American and stable. His hand, warm, dry and honest, held hers firmly. She loved, loved, loved him as she had never loved anyone.

She loved the way he looked. His eyebrows and eyelashes were so light you could hardly tell they were there. His hair had started to thin but not yet turned gray. His eyes were brown, kind and yet sardonic. He emanated intelligence, not the flashy, clever kind like Peter, but of an introverted, thoughtful kind. He had come to Hong Kong to study experimental programs to rehabilitate drug-addicted criminals through work and compensatory drugs. He was on a sabbatical from his hospital to look for solutions that could be applied in New York.

She told him about her mother's visit, and Peter not being home for dinner, and the children's exploits. Rider told her about how his work was going. He didn't talk down to Fanny. He seemed pleased that Peter had made no attempt at reconciliation.

He was due to leave in two weeks.

He wanted Fanny to leave with him.

She told him that her mother had invited them back to England. "I'm ready. It's even better now that Mother is here. The children will be fine. I have to leave."

He saw her desperation. He loved her. He knew she had no choice. He loved her.

He knew he was saving her life. He loved her.

Jean slapped her upper arm and startled Fanny. "Damn mosquitoes are starting up again. We'd better go inside."

Fanny peered at her through the darkness of the night, "I'd better get back to the hotel. I'm still tired out from the flight. It's been an emotional evening. I'm so glad you invited me."

Jean hesitated, then said, "Before you go there's something I want to tell you."

"Yes?"

When Jean didn't answer, Fanny said, "It's all right. I can take it, whatever it is."

"This isn't about you, it's about me. I've been married to that man in there for over forty years." She pointed to the house. "I'm thoroughly sick of him, but do you think I'd do anything about it? No. How many people who could make new starts, get new lives, actually do? A handful. You, my dear, are one of the brave ones. I admire you terribly for it."

Fanny couldn't help it; maybe the gin and wine were at last working their destruction. Her eyes filled up and tears streamed down her face. "It seems so long ago.."

They stood. Fanny put her arms around Jean and whispered, "Thanks. I missed them. My children." But, she thought, not enough. She'd gone through days when she'd barely thought about them. She wanted to go back to the hotel and look at the pictures. She was glad she'd had too much wine at dinner.

After a moment, Jean pulled back. "I know it's difficult. No hard feelings? Come back, if not tomorrow, then the next day. You know, I understand now, better than I did then. Peter was a fool. But all the same, leaving your children.... You haven't finished paying for that yet."

Fanny didn't want to talk about it. She wanted to run. She had paid more than anyone knew and Jean had no business preaching to her. She kissed Jean anyway.

Alan offered to drive her to the MTR, which would take her directly to the hotel. Fanny insisted on the ferry. She wondered if she was still a little drunk on Alan's wine. She liked Alan this time much better than she used to. He hadn't tactfully kept to the background when she'd known him before. She'd even suspected him of taking Peter's part. Now she sensed his sympathy for her.

In a daze, she walked off the ferry on the Kowloon side.

She knew that exhaustion must be playing a part in her mood. Rather than crossing the road and walking straight to the hotel, she took a detour along the waterfront again. Although it was late at night, she wasn't frightened in the least. She walked by the Cultural Center. Wherever she looked, young couples were holding hands. Perhaps Caroline was happy. She hadn't before, but now Fanny allowed herself to imagine her reunion with Caroline. Maybe it wouldn't be so bad. Maybe they could hug and kiss and Fanny would be forgiven. When was the baby due? She'd forgotten to ask.

She wanted to see her mother again; she wondered if her mother regretted all the horrible things she'd said when Fanny had left Peter. Fanny even wanted to see Peter again, Sir Peter, no less. She especially wanted to see Caroline, Will and Drew. Jean had opened up the floodgates.

In retrospect, visiting Jean hadn't been so bad. She wasn't as angry as Fanny had expected her to be. Jean had, in fact, welcomed her, and seemed to need to talk about it all. Wasn't it amazing that Jean had so many memories of her children—and she so few? Fanny reflected upon being a grandmother. Caroline pregnant. Did anyone as young as Caroline know how to marry sensibly? It was luck if an early marriage worked out. Caroline hadn't picked an easy course. Culture clash. She wondered where Caroline and her husband had met. Caroline had written from England, but Jean had said that her husband had been to school at Harvard and his father owned businesses here. What was Caroline doing in England anyway? Did Drew and Will like her husband?

She really had to see Peter. Mental cruelty wasn't something they talked about then. What kind of husband was he to that dreadful Ann? Peter wasn't capable of monogamy, of that Fanny was sure. How much of a mother had Ann been to her children? Had she really bequeathed her sweet little children to Ann, an ugly, cruel stepmother? Had Ann had children of her own? Stepbrothers and sisters for Caroline and the twins?

It was all too horrible to contemplate.

She looked at her watch.

One a.m.

New York was twelve hours behind. She had to call Rider and apologize for her earlier behavior. She'd forgiven Rider for telephoning all these people for her. He had let her make this journey. He had saved her life. How could she have forgotten? He was a good man and she still loved him. She smiled when she thought of Rider's American ways, something of a culture clash, too, but a sensible marriage nevertheless. The one she should have had in the first place. She wanted him to be here with her. This had to be the most romantic place in the world, the place where they had met.

She looked across the harbor at the gorgeous mass of twinkling lights beyond, the hills in their velvet blackness, a foil for the sparkle, the sky behind a deep indigo with a tinge of yellow and pink from the lights, the ferries continually plowing their way through the water. She felt that way right now, plowing back and forth, back and forth between her new life and old.

It didn't smell of Hong Kong here. It could be anywhere. It used to smell fishy and putrid.

She realized that she'd hardly thought of Nigel and Sarah. What kind of a mother deserts her children? She could as easily leave Nigel and Sarah as she had the others. She had hardly thought about them at all these last few days. She'd loved the others, too.

Fanny walked slowly to her hotel. At this time of night, Nathan Road was still crowded with all kinds of people even though most of the shops were closed. People spent so much time on the street because their flats were so small and cramped. Ironically, it was the only place to get privacy. She was glad of their company.

五

All systems go, Fanny thought. She had woken early with her energy level at full blast. No longer did she long to hit the bar in the room, no longer was she irritated with Rider, nor did she resent anyone or anything. She had lived with herself long enough to know that exhilaration and energy on the heels of exhaustion might not be a good sign, but she turned off a nagging warning light flashing in her head.

Although she'd promised to telephone Jean, it was more important to get to the house. She dressed in her hiking boots, thick denim jeans and her denim jacket over her T-shirt. The MTR to Tsuen Wan and the bus ride to Water Music went quickly in spite of her excitement. She didn't look towards the mutilated island. She concentrated on the road and the new buildings along it. She'd half expected the changes she had found yesterday to have been a dream. It was almost a relief to see the dense foliage she would have to make her way through to reach the house.

Scrambling through the undergrowth she tripped on the root of an old pine tree. The ground gave way under her—damp, warm, sandy loam. Startled, she lay on the ground for a moment rubbing her throbbing ankle. She could hardly hear cars on the road, and although she knew the house was ahead of her, she couldn't see it from where she had landed. She knew that she could lie there forever and no one would find her. It would all go on without her. She wouldn't have to see Caroline.

A sharp rock resting under her shoulder blade forced her to sit up. Then she thought about the snakes again. She stood, brushed spikes of pine needles off her jeans, and peered ahead. The outline of the house loomed before her. The whitewash had almost gone. It looked grimy, just how it was supposed to have looked during the war.

She shuddered. She remembered.

After they moved to Water Music in 1965, she and Peter established a routine. Eventually, they had six servants in all. A driver, Ah Fong, took care of Peter's needs. Sisters, Ah Lee and Ah My, came later, first one, then the other. They were baby amahs for the children. The highly paid cook, Chen; a cleaning/washing amah; and a fawong, or gardener. All the servants lived there except Ah Fong, who lived with his family in nearby Yuen Tun Village.

Peter and Fanny held dinner parties regularly. Under Penelope's guidance, Fanny learned how. She socialized with other wives at the beach, or sometimes she went for coffee mornings at their houses, or had them to hers. The days were filled with drinking: coffee, gin, cups of tea, then more tea, then more gin. The children played together.

There was no sense of trouble looming. Fanny was in her right mind mostly, though some days she'd canceled everything and stayed in bed all morning, or went to Tsuen Wan and wandered around aimlessly, but she never lost her bearings completely.

She and Peter had reached the point in their lives together where their passion had dissipated into tolerance and
they'd adjusted to each other's differences. For instance, Fanny
found Peter too fastidious, but she hated the way he became
sloppy when he had too much to drink. She knew that Peter
didn't care for her drinking, either, and wanted her to make
small talk to his superiors. If she had to talk to them, she
wanted to be able to talk about things of substance, but that
wasn't what was expected. He wanted her to be a political
wife, an asset in a difficult arena, the way his mother had been.
He wanted her to spy on the other wives for him, get information, let things drop. She never got the knack of it, never
learned to feign interest in people she thought foolish and
talk about small nothings.

It all flowed smoothly until one cool September day in
1968. Peter had risen early the way he always did. He dressed
in his clean, pressed khaki uniform and went downstairs to
get some breakfast. Sometimes the children were up before
him, but on this particular day, probably because it was cooler,
they slept late. Fanny lay in bed planning the day ahead, deciding on the preparations for the dinner party they were giving that night. Caroline had just started nursery school after
the summer and this started Fanny thinking about having to
send the children to boarding school in the U.K. Prep school
for boys started at age seven. With any luck, she might not
have to send Caroline until she was eleven. She didn't want to
give them up so young.

She heard doors slamming and Peter swearing. Then he
called her, not her everyday name, Fanny, but her formal name,
Francis, Francis, Francis, with an urgency she hadn't heard
from him before. Sleepily, she wrapped her red silk kimono
around her, slipped her feet into old rubber flip-flops and
clapped down the stairs.

She and Peter came face to face in what they called the breakfast room. He looked frantic. "They've gone. There's not a bloody servant in the house. Cleared out. Bolted. Done a bunk."

Fanny didn't believe him. It wasn't possible. She went to look for herself. The kitchen stood empty. The kettle wasn't on the boil for Peter's tea. Peter's egg hadn't been poached. No toast had been made. The marmalade was still in the cupboard. She went down the few steps and around the house to the servants' quarters. The louvered door to the cook's room was shifting in a breeze. She called out, reluctant to intrude, "Chen? Chen?" Only the waves below and the door banging answered her. She called out again, "Chen? Ah Lee?" She worried about what she'd see, but she pushed it open anyway. The room was stripped bare except for the mattress, the dresser and chair. Even the electric fan had gone.

She walked to the small room the sisters shared. One of them was supposed to be up with the twins. They took turns sleeping with the children. She called "Ah Lee? Ah My?" No answer. She turned the handle and opened the door, tentatively. Bare.

The worst possible thought flashed through her mind.

The children! What about the children?

She ran back into the house, past Peter, and up the back servants' staircase into the twins' room. Will sat in his crib happily playing with some plastic blocks, and Drew stood whimpering, but they were whole and alive. She flew into Caroline's room. Caroline was sitting at her desk looking through a picture book. She'd tried to dress herself and wore mismatched socks and her dress was backwards. Tenderness flooded Fanny. She lifted Caroline and hugged her and carried her into the twins' room. "My little ones, my babies."

Caroline said, "Where's Ah My?" Fanny didn't let herself get flustered. "I don't know, darling."

Drew pulled himself up to the side of the crib , "I want Ah My!"

"Well, you'll have to put up with Mummy." Fanny hugged him. Peter came into the room. He stared at her over the children's heads. "Thank God they're all right. I'm not sure what prompted this. I'm worried. Maybe there's trouble in Tsuen Wan."

The previous year during the riots, the police station had been barricaded. The residents from overseas had been jittery. The Cultural Revolution was going on only a few miles away, separated from them by a few rows of puny barbed wire. Not a lot of damage had been done, but it was enough to stir up hatreds and concern the government. Peter hadn't been home for days trying to sort out the mess.

"Has anything been brewing you haven't told me about?" she asked.

"Nothing. I'll give the Meades a ring."

The Meades lived a few miles away. To Peter's enquiries, they answered that didn't know why the Ardel-Rhys servants might have deserted, as theirs hadn't. Alan said he'd interrogate his cookboy. Jean said she'd approach the amah.

Ah Fong, the driver, came to drive Peter to work. Normally Ah Fong, an unusually tall, gregarious fellow, would make his presence known in the kitchen while Peter ate his breakfast. Ah Fong flirted with the washing amah. Fanny and Peter would hear them laugh together. Once when she was in the kitchen Peter heard Chen tell the washing amah that Ah Fong was a married man and to get to work.

That particular September day, Ah Fong sat in the car, wearing sunglasses, reading the paper. He made no move to come into the house. Fanny could tell Peter was furious. Just above his left eye, his eyebrow twitched.

Peter leaned on the car, casually, and asked Ah Fong in Cantonese if he knew that the servants had left. Ah Fong said he knew nothing, and looked away. When Peter asked him why he hadn't got out of the car, he said that he was late and there wasn't time today.

Peter turned and growled to Fanny, "Evasive bastard." He gave her a soft kiss on the cheek and walked around to the passenger side. Usually he sat in the back, but today, he sat next to Ah Fong.

Fanny was upset. She was at a loss. Now what?

Earlier Peter had looked at her as though she had something to do with the absconding of the servants. He questioned her. "What happened yesterday? Think back."

It was a mystery. Yesterday had been like any other day.

Meanwhile, Fanny had to wash and dress the children, feed them, make out her shopping list for the next morning, accept grocery delivery from the Asia Company, drive Caroline to nursery school, and get organized for a dinner party of twenty which she would have to manage alone. Peter had told her the party was too important to cancel. There was no way to get in touch with the guests of honor at such short notice: an M.P. and his wife, out for a visit from the U.K., old friends of Peter's parents.

She thought quickly. She couldn't impose on Jean Meade or any of Peter's other associates' wives, so Fanny did what she would only do in desperation; she rang her mother-in-law for help.

All that morning, Fanny tried to cope. She tried not to think about why. Why they would have left. Why they didn't say they were going. Where they had gone.

Chen had lived with them for five years. Why hadn't he spoken to her? He'd betrayed her and people would blame her.

She needed to have a rational conversation with another adult; she was beginning to think that perhaps it had been her fault. She called Jean Meade, who wasn't home.

She missed the servants. She was used to them. Even with the children, the large house seemed empty without them. By the time she had taken Caroline to nursery school, cleaned up after feeding Peter, Caroline, and the twins, by the time she had dressed the boys, picked up Caroline from her morning session, it was time for lunch. The twins, knowing a crisis was at hand, demanded extra attention and fought each other relentlessly. Caroline never stopped talking.

Penelope had managed to arrange for two chauffeured cars to carry her and her entourage to Water Music. She arrived in one and her cook and amah in another. The servants traveled with a carload of polished leather suitcases.

When they arrived at the front door, Caroline was crying, the twins were throwing cereal at each other, and Fanny had burned the toasted cheese. The Beatles sang "Lady Madonna" on the radio. The satisfied way Penelope flounced in, turned off the music, and ordered her amah to tidy up the mess, humiliated Fanny, but she was grateful nonetheless. Ten minutes after Penelope arrived, Peter walked through the front door with a very British police superintendent, two Chinese policemen and Alan Meade.

The British superintendent, Peter, and Alan sat Fanny down on the settee in the main room. When the Superintendent introduced himself as Ross McDonald, Fanny knew she'd heard his name last year in connection with the troubles in Tsuen Wan. He was small and had the kind of moustache that had to be waxed. Fanny wondered what it would be like to kiss someone with a waxed moustache.

He questioned her at length while the Chinese policemen wandered around the house. Fanny could hear them

stomping around and talking. It was still summer and hot
during the day. She couldn't stop watching his moustache because it didn't look real. She couldn't look him in the eye.
Her mind traveled. She worried about the children and the
party later and kept wondering what Penelope and her cook
were up to. She asked Peter if he would see to the children,
but Peter was too interested in the proceedings to leave.

Ross McDonald and Fanny went over and over the events
of the day before, of the week before, of the month before.
She tried to concentrate. She described the servants, not surprised that Peter couldn't. The servants had needed very little
managing. They were experienced in running a house and
taking care of children and she let them. They all deferred to
Chen and he'd been honest and loyal. She'd liked the baby
amahs and mildly disliked the washing amah. Even though
they had lived together for five years, she knew surprisingly
little about them. She knew that Ah Lee and Ah My had a
family in Hung Hom and went there on their day off. She
knew Chen had some kind of base in Yuen Long, but most
of his family still lived in China. She knew nothing about the
washing amah. She knew where Ah Fong lived and told them
that they could ask him.

Caroline ran in, her face very flushed. "Come down,"
she gestured. "Come down to Chen's room."

Alan and Peter stood up, instantly, reflexively. Fanny
was slower, but stood and straightened out her skirt. Ross
McDonald frowned.

They all followed Caroline out the French doors, around
the corner, and down the concrete steps to the servants' quarters. A slight breeze rustled the evergreens. Fanny was right
behind Peter and saw the Chinese police speaking conspirato-
rially together by Chen's bare mattress arguing and exclaim-
ing. The older, taller policeman was pointing something out

to the younger. As soon as the policemen became aware of the party from upstairs, they stopped talking. McDonald addressed them in Cantonese. The taller one answered evasively. He didn't look directly at McDonald as he spoke. McDonald turned to Caroline, "Why the hell did you bring us down here?"

She burst into tears. Fanny stroked her soft hair to comfort her.

While Alan talked with the police, Fanny watched Peter. He had been walking ahead of the others leading the way. He'd heard what the police had been saying. She knew that whatever it was, he knew. He'd turned from them and was staring out towards the sea. She could tell from the stiffness of him and the whiteness of his face that he wasn't going to share what he'd heard with Alan or McDonald.

She said to McDonald, "I'm taking Caroline upstairs. There was no need to talk to her like that. Obviously she thought they'd found something." She took Caroline by the hand and they went upstairs to the children's bedrooms, where she tried to convince the tired little girl to take a nap.

By three o'clock, Fanny was depressed and angry. She'd had no lunch, she'd felt accused, the children were whiny and tired, her bossy mother-in-law was in charge of her house again, and the servants had betrayed her. Caroline was too excited by the commotion below to sleep.

Her anger enveloped her. It suffocated her. For the first time, Fanny felt herself float away. She wasn't sure; perhaps this wasn't the first time it happened. Before when this feeling came over her she had forced herself to stay grounded, but this time she lost control. She actually saw her anger swirling around her in a red and green cloud. She saw herself floating over the room where Caroline was setting up a tea party.

She screamed.

Peter and Penelope ran up the stairs and into Caroline's

room. Fanny was shaking and flaying her arms. Caroline watched her with interest. "Mummy's fed up. Let her go to bed and sleep. She's sick."

Penelope muttered, "Out of the mouths of babes." She scooped Caroline up and gestured to Peter to help Fanny.

The rest of the day she'd lain on her big double bed on top of the pink quilted bedspread. She had no idea how the children were cared for. Penelope played hostess at her party.

Sometime during the evening, Jean Meade walked upstairs to see her briefly and brought her a drink and a plate of food, but no one else bothered. Peter came up late and drunk, pronouncing it the best party they'd ever had in the house. "We don't need so many damn servants anyway."

Fanny had recovered by morning of everything but a dull sense of oppression and foreboding. She got up at the same time as Peter, showered and dressed. Peter acted as though everything was normal. Nothing had happened. He hummed as he shaved; he shook out his trousers before he stepped into them the same way he always did. But he didn't kiss her. His manner towards her was distant.

She took his lead. She pretended that she hadn't lost control the day before. A little adversity, the loss of the servants, was not enough to destroy her. Peter would forgive her. It would be all right. There would be plenty of time to think about yesterday. She determined not to let Penelope run her life.

She checked on the still sleeping children and went downstairs before Peter, the back way, to the kitchen.

The place was a mess. No dishes had been washed from the party the night before. Half-filled glasses, empty glasses with lipstick on the rim, plates, napkins were scattered everywhere. No effort had been made to clear it up. Someone had spilled something sticky on the parquet floor and a swarm of large black flies were feeding from it. Worst of all, half-filled drinks, crumpled napkins and cigarette ashes littered the top of her piano. Penelope had boasted that her amah and cook would between them make the house look better than it ever had before. Neither Fanny nor Peter were used to this. They expected, as a matter of course, that when they came down in the morning the house, would be perfect.

Peter walked behind her. He said nothing. Fanny decided that if she didn't start doing something she'd have to go right back to bed. She walked to the kitchen and set about boiling an egg and toasting bread for Peter's breakfast.

Peter brought in a pile of dirty plates. He came back with glasses. He said nothing. She knew he was worried and didn't want to upset her further. He knew more than he was saying. She wanted to insist that he tell her, stamp and have a tantrum, but she didn't, more for fear of waking the children than worry about Peter.

They heard Penelope's high heels clicking down the main stairs. Peter and Fanny went into the living room to meet her.

Before they could say a word, Penelope's cook and amah entered the room from the outside French doors. They must have been waiting for Penelope's entrance. Neither of them were dressed in their black and white uniform. He wore brown trousers and a sporty blue short-sleeved cotton shirt; she wore brightly patterned cotton pajamas. Both appeared extremely agitated. She fidgeted and he twitched. Penelope, Peter, and Fanny stared at them in amazement.

The cook said, "Me no sleep here. Go home." He addressed Penelope directly. "Missie, go back Hong Kong." The amah nodded her agreement.

Penelope's voice cracked in fury, "Nonsense. Why haven't you cleaned up?" She pointed around the room.

The cook answered, "Go home now."

Penelope wouldn't accept it. "What are you talking about? Put on your uniforms and start clearing up this mess. If you get right to it, we will forget this." She glanced at Peter and Fanny. "We are staying right here until this is resolved."

The cook stood his ground, "Go back, Missie."

Penelope's voice sounded tight and dangerous, "Don't be ridiculous. That's the last I'm hearing of it."

The cook shrugged his shoulders, "Bye-bye, Missie."

Penelope saw he meant it. He was a good cook; she'd hired him away at great expense from a French couple who'd taught him Cordon Bleu. He had a wide repertoire, was reasonably honest, and spoke English better than most. She didn't want to lose him. He could get another job in a minute. Just last week, someone had made overtures to him. She gave an inch, "Why?"

The cook pointed at the ceiling and then at the floor and then at the door. "Me no like. Me no like. Bad, very bad." Fanny had watched him carefully. He'd metamorphisized. He'd always held himself with an air of confidence and snobbery. Today he stooped, pale and nervous. In spite of the heat, she felt chilled. He turned and walked towards the door, the amah close behind him. "Go, too. Everybody."

Peter marched after him into the hallway and told him to wait. He made a call from the black phone on the mahogany hall table. To the cook and amah he said, "There are two spare rooms upstairs. Would you like to stay there?"

They were adamant. They were not going to spend another night in the house in any room at all, but they agreed reluctantly to wait a few minutes.

Caroline wandered in sleepily. Fanny noticed that her nightgown was too small. She could hear the twins upstairs fighting. They must have climbed out of their cribs again. At first they always fought playfully, but in the end it turned murderous and they had to be separated as neither one would give in to the other.

Caroline handed Fanny a filthy ashtray. Fanny could hear Drew howling upstairs. She looked at Penelope, then the servants. It came to her, a sudden flash of insight. What else would explain it all? Ghosts. The ghosts, she thought.

She'd felt them often. Especially when she was alone at night waiting for Peter to come home. She knew it was nothing evil or frightening, just a wisp of something. She'd never told Peter because he would have dismissed it. Say that she'd always been a little on edge, imagining things. He was always so matter-of-fact. Everything to him was very solid and real and explainable.

Fanny put the ashtray down, took Caroline's hand and led her upstairs.

Nothing was normal that day. Peter didn't go to work. Caroline didn't go to school.

Later that morning, Fanny made a game of having Caroline bring dirty glasses into the kitchen while she filled the basin with hot, soapy water. Caroline remembered their last treasure hunt and liked the game. Fanny, relieved to have something to do, washed and rinsed each glass that Caroline found for her. As she stacked them on the drying rack, she thought back through the last two years. The servants had never seemed nervous. What was it about the night before last that changed everything?

Peter brought in a stack of plates. "Sorry about this, darling. This is a damn nuisance. We're on the right track now. We'll get it sorted out."

Fanny dropped the plates into the bubbles, one at a time. "It's very strange. I'd really like to talk to Chen. He had a lot of nerve leaving without even telling us. What a coward."

Peter said nothing, but rubbed her back, the first time

he'd touched her all day. She turned to him and hugged him. "It's all right, you know. I know all about it."

He pulled away. "What on earth are you talking about?"

"It's the ghosts," she said.

Peter stared at her. He pulled her towards him and, in spite of her soapy hands, hugged her again. "Who told you?"

Fanny never had a chance to answer him.

The doorbell rang and Alan Meade let himself in. They could hear him interrogating Ah Fong. "We all need to have a little chat. Come onto the terrace."

Peter pulled away.

Peter, Alan, Ah Fong and Penelope's servants went in convoy through the French doors. Penelope wanted to join them, but Peter held up his hand. "There are enough of us here already. Go help Fanny in the kitchen."

Fanny watched Penelope, wondering whether she'd make a scene and insist on going with Peter, or come into the kitchen. For a moment Penelope wavered, then she strolled into the kitchen and pulled a drying up towel from the rod on the wall. "Haven't done these for a long time. I'd be back in the U.K. if this sort of thing appealed to me."

Fanny laughed. "Strange, isn't it? Ghosts of all things. Who would have thought it?"

Penelope took a step back. "Peter wasn't supposed to tell you. We worried it would upset you."

Fanny stopped herself from slapping Penelope. Nothing would give her more pleasure. "I know a lot more than you think I do."

Penelope walked out of the kitchen and returned a few moments later with more things to wash. She ignored their last discourse. "I don't believe in ghosts, of course, but these damn Chinese, so superstitious. Jumping at their own shadows. Probably just found another position that paid better and then the rumor got out."

"They all got other jobs?"

"Someone might have hired them *en masse*. These things happen when they're not being properly managed."

Peter walked into the kitchen and spoke directly to her, ignoring his mother. "It's definitely ghosts. Chen and company got scared out of their wits the other night. They think someone was murdered here. It's ridiculous—they say these ghosts want revenge. They think that they are in danger."

"Stuff and nonsense," Penelope said, "We're not going to be intimidated by a flock of ignorant Chinese. Stick it out. They'll see that nothing will happen. They'll be back before you know it."

"But what are we going to do in the meantime? If your servants found out so soon, Penelope, we won't be able to get servants anywhere," Fanny asked

"Can't someone talk some sense into them?" Penelope sighed. "Of course, it's like dealing with the Irish. Once they get an idea into their heads…."

六

Most of the time, memory is unreliable. Incidents meld together, people take on tints of their later selves. Twenty people can be in the same place and see the same thing and ten years later have entirely different versions of what happened, if they can remember it at all.

This wasn't like that.

Fanny knew she remembered it exactly right. Perhaps she didn't remember every sound and every taste, but close enough. She found it easier to recall that time than three weeks ago when she'd been at work, at her new PowerMac, designing a Bresso box.

The past hadn't become buried It was as though she had stored it in her brain like an unread book. Everything that had happened since had been piled on top of it, burying it deeper.

Caroline's letter had wiped away the debris, and exposed Fanny's unexamined past. She wondered if it was the madness that had made her memory so clear. The lapse of thought.

Fanny stepped around the outside of empty house, remembering the ghosts and trying to conjure them up again. It was a sweltering day for April. She peeled off her denim jacket, which was glued to her back with a layer of sweat. The strangest things were flooding her mind. How people looked. A sandbox she had nailed together for the children. A typhoon.

She didn't have any fear in this most familiar of places, but she still, unmistakably, felt the presence of something else. Spirits, but care-taking spirits, friendly spirits who liked her. It still puzzled her that what was comforting and friendly to her had been terrifying to the servants.

Waves still attacked the rocks below, over and over again. The same rhythm, the same water? The same molecules? Sea had evaporated into clouds and dropped down again how many times in the last twenty-two years? Yet still the house was here. Incredible.

She fought her way through the overgrowth, cutting her bare arms on coarse bamboo leaves. She put her arm to her mouth and tasted the blood. The same. She tasted the same.

Snakes. Snakes, she kept thinking. Snakes guard this overgrown place. Snakes keep the spirits safe. Bamboo snakes. You can't see them. They strike if you frighten them. She'd encouraged the bamboo growth when she'd lived there. She'd forbidden the gardener to cut it back. It had matured into a dark, thick grove with an order to it. It divided itself neatly into sections. Some of the canes were several inches diameter now. She tried to picture herself in the heart of China somewhere and a panda crashing through the stalks, or a panda watching her while he chewed the fresh young bamboo shoots.

She came to the place where the stream had wound around and dropped to the sea below. Its path was tangled in weeds now, dry and sandy. She paused at the concrete pond where the goldfish had swum, cracked and filled with nature's litter and food wrappings. The goldfish were really carp, and some weren't even gold, but silver with patterns and dark spots on them. She and Peter, with expert advice from the fawong, had planned and stocked it. They had worried together about wildcats and frogs and freezing conditions and parasites. She wondered about the goldfish. Had Peter kept up the collection after she'd left? He'd probably sold them, or given them away to one of his rich Chinese friends. When she'd gone into the hospital, she knew the fawong had come back to care for the fish. He was unfazed by the spirits that terrified everyone else, perhaps because he never went into the house.

Fanny walked around to the French doors on the sea side of the house. They were nailed shut, boarded with plywood. Large, red, Chinese characters had been painted on them, which she couldn't make out. She tried pushing at the boards but they didn't move.

She walked down a few steps and around the house to the servants' quarters. This time she saw what she least expected and it gave her a terrible fright. Signs of recent habitation were everywhere. Probably caretakers, she thought, a family. Plastic slippers and three matchbox toy cars and a small red metal bus were parked in a row in the dirt. Several pairs of flowery women's cotton pajamas, a man's white t-shirt, and pair of shorts hung out to dry, strung between the corner of Chow's room and a pine tree. Clean rice bowls waited for the next meal. Old Gordon's Gin bottles, filled with what Fanny guessed was drinking water, were organized untidily on a windowsill. A covered bowl sweated condensation. She heard a radio playing and voices down the slope towards where the rocks met the sea. These people didn't appear to be afraid.

Fanny didn't want them to see her. She was afraid they would resent her intrusion and shoo her away. She backed up the concrete stairs listening to footsteps and a dog barking. It occurred to her that the dog must have been the reason why she hadn't disturbed any snakes. Dogs and snakes respected one another, even if in battle the dog usually lost.

The worry that these tenants would try to stop her made

Fanny especially anxious to get inside the house. She had a plan. One side of the house was partially built into a huge rock, or hillock, although someone had planted a shield of fragrant camphor trees for camouflage.

The side of the hill was rock, sheer and unclimbable, but there was a narrow place between a pair of camphor trees that could be scaled. She and Peter had found the place when they'd been planning the goldfish pond. The trees were still there. They'd grown huge in the time she'd been gone. Clutching her jacket, Fanny clambered up the stone slope. Woody azaleas grew out of rock, blooming around her in tacky, clashing colors, bright purple and orange. Good luck colors, Peter would say. The top of the rock made a private lookout for the master bedroom. The tops of the camphor trees reached up there now, partially blocking a view of the sea. She was glad; she'd wanted to avoid seeing the new bridge and the amputated island. Fanny had sunbathed up there when they'd first moved in and she'd had little to do. For old times' sake, she plucked a few glossy, new leaves off a tree and crushed them in her palm. They smelled musky and pungent.

The people living below blocked her from the stairs down to the sea. She'd envisioned herself sitting on the bottom step watching the defacement of Tsing Ye Island and the building of the bridge. How could the Chinese so concerned with harmony and all the elements in perfect balance have agreed to this? Here the world was askew, as far from serenity as she could imagine it. Well, Fanny thought, it's better not to be watching it.

She leaned with her full weight on the glass door to the bedroom while holding down the door handle and then kicked the metal support at the bottom. Just as Fanny had known it would be, the door was easy to force open. It had been a worry when they'd lived there. She'd often thought that someone could break into the bedroom without a struggle. Peter had told her not to worry, no one would think of climbing up there when there were plenty of better, more obvious, places to break in below.

At first she was dazed by the warmth and darkness. She closed the door behind her. Spiders' webs brushed and stuck to her face and hands. She wiped them away. She stood in her old bedroom, empty now of furniture, relaxing her eyes into the dim sleep of the room. The place smelled musty and tropical, partly rotting fruit, partly mildew.

This was the ultimate in privacy and peace. She thought of killing herself. Here and now. Rider and the children would survive without her. Caroline would never have the satisfaction of hurting her. The sadness filtered out of her gradually. Fanny concentrated on all the reasons why being alive was good.

She looked around the room. She'd almost killed herself in it several times. Some of her most unhappy moments had been spent here, her head spinning with too much drink and sun. This is where she had retreated when her confidence was at its weakest, curling in the corner with her bottle of gin. She remembered Peter. Sleeping with him. Listening to the waves, the radio from the servants, crickets from the bushes outside. What was it about this room that had always been so oppressive? Perhaps the spirits here were not kind after all. She would need to fight the lethargy and the self-destructive impulse it smothered her in. She could see her footprints clearly on the dirty wooden floor. No one had been in here for a long time.

Fanny listened. She heard the outside dimly, but the house itself was silent. She decided to explore.

The ceiling in the hallway had partially collapsed. Piles of plaster and shards of concrete littered the floor. As she walked through what was left of the upstairs, her former existence returned to her vividly. In Caroline's room, about a foot from the floor, under the window by the airconditioner, she recognized the graffiti that Caroline had drawn with a pen: her name, "Carrie," an elongated version of a giraffe and some scribbles. The house hadn't been painted inside since they'd lived there. She wondered if Caroline had grown into an artist. In the hallway, she retraced where she'd walked up and down for hours with her colicky twins. This was where she and Peter had argued about Genevieve. This wall was where her first attempt at abstract painting had hung, crimson, primrose, emerald and ice blue. They thought it good therapy at the hospital, making her paint. She wondered if Peter still had the painting. He'd liked it. In a generous moment, and to her absolute amazement, he'd said that it didn't remind him of her illness, but of her beauty.

Fanny didn't feel sad, or even sentimental, walking through the rooms. In fact, it cheered her up. It doesn't all come to an end, she thought, hard to imagine, but it does go on. There is always an answer. She hadn't killed herself, and she'd been happy since, though she never thought she could be happy again. She easily recalled the desperation she'd felt and her intense love for the sweet little children.

She leaned against a doorjamb. Curious about the systems in the house, she wondered what would happen if she flipped a switch. She decided not to risk it. How could she have forgotten a flashlight? She walked back to the bathroom that she and Peter had shared and flushed the toilet to see if it still worked. It coughed, wheezed and clanked, but eventually it released a torrent of brownish water and a swarm of beadlike, winged, black insects. She twisted the cold-water tap. It resisted and then disgorged a thick ooze of rusty liquid. She let it run a few moments, then rinsed her hands. She heard the pipes clang throughout the house. She wondered if the family living outside could hear it. It took all her strength to turn it off again.

The staircase received very little natural light. A lot of debris had fallen from the ceiling. She had to walk around and down the mess carefully and slowly. It wasn't the same house in smell or looks and yet the graceful proportions and elegant atmosphere were still apparent. Details she had forgotten struck her: the varnished wood banister, still gleaming when she wiped the dust off with her fingers. The almost Islamic geometric pattern of the tiles on the stairs had been cracked and separated in places. It reminded her of a marquetry table she and Peter had bought. Had that warped and separated too?

Still, Fanny wasn't frightened. Although she did think about the ghosts or spirits that lived there, she knew they weren't threatened by her. "See," they were saying, "see what happened because you left?"

The downstairs rooms were too dark from being boarded up to be inviting or of interest. Fanny envisioned snakes, large flying cockroaches and rats living there, feeding on each other. She found what remained of an old broom in the kitchen and trailed it behind her, disguising her footprints on the floor. She thought it might make a weapon against a creature should one threaten her.

She kept thinking about her piano. Would Peter have left it there in the main room to decay? It wasn't there, though. The room, even in unnatural darkness, looked lost without it. She wondered what had happened to the piano. Had Peter sold it, or who had taken it? He wouldn't have wanted to keep it.

The door to what had been Peter's study was closed. She tried the doorknob, but it was locked. It was the only room in the house with a heavy working lock. They had inherited the room that way. The fact that it was locked made her curious about it. This room had been where the feeling of spirits had been the strongest. She'd sometimes sat in there in the evening in an easy chair while Peter worked at his desk writing and reading reports. She'd pretend to be reading, but she'd felt strongly that they hadn't been alone.

She had the impression that forces were working there. On quite another level, the spirits agitated. She'd attempted to arouse Peter's interest. "Doesn't it give you the creeps in here?" Or "this room feels uncomfortable." He'd always laughed and tell her to go to bed, saying she must be tired or had too much to drink. It hadn't bothered her, though. She'd thought it was interesting. She'd tried to work out where in the room it was coming from: two or three wisps of something struggling together. She thought it moved. Then it was gone. Peter still writing his reports, a baby crying upstairs, and a breeze outside. Instead of taking Peter's advice and going to bed, she'd walk out to the verandah and watch the lights of the fishing boats until Peter was ready to go upstairs with her.

Once the servants left, it became local knowledge that Water Music was haunted. The ghosts became a serious problem, not because Peter or Fanny were afraid of or threatened by them, but because the house was too large to be managed without servants. Warnings had spread and servants refused to live or work there.

Peter didn't believe in the ghosts, full stop, end of discussion. He called it "superstitious nonsense of the most pernicious kind." His attention was taken with how to prevent everyone else believing in them. Fanny, not only believed the spirits were real, she was allied to them. They had made themselves known to her and had, she felt, protected her in some strange way. The evening Penelope's servants had left, Fanny and Peter talked about it, while lying in bed. She couldn't take his side and tried to defend hers. "You see, something must have *happened* here. There's more to this than meets the eye."

He nuzzled her hair and kissed her. "Yes, but what? It's ridiculous."

She tried to convince him. "Let's go down to the study now or the servants' quarters. If you make a special effort to concentrate you may see what I mean."

He said, "But if we go down, I want you to make a special effort to see that there is *nothing* there. *Nothing*. This isn't real, Fanny. You are so highly strung. You've become like the servants. You are susceptible to things like this." She felt him stiffen beside her, irritably. He turned over. "Time for sleep. We are both overtired."

Of course, Fanny felt rejected. Of course, she stayed awake for another half hour trying to decide if he was right. He might be. After death is there nothing, a big blank empty space?

She had once thought that if there were such things as ghosts, they would be threatening. They didn't frighten her now. Why were the servants so afraid?

The days following the leaving of the servants were filled with household activities. Fanny's hours were taken with the boring, but necessary, chores that keep life on an even keel: cleaning, dusting, making beds, washing clothes, caring for children. She'd never appreciated what her mother had done for her. Things she'd never had to do in her life before. Penelope stayed for a week and watched the twins. Sometimes she helped with meals. Fanny could tell that Penelope was itching to get back to the Peak where her servants had returned. Fanny had no idea how she was going to manage when Penelope left. There was no time to play the piano.

She wasn't able to leave the house. The Asia Company delivered the groceries she ordered each morning and afternoon. The flower lady brought flowers: gladioli and lilies; the vegetable lady brought vegetables and fruit: water chestnuts, bak choi, limes, melons, string beans, mangoes and sometimes tomatoes; the fish man brought fish: eels, sole, prawns, grouper; the shoemaker repaired their shoes right at the front door. These people would walk carrying twin wicker baskets strung from a bamboo pole balanced over their shoulders. When they arrived, they would spread out their wares for Fanny to choose. And she did. The flower lady even had a baby strapped to her back. Fanny had seen her nursing the baby under a shade tree with her yellow and white chrysanthemums beside her. For the first time, Fanny envied these poor people who lived at subsistence level. Everyday they walked. Everyday they saw different things and different people, whereas she, Fanny, was confined to the house.

That first week she didn't even get the opportunity to drive Caroline to school, because Penelope insisted on doing it. Penelope was watching to see how she bore up under the strain but Fanny mustered all her resources and coped.

The chores gave Fanny structure, and uninterrupted time to think. One day when Jean telephoned, Fanny asked her to find out the history of the house. What could have happened there to spawn phantoms? When was it built? Who by? Why? Jean promised to ask Alan to investigate the records.

Jean reported back that the house had been built in the 1920's by Chinese laborers for the British government. It had been built on empty, unfarmed land. It had been in British hands ever since, with nothing on the records of any interesting incident at all, certainly nothing criminal like a murder. The tenants were listed with quite ordinary British names, mostly Mr. and Mrs., but once or twice just names like Dawson,

Whittaker and Highcliffe. Only in the 1950's had it been called Water Music; before that it had been known as Flower Villa.

Fanny thought a lot about this. What could have happened that would be serious enough for ghosts to linger, but wouldn't be reported in the official record? An incident among the servants would not have likely been officially reported. One might have murdered another, a love triangle, a family feud. How to find out? Whatever it was must have happened since the house was built. Sometime between 1922, when it had been built, and 1965, when they had moved in.

A possible answer came to Fanny several weeks later, about the time that Peter was coming to his own conclusions. Penelope had returned home to the Peak, which had increased Fanny's workload, but decreased her frustration. Fanny decided to take a break and get out of the house, no matter how messy it was. She packed a picnic lunch, and after picking Caroline up from nursery school, she drove all of them to Tai Lam Chung Reservoir. There, sitting on a blanket on a patch of grass over the high dam, Fanny, Caroline and the twins ate their sandwiches and drank lemonade. They were all in high spirits, the twins running to and fro, Caroline keeping order.

A well-kept, white-haired European man, at least sixty years old, distinguished, carrying a walking stick, paused to watch them. He seemed fond of children and asked whether the boys were twins. Sociable Caroline, always incensed at the attention given to the tow-headed boys and their twin-ness answered, "Yes, they are. They are my brothers. They don't run very fast, do they? My name is Caroline." She sat down.

He laughed and said that he used to have twin brothers, so he understood, "Long since dead, my brothers, God rest their souls. Killed in the war. Younger than me, they were. Well, I've finished walking for today."

Fanny offered him her uneaten ham and mustard sandwich. To her surprise he accepted it and demolished it quickly. She then offered him a banana, which also disappeared. He eased himself down onto the blanket next to Caroline and asked what they were doing there and where they lived. Fanny told him.

"Well, well," he said, "Connie and John Martin lived there in my day. Very nice it was too, yes, very nice. So your husband is Ardel-Rhys. I've heard of him. Well, well. Small world, what?"

He introduced himself as John Carr, said that he was retired, lived in Kowloon now but had worked for the Public Works Department for many years. His wife didn't come on his afternoon jaunts to the New Territories. She played bridge most afternoons. After a few moments of conversation, Fanny gathered he'd been pretty high up on the ladder and had butted heads with district commissioners on several public works, roads, mostly. Sensing an opportunity, Fanny said, "I'm terribly interested in the house we're living in. You wouldn't know anything about its history, would you? Or do you know anyone who might?"

"Only a few things. I didn't know all the people who lived there, of course. Very good people, the Martins, never skimped on whiskey. Some of the others didn't last as long. Especially right after the war. A problem really, keeping people in the house. A beautiful spot, mind. Quite the thing…view of the sea like that. Something to see with the Union Jack unfurled. I'm not surprised that it suits you. I've seen young people water skiing there fairly recently. Was that you?"

Fanny smiled and tied Caroline's shoe. "Perhaps. I suppose we'd do more of that if we didn't have small children."

"Yes, yes. Well…." He said, "Wish I had a kite with me. I used to come up here with my boys and fly kites. Yours are a bit young, yet. Well, well."

Fanny tried to get him back on track, "Our house?"

"Yes, yes. The only thing I remember of any historical interest about your house was that during the war, bad time that, some Japanese requisitioned it, Kempeitai actually, the worst of a bad lot. Some appalling atrocities, I understand. Not firsthand, of course, having been thrown into a flea pit of a camp myself, but I was told. Probably better off not knowing, wouldn't you say? Tenants at the time were said to have shipped off to an internment camp in the New Territories somewhere. Wife and child got very sick, I heard. No one ever said what happened to them. Nothing would have surprised us. Nasty business."

She should have guessed. Now she'd heard it, it seemed obvious. The ghosts must have been there for over twenty-five years: Kempeitai, the brutal and merciless Japanese military police.

She watched the children. They had taken Caroline's lead and were spinning around and around, their arms above them, showing off for the stranger. She called out to them, "Stop it this minute. You'll get dizzy and be sick. Let's go look at the water and see if we can find some birds to feed our crusts to." She gathered up the papers and cups. "Anytime you'd like to stop over, John, you'd be more than welcome. I'm quite generous with gin myself."

John Carr forced himself up. "Might just take you up on that. Would be good to see the house again. I'd like to meet your husband. Heard a bit about him, actually, interesting young man, I hear. Going places. Well, goodbye, and thanks for the sandwich. Hit the spot."

Fanny watched him walk towards his car. Then she took Drew and Caroline by the hand and walked them towards the water, William following.

That night after dinner, after the children were in bed

and the dishes were done, she and Peter sat out with a couple of brandies. She shared what she'd learned from John Carr. Peter nodded, "I'm not surprised, that explains why they gave us the house. You know, I'm relatively junior to have received such palatial lodgings. I'd assumed it was a sign of good favor, but obviously it was backstabbing trickery. Good work, Fanny, cheers." He lifted his glass and she bounced hers against it. He continued, "Actually, I've been making some inquiries myself. I've decided to get rid of them."

"Get rid of what?"

"Whatever it is that's making people so jumpy. I've arranged for the British government to pay for a Buddhist exorcism right here. With any luck, and enough cumshaw, we ought to be able to get it arranged in a week or two. Then we can get the damn servants back."

The exorcism became Peter's obsession. He thought he'd hit on the only thing that might work and he was determined to have it done properly. As far as Peter and Fanny knew, Buddhist exorcisms weren't often done in European buildings. There were a few, very well publicized exorcisms a few years back, one at the Jockey Club and the other at a government building in Central. The only problem was, that although Peter wanted the servant network and the local Chinese to know about the ridding of the ghosts, his superior, David Mulgrave, agreed to foot the bill on one condition. "For heaven's sake, Ardel-Rhys, keep it out of the English-speaking papers. God knows what sort of stampede of superstitious nonsense we will unleash, not to mention ridicule, unless we keep it muzzled. I'm not only thinking about the department, but you and your family. Fame of this kind is a two-edged sword. These things can get quite out of hand, take it from me. Get it done properly, with the minimum of fuss. I don't want to hear another word about it."

This prohibition put Peter under a great deal of stress. First of all, arranging such an event was a time-consuming, difficult matter and cut into his normal duties. Secondly, the whole purpose of the show, in his opinion, was to get the word out and have people believe that Water Music was cleansed of its ghosts. The idea wasn't to rid the place of ghosts, because he didn't believe in them.

How to keep it all within the confines of the Chinese community? Such a thing was impossible. Servants would tell their masters and word would get out and one way or another he would be in trouble. Because he was Peter, and intent on furthering himself, he had made contacts among the press. Some had even visited for dinner parties. He doubted that they were friends enough to let a good story go if they heard of it. In fact it would anger them that Peter hadn't tipped them off and favors in the future would be sacrificed and all his hard work cultivating them would be in vain. He had to be very careful.

The first thing that Peter did was enlist Ah Fong, who he knew would let it be known among the servants when the threat in the house had diminished. At Ah Fong's recommendation, he hired a spirit-medium from Ting Kau, the closest fishing village. This sing-gung arrived on foot with an entourage of interested old men and women. After messing about for a while, he went into a trance. He confirmed with dramatic gestures and energetic twists and turns of his body the presence of unhappy spirits in the house.

Then Peter arranged the exorcism with the abbot of a small, relatively impoverished monastery outside Yuen Long. Once he had set things in motion, it was impossible to stop them. There was a small chance it wouldn't become a colony-wide sensation. It was in his favor that the house was isolated from the main pulse of Hong Kong, in a place more rural than bustling.

The abbot saw this as a way to aggrandize his monastery. It was clear to him that being asked to do an exorcism was an honor and should be publicized to the fullest. He wanted to wait several months, he said, for an auspicious date. However, it became clear that he also wanted to wait in order to give himself enough time to organize a really impressive spectacle. Peter began to understand why Mulgrave had insisted on a low-key operation when he discovered that the abbot was in the process of recruiting thirty monks from one of the big important monasteries on Lantau to help. Although he put a stop to it in time, it worried him.

He told Fanny, "That was a close shave. I'd envisioned a couple of bony fellows lighting a pot of incense, walking around a bit, saying a few prayers, passing the word and that be that. I had no idea it would create such a palaver." The abbot asked for transportation, and Peter arranged for the monks and their assistants to travel in the back of several veg-etable lorries along Castle Peak Road. Peter and the abbot were to ride in Peter's car driven by Ah Fong up front. The abbot negotiated hard with Peter. He insisted on all sorts of provisions being laid on, and stopping at villages along the way. Peter didn't want them drawing attention to themselves in this way, but gave in when Fanny convinced him that Euro-peans noticing the cavalcade would think it was for a farming or fishing festival that they traveled. Peter's only requirement was that in return for the payment of a hefty sum of money and the providing of food, firecrackers and other essentials, servants would be willing to work in the house again. The abbot assured him that this would be so.

Fanny hadn't told Peter that she didn't believe that the exorcism would work. She felt that whatever it was that the ghosts were doing in the house, they would continue to do until they felt like stopping and no amount of firecrackers and pleading would stop them. On top of it all she wondered if the ghosts were Buddhist, Confucian, ancestor worshipers, or Taoist. If they were Japanese, they might be Shinto, whatever difference that made. She wondered whether Roman Catholic ghosts would leave a house exorcized by Buddhists and decided not. It was more complicated than that. That particular worry need not have concerned her, for as Peter told her later, the Buddhists were not the only ones there. The Taoists didn't want to miss the fun, Peter counted five Taoist monks among the Buddhists and "who knows what else."

On the day, nineteen monks showed up, with as many novices and assistants, and a small crowd of onlookers, mostly drawn from the villages along the way. But there were a few smartly dressed Chinese among them who didn't look like farmers or fishers and were clearly educated and highly interested. Peter was terrified that one of them would whip out a camera and a notebook, but couldn't send them away.

Alan and Jean Meade insisted that Fanny and the children stay with them for the duration of the exorcism, which they'd been told would last three days and two nights. The night before the lorries of monks were due to arrive, Fanny packed suitcases. Peter stood by with a drink in his hand watching. "But Peter, this is the most interesting thing that's happened in years. I don't want to be shunted off to the side. I know these spirits better than anyone. I want to see them leave. Say goodbye or something."

Peter, although anxious that the next day would be a success, was in an unusually good mood. He answered dramatically. "Say goodbye tonight, my friend." When Fanny didn't respond, he modulated his voice, "You're right. This isn't a joking matter. There will be gongs and firecrackers, a lot of them, loud enough to scare off the living and the dead. I'll tell you all about it. You know you've got to take care of the children. I imagine the whole thing will be pretty terrifying, actually."

He took a swig of his drink. "The children don't appear to be nearly as unhinged as their parents by all this." Fanny cursed the gods one more time for giving her three children, instead of the two she'd bargained for. There was always someone willing to take care of two children for you, but three seemed just over the limit of what you could ask of people, no matter how well behaved the children were. More than anything, she wanted to be able to watch the excitement.

As though he could read her mind, Peter said, "You know, you could give the children to my mother for a few days."

"Never," said Fanny, "it's not a good idea." They hadn't told Penelope about the exorcism for fear that she'd let the cat out of the bag at one of her parties and the whole English-speaking world be rapidly informed.

Peter drove Fanny and the children over to the Meades early the next morning. He kissed them goodbye and promised to join them that evening and tell them all about it. So as not to frighten the children, they hadn't explained anything to Caroline except that they were all going to stay with Auntie Jean and Uncle Alan for a few days.

Fanny and Jean and the children walked down to the road from the Meade's driveway when they expected the lorries to be driving by. They only waited about ten minutes before Peter's car, and then the lorries, appeared. Fanny desperately wanted to go watch. As the lorries rumbled by, she got a glimpse of saffron-robed Buddhist monks with amber necklaces, red-robed Taoist monks and several white-robed, gray-bearded characters.

Although Jean and Fanny didn't see much else, they heard

it. From the verandah of Jean and Alan's house, about two miles towards Castle Peak from Water Music, Fanny and Jean could hear the firecrackers all through the afternoon and night. Alan and Peter described later what they didn't hear and see: the candles and incense, the red streamers and gold calligraphy, the gongs beating and the droning chants. He and Alan left the house in the possession of the monks when they returned to the Meades, exhausted at three a.m. Apparently the monks worked in shifts around the clock.

Fanny had been right. After three days and two nights of rigorous work on the part of the monks and their followers, after a sizeable amount of money had exchanged hands, after a layer of thick gray ash was deposited all over the house, the spirits hadn't budged. Fanny knew it at once and knew the sing-gung, spirit-medium, knew it too. He wasn't telling and neither was she. He avoided her stare. He knew she knew. He was, however, in the pay of the abbot, and knew which side of his bread was buttered. He pronounced the house free of spirits and disappeared quickly, to the annoyance of the abbot who wished to exhibit him to the curious. Fanny was surprised that the abbot seemed oblivious to the ghosts, but then she knew he was the business manager of the monastery, not the one closest to the spiritual side of things.

She left the children playing outside with Jean while she wandered through the house in a daze. It was filthy. There were food offerings everywhere, ash, shreds of red paper and candle wax. She was glad they'd rolled up the carpets and locked up their valuables. The house smelt of incense, dried fish and smoke. It permeated the curtains in the bedrooms, it wafted from the pillows in the study. Little piles of hard-boiled eggs, dried flowers and cakes had been left in corners. She knew it had been hopeless. If the servants hadn't wanted to work there before, they wouldn't now.

She decided on a preemptive strike.

She ran outside onto the grass in front of the house where the abbot and Peter were making their goodbyes, hands clasped together, heads bowed and she interrupted. "Peter, just a minute, don't let him go. We need people to clean the house. We need them now."

He threw her an angry look. "For God's sake, Fanny, not now. We will see to that later."

She didn't back off. "No Peter, get him to designate someone now. It's important."

Peter turned to look at her. "No. Absolutely not. It's not his job."

She blinked back her tears. "Then, my dear, you are going to have to clean the house yourself, because if he can't make them, we certainly can't. This was your idea and hasn't helped a bit."

Jean walked over from where she was standing under the trees and took Fanny by the arm. "I'll ask Ah Soh to get all the amahs to help. She'll have an army here cleaning in no time flat."

Fanny said to Jean, "You don't understand. They won't stay. The place is still as haunted as ever."

Jean said, "You don't know that. You're upset, I know. Who wouldn't be? I'm ready for a good strong drink. These are the experts, dear, it must have worked. Come along, children." She gestured to Caroline, Will and Drew who were playing by the goldfish pond.

Jean's amah, Ah Soh and a number of other curious amahs came that afternoon to tidy up. It took them until six to put the house to rights, and, except for the smell, which Fanny didn't think would ever disappear, they did a commendable job. They waxed the parquet floors, they mopped, polished and shined, and then they went home.

Sitting in the study that evening, Peter described it to Fanny. He was pleased with himself. He hadn't spotted anyone from the newspapers, the police or local government. It seemed to have gone off without a hitch. It had been fascinating and a good story to tell his mates when they drank together. He rewarded himself with expensive old brandy that he saved for special occasions.

Fanny sat quietly, listening to his self-congratulation. She thought the ghosts were listening, too. She wondered if they understood English.

七

Being back in Water Music, thinking about the exorcism and its aftermath, left Fanny with a strange echo of her old sickness. Her head felt empty and a little dizzy as it did when she'd attempted something rash and uncharacteristic. Her anger with Peter was immense. Immediate. Black. Perhaps her sickness had been anger, after all. Not hereditary, not a mental defect, just simple anger. When she had suggested this so many years ago Dr. Greenwood had said patronizingly, "Lots of people feel anger, my dear. It is a normal human reaction when things don't go quite your way. But your recent furies aren't normal. It's just not within the scope of what we are used to dealing with. It's antisocial. That's why we think you need a bit of a rest. Think of it as a change."

She felt herself getting as angry again here and now. A familiar, not altogether unwelcome, anger building up in her, layer upon layer, like sedimentary rock in her head. Why hadn't she felt this rage in between? With Rider, it never surfaced. Her head never felt light. Her movements were never unpredictable and rash. Sometimes she was angry with him, furious, even, but never like this. No matter what frustrations she encountered with clients or employees at work. With Rider

,with her new life, she'd never been as angry as she was today, standing alone in Water Music. She'd only felt like this before she left.

Fanny tried to open the study door again. It wouldn't budge. She leaned on it and kicked, venting her fury on the door. Then, she gave up. She took deep breaths. She lowered herself onto the cool tiled floor, forgetting insects, snakes and rats, not caring how dirty the back of her jeans became. Her anger subsided in waves.

One night, remarkable because it was so unusual, Peter had talked to her about his work. He'd been working late in his study, reading reports, making corrections. Fanny came and sat with him, and when he was finished with his reports, he put down his glasses and talked to her. One of his men had been killed when he'd discovered, completely by accident, a triad-run heroin refinery. To top it all off, Julia Wo had come to see him. Her mother-in-law had made life horrible for her and, according to the old ways, demanded obedience and grandchildren. Julia, who had tasted freedom at the district office, was rebellious and hadn't, despite foul-tasting potions and petitions to the Gods, conceived children. Jimmy took his mother's side against her.

Julia had come to Peter to ask him to intercede for her. She wanted a divorce. Peter didn't feel he could possibly help her, for fear of reprisals from Jimmy's influential family whose goodwill he counted on.

Peter shook his head, "I can't possibly interfere in the machinations of such a family. He defied his family to marry her in the first place. Besides divorce is unheard of. Under Chinese law, only a man can seek divorce."

Fanny thought of her own mother-in-law and felt desperately sorry for the girl she had named. Nevertheless, she didn't yet see her own situation as desperate as Julia's.

One evening he invited the Grahams, the Taylors, and the visiting double-barreled Chelmsford couple for drinks without even asking her. She'd had the children underfoot all day, the house was a mess, the air was still and hot and he expected her to cleanup both the house, herself and the children and serve chilled, perfectly-made cocktails with cocktail snacks. He went upstairs to cool himself down with a shower. Fanny retreated into the kitchen and ransacked the cupboards and refrigerator for cheese and biscuits, which she put on a platter with grapes she had intended as a treat for the children. She emptied peanuts into glass bowls and placed clean glasses on a tray. When the doorbell rang, she was busy picking up Matchbox cars from the floor and puffing up cushions. Peter came down the stairs, three stairs at a time, fresh in khaki shorts and white shirt she'd ironed only that morning.

He'd come into the kitchen a few moments later to ask her to join them and was furious that she hadn't changed her clothes, the kitchen such a dreadful mess, the children were disheveled, noisy and in the way. "Bloody hell woman, you look like something dragged out of the gutter. Get these children under control and into bed, and put some decent clothes on while I act as host."

As there was no babysitter to be had, that night Peter went out to the floating restaurant for dinner with the Grahams, Taylors and double-barrels from Chelmsford. Fanny stayed home with the children. Mary Graham did offer to stay with Fanny, but Peter talked her out of it. "Oh, Fanny will be all right. There's plenty here for her to do."

Sad and left out, Fanny cried for most of that evening, tears falling as she washed the glasses the guests had left behind. So many glasses. She nibbled at bits of cheese left on the plates. She would never be able to please Peter. She slumped over the kitchen counter and banged her head against it until

it throbbed. She blacked out. She'd woken up there on the
floor much later, and, when she dragged herself to bed, she
found Peter already asleep.

A smell of fungus and forest rot permeated her memories
and swept her back to Water Music and its dilapidation.

Fanny returned upstairs using the concrete servants' staircase steps. It had fared better than the wooden staircase at
the front of the house. She considered leaving her hotel room
and camping in the deserted house for the rest of her stay.

It wasn't really an impractical idea, she thought. It would
save on hotel bills, she would be where she wanted to be, she
would be out of the way of destructive forces like alcohol,
and intrusive forces like the telephone. She wouldn't have to
see Peter. She discarded the idea. It would be regarded by
everyone else in the world as crazy not to mention illegal.

She wanted to be able to return to Water Music, so didn't
want to alert the family living outside that she'd visited. She
listened at the bedroom door to see if they had returned to
their living quarters. She couldn't hear much. She set the
broom against the wall in the bedroom.

She opened the door from her old bedroom and slipped
outside onto the rock patio. Only from one point up there
could she see or be seen from the servants' area. She sat cross-
legged in the sun, taking care to stay out of sight, leaning
against the house, plotting her next maneuver.

The house had clearly been condemned. It was unthink-
able that in this property boom, and in such a prime location,
it would be left vacant for much longer, even if the view had
been ruined. Whoever built here wouldn't have to live here.
It could be sold to some unsuspecting person before the ghosts
were discovered, but she knew it was common in Hong Kong

to have a feng shui expert inspect a house before its purchase, the way they would have a termite inspection or a radon inspection in New York. The experts had said the main entrance of the house should face the sea, not the road, and the driveway should wind around there. The sea at the back of the house dragged the life force or ch'i from the house. The rock on the side of the house was a dragon, not guarding the house as dragons normally do, but overpowering the house, breathing noxious fumes into it. Feng shui practitioners (Peter had consulted several after the exorcism failed) told him that the house was obviously designed for Europeans by Europeans who didn't know any better.

A high, excited child's voice squealed outside. It reminded Fanny that she wasn't alone. She needed to think about the family living below. Who were these guardians of Water Music? Paid caretakers or squatters taking advantage of others' fear of the place? How could she find out? If they lived there illegally, her visits would be ignored. If they were squatters, wouldn't they go the whole hog and live in the house? If they were caretakers, why would they be willing to live here if no one else would? Weren't they frightened?

She smelled fish cooking. Although the whiff wasn't appetizing, her stomach tightened and her mouth tasted dry and dirty. She had had anything to eat or drink all day. Tap water would be unsafe. There were three things she'd forgotten: food, water and a flashlight. The sun was up behind the road now, pink and gold. Her watch read three. Although it wouldn't be night for a while, it was time to be setting off home to the hotel. Except this felt like home to her.

Getting down the rock slope proved harder than climbing up it had been. She clutched bushes and slid, her shoes tearing at the roots. Reaching the bottom, she dislodged a patch of sandy soil that slid down with her in a crash, leaving evidence in front of the trees that someone had been there. She stood still for a few moments listening, but nothing moved around her except the tops of the pine trees in a wispy breeze. A cuckoo pecked at a dead cricket. She kicked the soil back. She realized she was ravenous.

The panoramic view of the destruction of Tsing Ye Island and the building of the bridge forced her attention away from her hunger. Barges chugged back and forth as a hydrofoil zipped by. This patch of the South China Sea was never this busy when she'd lived here. The only hydrofoil in use then was the one to Macao and it didn't pass this way. Years ago, only fishing boats, oil tankers and rusty old water tankers from China motored through these waters. There wasn't one fishing junk or sampan in sight. Just boats in the business of construction, earth moving and human transportation.

She ducked around the side of the house through the bamboo and onto the road, and trudged along the hot asphalt in the direction of Tsuen Wan. She'd sometimes done this in the old days, when the road had been busier. After she had walked about half a mile, a pak pai with a red stripe down the middle drove by. She waved her arms at it self-consciously. It stopped for her. The driver gave her a leering smile. She handed him five dollars without looking at him directly. She'd learned that trick in New York. When he didn't give her change or ask for more, she walked back around plastic bags filled with vegetables and sat down next to a young woman in black pajamas who made it clear, by the way she shifted in her seat and turned away, that Fanny was unwelcome. But Fanny didn't care. She was worn out.

When the van reached Tsuen Wan, she walked to the nearest grocery stall. The proprietor's son was practicing his calligraphy in an exercise book lined in squares. Fanny scanned the dusty shelves and pointed out a package of dried beef,

some Peek Freans Rich Tea Biscuits and a 7-Up. They didn't
sell bottled water. She ate the beef and biscuits steadily, one
by one. Then she bought another 7-Up. There was nowhere
to sit, but she didn't care. If she sat, she thought, she'd never
be able to stand up again. She leaned against a dirty postered
wall, exhausted and still thirsty. She wanted to see Rider and
the children, to hug them. She wanted to go home and forget
she had come. But it was real now, her memory exposed,
ready for serious analysis. She hoped she had the courage.
She bought a string bag of six California oranges and walked
towards the Metro.

Sarah and Nigel would really like living at Water Music.
They would appreciate being so close to the beach, the goldfish and the sun. Rider had like the house, too. The times he
had visited there he had been mesmerized by the grandeur of
it all.

The first time Rider had visited, she had invited him, Dr.
Greenwood and Lily Chen from the hospital. She wanted to
repay their kindness after her breakdown. Peter discouraged
the party, irritated to be reminded of Fanny's infirmity. "One
just doesn't invite doctors and nurses to one's house." Fanny
ignored him. She missed the hospital. She missed being cared
for so closely. She wondered if Peter resented her being the
center of attention. She'd begun to assert herself in small
ways after leaving the hospital.

Fanny tried to make the evening special. She'd invited
the Meades because Jean had come to see her in the hospital
once or twice and had met Dr. Greenwood and Lily. Her
other friends hadn't come to see her. She suspected they'd
been repulsed by her incarceration. Jean wasn't afraid. She'd
brought flowers, books, and grapes. Still Fanny measured Jean's
friendship and thought it had diminished. She hadn't told Jean
about Rider.

She didn't yet know she was in love with him. He said later that he'd been in love with her almost from the start. She was amazed to hear that it was possible for someone to be completely head over heels in love with you and you not know it. Also, that anyone could have fallen in love with her who knew her so well, who had seen her first at her pathetic worst. That, of course, was part of her appeal to Rider. He had found her broken and helped mend her. He liked delving into her complicated insecurities. He told her she was a "nice" person.

A "nice" person. She contemplated that. She'd had a teacher when she'd been about nine who'd told her never to use the word nice." "It doesn't mean anything. It's not specific enough." She presumed that by "nice," Rider meant that she was a bland person in a pleasant sort of a way. He knew everything there was to know, and he still liked her. Certainly, by then, he knew her much better than Peter did.

That night, at the party, Rider was different. Meek almost. Peter intimidated him. Peter liked intimidating him. Peter had identified Rider as a threat long before that evening and his usual suave, charming reserve had evaporated into sarcasm. More than one person remarked on it. Jean asked him, "Are you feeling a little off-color?"

Fanny tried to deflect his attention, but she only made it worse. He mocked psychiatrists, calling them worthless and demeaning, pseudo-doctors, penis-obsessed. He belittled Americans. He talked incessantly about them not being able to manage their own affairs and meddling in governments that were none of their business. It was August 1968, so he had ample ammunition. He droned on about assassinated Kennedys, race riots, student riots, and the war in Vietnam.

Lily Chen, straight-laced, American-educated, and a matron at the hospital, made several attempts to defend Rider.

Fanny thought Lily was a little in love with him. Dr. Green-wood got thoroughly drunk and ignored the whole business. He was too old and too jaded to pay any attention to Peter's slights and, anyway, probably shared some of Peter's preju-dices. Fanny tried to take Rider aside and change the subject, but her attentions only irritated Peter further.

The guests left soon after dinner.

Dr Greenwood discussed it with Fanny at their next meeting. "I'm not sure why he was as rude as that. William Rider is a good chap even if he weighs in a little more heavily than he ought on the sentimental side. Ardel-Rhys on the other hand…I know he's your husband, but can we talk frankly?" He glanced at Fanny and scratched his chin, "…Bloody minded, if you don't mind me saying so. Honor and obey, what. Stuff and nonsense. Think I'm a bit more sympathetic to your dilemma, my girl. Though I suppose what you've got to do is grin and bear it. I don't take sides in these matters, you know…husband and wife, and all that."

Fanny thought he was trying to say that Peter didn't love her.

Jean knew it, too and on one of her rare visits, she bluntly said so. "Sometimes I just want to bash his stubborn idiotic head in. He has no idea how lucky he is. You've put up with a lion's share, with no thanks from him, ignoring what cannot be ignored. He has no business running around with other women while you are coping valiantly at home under such adverse conditions."

She had never alluded to Peter's unfaithfulness before.

Fanny had known about Peter's other women long be-fore her illness, even before Caroline had been born, before they'd moved to Water Music.

First there was Ellie—Eleanor McGrath. Fanny worried for months before she met Ellie. She knew her by reputation. Acquaintances on the Peak said, "She's a horsewoman," or "She has a flair," and, worst of all, "She's the best tennis player out here in years." Peter worked with her husband sometimes.

Peter never withdrew his affection from Fanny during his dalliances. She learned the truth in an instant at a diplomatic function. The Governor was there and Eleanor with her husband. Peter, in formal dress, smooth and aristocratic, never behaved skittishly. When he saw Eleanor, he'd flushed very slightly, leaned towards her, took her hand and kissed it in an intimate, teasing way. No one would have noticed but his wife.

How could Fanny compete with Ellie? They were as different from each other as a mountain and a tree. Fanny felt small and insignificant beside Eleanor.

Fanny had herself invited to places she thought Eleanor would haunt. The Ladies Recreation Club. Peter played tennis there twice weekly before they'd moved to the New Territories. Fanny never played. Her tennis lessons had not been a success. Then when she found out that Peter was partnering Eleanor in mixed doubles, she began to worry in earnest. She watched the match, drinking gin and tonics in the shade, not caring who saw her. She evaluated Eleanor stalking out onto the court, her long brown legs gleaming in the sun. She'd borne three children without any sign of it. Eleanor never seemed to sweat, and Fanny sweated just watching her.

Fanny couldn't find a strategy that made her feel better. She made an effort to make friends with Eleanor and asked her to lunch. Eleanor answered, "I'm sure it would be very nice, but we have so little in common. What would we talk about?" Fanny didn't say what leapt to mind: Peter. Peter.

Peter.

When they first moved to Water Music, Peter would pretend to have visited distant villages, but Fanny found out that
he'd not been working at all, that he'd gone to the Island to
play tennis with Ellie.

Some afternoons when Fanny was trapped in the house
with the children, she would dial the McGrath's number on
the telephone and then hang up if someone answered. She
tried to keep it to herself, but failed. She asked Alice, who
played a lot of tennis, to find things out. Where was Eleanor
from, exactly? What kind of perfume did she wear? She found
herself following Eleanor around Shui Hing one afternoon,
past the French silk scarves, the stockings, the housewares.
She watched her purchase a can opener.

Then, one day, she realized it was over. She could account for Peter's every movement. No one talked about
Eleanor any more. Peter stopped going to the Island to play
tennis. Fanny relaxed. The affair had lasted nearly two years.

Genevieve Maurier appeared on the scene six months
later. She was French and wore tailored suits with matching
handbags and shoes, her blonde hair tied back tightly with a
black velvet ribbon. Fanny estimated she was at least ten years
older than Peter. She had two studious teenage children, a boy
and girl, who both spoke four European languages fluently.
She had a courteous amah and an intimidating French chef.
She lived in an immaculate, whitewashed house on Kadoorie
Avenue with a boring banker husband, Jacques, who was even
older, and didn't look as well-kept as the rest of them. He had
a paunch and a bald spot, and always wore monogrammed
shirts and loud Hermes ties.

This time Fanny didn't follow Genevieve, but she confronted Peter after a dinner party at the Maurier's. He and
Genevieve had sat next to each other and, engrossed in quiet

conversation, had ignored the rest of the party. Peter drove home through the hot and humid, rainy night. He and Fanny had both had too much to drink. "What on earth do you see in her?" Fanny asked.

"Who do you mean?" He didn't turn to look at her.

"You flirted with her all night. Don't deny it, Peter, for God's sake. Are you in love with her?" Fanny rolled down the car window and felt the warm rain splash on her face. She watched it change the color of the silk sleeve of her dress.

He still ignored her, pretending to concentrate on driving.

If she hadn't had so much to drink, she might have controlled herself, but thunderous sobs of self-pity shook her. Peter drove about five minutes longer, staring straight ahead at the road, and then he pulled the car over into a bus stop.

He leaned over, turned Fanny towards him, pushed her hair out of her eyes, took her face between his hands and kissed her on the forehead. "Don't be jealous, darling. It's nothing. Nothing at all. I just think the French are fascinating."

Fanny sobbed, "Why can't you be more discreet?"

He answered seriously, "Remember this. I could have married any number of women. I chose you and I would choose you again. This is just the way men are."

"All men are not like this."

"Yes, they are," he laughed, "Take it from me."

Fanny couldn't stop her tears, "I want you to love me. I want to be fascinating."

He laughed. "I know you too well for you to be fascinating to me now. Cheer up. It'll blow over before you know it. Right as rain." He straightened back up and started the car up again. He smiled, "For a start, Jacques thinks you're fascinating."

Fanny didn't pursue it farther. She was sure Jacques didn't find her any more fascinating than she found him, but she let herself be pacified.

Occasionally she'd cry herself to sleep after an evening when Peter had slipped up and used an unfamiliar French phrase, or talked about French wines she'd never heard of, but she gradually trained herself to ignore it. It didn't mean that she liked it better, just that she came closer to accepting it. He'd said "it's nothing, nothing at all" and "over soon." That was at least something. He wouldn't leave her. It was considered bad form to leave your wife without provocation. She told herself, "It could be worse." She wasn't sure who else suspected and she never discussed it with anyone.

She bought herself a bell-bottomed, psychedelic, fluorescent-swirled catsuit which zippered up the front. Peter hated it. She wanted to dazzle. He didn't want a dazzling wife. When she wore it one evening, he said, "Take that bloody thing off. What's the matter with you? You look ridiculous. It's not the sort of thing that the mother of three children wears."

She refused. He finished his drink, walked out to the car, and didn't come home until the following night.

Carla and Roberto, a well-shod, leather-clad Italian couple, joined their circle of friends. Fanny knew immediately when Peter started romancing Carla. It was after Roberto had issued the declaration, "Women exist merely for man's pleasure." Carla had giggled, flipped her short glossy brown hair out of her eyes, and lisped, "'E is tooo see-llee." About that time Peter gave up French wines for Italian, and mysteriously acquired some wide Italian silk ties. The affair didn't last more than a few months. Fanny got some satisfaction thinking that Carla hadn't lived up to her billing when Peter went back to French wines and the ties disappeared.

Several others came and went but none lasted nearly as

long as Eleanor had.

Later, after the servants left, Ann, the extremely bored seventeen-year-old daughter of the Grahams, offered to help Fanny take care of the children every now and then. Fanny welcomed the relief. She had to admit that Ann handled the children well. They loved her and behaved for her. She matched their moods, had endless patience for them. She spoke their language and coddled them. She tumbled with them and went on picnics with them. Fanny found herself becoming dependent on her and disliked her for it.

Fanny liked her even less when Ann, always a little boy crazy, fell wildly in love with Peter. Alan Meade joked about it. Fanny knew that Peter, although flattered, did nothing to encourage her. Ann was too young and too in love to be subtle, or even interesting, to him. She followed Peter around. She bought him presents and she made no secret of her jealousy of Fanny. She wore revealing bikinis when she thought Peter might be there to see her. When Fanny went into the hospital, Ann volunteered, and was hired by Peter, to stay with the children.

Discovering Peter's affairs hadn't happened the way it does in films. She never caught him kissing or ever surprised him in bed with someone else. The worst she ever saw was a glance here and there, secret smiles, jokes. She knew for sure from the smell of the other women, and his heavy-handed use of aftershave. She timed Peter's movements, trying to find him during the day, catching him in lies about his whereabouts. She tried to imagine, but never found out, where he met these women—a flat somewhere? It couldn't have been the office where he worked because it was too peopled and public. It couldn't have even been the New Territories, because Westerners stood out noticeably. Word could get back. If they met in a hotel room in Kowloon or Hong Kong, the money would have to be accounted for. Fanny saw all the statements from the bank. She knew how they spent his salary down to the last penny. So when Fanny saw how jealous Peter was of Rider, she was surprised. Sometimes Fanny thought that she had fallen in love with Rider of all people because Peter was jealous of him. It was hard for her to understand Peter's double standard. After all, he had freely helped himself to other people's wives.

Seated on the MTR, barreling through the tunnels carved under the streets of Lai Chi Kok, Fanny's thoughts of Rider wound their way back to Sarah and Nigel. She was glad she hadn't succumbed to Water Music's temptation and her self-preservation instincts hadn't failed. She concentrated on her life in New York. Sarah was so sensible, so much like Rider in looks and personality, redheaded and stable. Nigel was like her, Fanny, temperamental and highly-strung. She thought too about the studio. How far away work seemed now. She glanced over a suited man's shoulder. Instead of reading the Cantonese newspaper she expected, he was reading an American industrial trade magazine, *New Equipment Digest*, tabloid size. She'd actually placed advertising for a client in it. She had been thinking of expanding the studio into a full-blown advertising agency. She thought that she knew enough now. The anger in her had diffused, and though tired, she was sane.

As soon as she got back into her cool, tidy hotel room, Fanny stepped out of her clothes and into the shower. Feeling the warm water wash away the dirt of Water Music, she hummed. She hadn't been discovered. She knew how to get there without anyone knowing and she could be there alone. She could go back anytime. She hadn't gone mad. She hadn't stayed there. She had survived.

She dried herself off using every towel in the rack. The phone rang. It was Jean.

"Blast it, Fanny, I've been ringing all day. Where have you been? Have you been seeing anyone?"

"No. Just delving into the past, and, amazingly enough, surviving it intact."

"Don't be so cryptic. Did you see Peter?"

Fanny stood on the carpet, stark naked, and felt herself start to shake. First a tremor, then a serious teeth-chattering coldness. "No, of course not."

"I didn't think he was that devious. I just so happened to bump into him today at the Hong Kong Club. I went on and on about how marvelous you look and what a businesswoman you are and how there mustn't be any hard feelings. Everything has turned out for the best which it always does in the end, doesn't it?"

Fanny's teeth were chattering so fast, she could hardly speak.

"I say, are you all right? You sound awful. What's wrong?"

"I just got out of the shower and the airconditioning is blowing on me. I'm freezing to death. Hang on."

Fanny lay the phone down on the bedspread and ran to the closet. A pair of sweat pants and a blue stone-washed sweatshirt were on top. She pulled them on, not caring which was the front or back. She paused for a moment before picking up the receiver. "OK, I'm back. I'm slightly warmer. How did he react?" It was like talking with Jean years ago. It was difficult for Fanny to remember that she had to be careful. She used to trust Jean—and didn't know how she felt now.

"I knew he was surprised, but he took care not to show much of a reaction. He changed the subject. Let him think about it. After all, everything has turned out for the best, hasn't it dear?"

Fanny hardly knew how to answer. She didn't philosophically agree that everything always turns out all right in the end. Mostly in her experience, it didn't.

Jean continued, "I rang Will. You see, I suspect he's the one who put Caroline up to contacting you. He wasn't a bit surprised you've come back and he's desperate to see you. He's invited us to dinner at the golf club tonight. He wants you to come to his flat for Easter lunch, tomorrow. He's inviting Peter and Ann. Peter's always so busy. He might have to go off to Beijing at the beginning of the week, so it's probably your best opportunity."

Fanny blurted, "I'm not sure I want to see him. Are you sure he's so anxious to see me?"

"They all are, positive. Curiosity probably. I can't wait for you to see what Ann has turned into. You won't be jealous at all."

"Jealous?"

"Weren't you simply green-eyed about Ann? So young and dewy-eyed? She's had everything money can buy. She's years younger than he is. She's an efficient housekeeper and hostess, but, God, she has absolutely no sense of humor. Never sees the light at the end of the tunnel. Everything's uphill. She's always worried and it's aged her. Of course, Peter hasn't ever noticed. Remember how you used to say that he treated you like a piece of furniture? Nothing has changed. She doesn't object as strenuously as you did. I doubt he's ever taken a good look at her in all these years. I am rambling on. How was your journey down memory lane?"

"I don't know. I don't know. Tonight is awfully soon. I

think I'd rather see Will alone."

"Alone?" Jean seemed finally silenced. There was a long pause.

Fanny tried to explain. "You see, it's so embarrassing. I'll probably cry. I know I will. I have things I want to say to him. Don't you understand? It would be excruciating for Alan to watch me cry."

"Oh! If that's what you're worried about, don't. Alan's used to dealing with crying females." Jean paused a moment and then said, "William wants us to be there. He said specifically that he wanted us there. We don't really want to get in the way, and we will leave gracefully if it's appropriate, but I honestly can't let Will down."

Another silence hung between them.

Fanny broke it. "That's not all that's worrying me. If I have to see Peter, I think I'd rather meet him on his own, at least at first. Ann will just muddle everything up. She'll be protective and petty—that will only confuse things."

Jean sighed. "I'll give you his telephone numbers, but he's terribly busy. He won't be in the office now. It's Saturday night. Just a mo…here it is." She gave Fanny the number. "He'll be home and you'll have to speak to Ann. I'm sure it's worse than trying to reach the Prime Minister. You're up against newspapers, favor seekers, and so on."

"Don't worry," Fanny said. "I might not ring at all."

Jean responded. "By the way, in case I forget to tell you later, if you're at a loose end on Monday, come with me. I've ordered some furniture from a little shop off Canton Road, so I'll be coming over to Kowloon side. I'll pick you up and we can make a day of it. There's a top-secret factory where they make Ralph Lauren trousers. The most gorgeous stuff, dirt cheap. No ifs, ands, or buts."

"I've tonight and tomorrow to get through first." She

couldn't think of anything else to say. She was exhausted again. She said she'd take a taxi to the golf club, said goodbye and replaced the receiver.

Hadn't she felt lonely traveling back on the MTR? Hadn't she wanted company? Now that she had no choice, she didn't want it at all.

八

Although Fanny decided to arrive early, she dreaded her dinner with the Meades and Will. By six o'clock, she'd ridden the Star Ferry and walked over to the buses at Exchange Square. She boarded the air-conditioned #6 marked STANLEY via REPULSE BAY.

She'd worried about how to dress for the evening and had decided on a comfortable, conservative navy blue dress with gold buttons she often wore to work. Now it didn't seem special enough. Should she have chosen her tan skirt with a jacket? Should she have worn her turquoise pants, embroidered blouse and Zuni jewelry? What about her shoes? This would be Will's first impression of her. He would relay it to Peter, and probably to Caroline, and definitely Andrew. There was still time to get off the bus, go back to the hotel, change and not be late. She forced herself to relax. She told herself that Will would expect his mother to look like a fifty-year-old woman, not a fashion plate. Ann, no doubt, always looked stunning. Hadn't Jean said something about that? When Fanny had seen Ann last, Ann had been eighteen. Even Caroline was older than that now.

The bus traversed roads from Fanny's former life. She recognized blocks of flats, gardens, and garages. She and Pe-

ter had enjoyed good times before Water Music, before the
children were born. Peter had been different then. Still driven
by his desire to succeed, but willing to waste time hiking with
her, exploring little known paths on the hillsides.

She stepped of the bus at the eastern end of Deep Water Bay and looked at her watch—quarter to seven. The
evening had remained warm. Children played in the sand.
She crossed the road and walked on the path by the beach.
Her stomach turned over and over; surges of anticipation
knotted her shoulders, arms, and legs. She tried to overcome
her panic. She was hoping for too much from this meeting
and wanted it to be over. In four hours, she thought, I'll know.

The beach looked cleaner than when she'd lived there,
and more crowded, even for an April evening, the night before Easter. Not that Easter mattered here. When China took
over, Easter wouldn't exist at all.

Fanny hardly recognized the Royal Hong Kong Golf
Club. It had been a handsome, dowdy old building in need of
repair, not used for much other than the bar and showers.
Now it loomed bigger, glossier, bustling and surprisingly modern. Nothing ever stayed the same in Hong Kong. She watched
a steady stream of expensive cars arrive. She was amazed to
see well-dressed Chinese stepping out. Twenty years before,
Chinese were few and far between in this place, rarely, if ever,
invited to membership. Fanny smiled to herself—some things
had changed for the better.

She looked at her watch: seven p.m., still half an hour
early. Her insides played a jig, invisible fingers clutched inside
her throat. She nodded boldly to the doorman, who hardly
glanced at her as he opened a car door for a dark-stockinged
woman. Fanny entered.

The skeleton of the lovely old colonial building remained,
but around it glass doors, new floors and ceilings had been

erected. She no longer belonged here. Walking through the hallways, she expected to be challenged by an officious sentinel, but no such thing happened. No one tossed her a glance. She wondered if she had become invisible. She had worn the right costume after all.

She walked a few steps through the hall to the bar. The golf course had been closed for the evening and a driving range set up and floodlit, in full view of the bar. She sat down at an empty table and watched. A white-jacketed waiter hurried up and asked for her order. She told him that she was waiting for someone and would pass. The tightening of his lips and the twist of his expression gave Fanny the full brunt of his disapproval without his having to say a word to her. He didn't ask her to leave though, or wait outside, so she put her handbag on the floor next to her and tried to concentrate on breathing steadily to calm her nerves.

Voices to her right intruded on her worries. She turned to see three young men at the bar, dressed as though they had come from the office, even though this was Saturday. Yuppies, Fanny thought; they even have them here. She was startled to hear the tallest one say, "She walked right out with her doctor, if you don't mind. Absconded and left the three of us quite small children to fend for ourselves in a haunted house. Still mad as a hatter, I shouldn't wonder. Fucked us all over. Poor Dad, it was quite a humiliation. Not quite sure how he managed, really. Married Ann soon after, silly cow."

His much smaller dark-haired companion loosened his tie and said, "My word, what a story. I'd no idea Peter had such a comeuppance. Now you say it, I do remember my parents saying something about it. The bets were on that you'd have a stepmother the minute the divorce came through. They didn't guess it would be Ann, though. There was speculation about an Italian woman or a French one, I can't remember."

The original speaker poured the rest of a bottle of beer into his glass with a flourish. "So, boys, that's what I'm doing for dinner tonight. Top that or I win." He grinned at the other two.

"Can't," said the small dark-haired young man. "I'm meeting Sophie."

"Neither can I," said the other and took a swig of his beer. "You win. We pay tonight."

Will continued, "The sentimental reunion…mother and son. I'm supposed to ring Drew and my sister as soon as it's over and report fully. My sister says I've to ring England any time day or night. This mother of mine is arriving here under protection of the Meades. Not quite sure what Jean thinks I'll do to her. Supposed to be here half past seven. Stay, and meet her, fellas. Ten minutes to go. I can't imagine what this is going to be like. What an ordeal, as if the early part of the day wasn't bad enough. I do hope she turns out all right. It would be awful if she's cuckoo."

Fanny was slightly relieved. He didn't know the worst; he just knew she'd abandoned him. It was now or never. The longer she left it, the more chance that she'd panic and leave. She had to get it over with and confront him. He had expressed no other desire than that she be sane. If he'd have wanted her to be extraordinary, she could never have managed it. No matter what happened, she was determined to prove to herself that she could handle meeting him. She stood up dizzy-headed, took a deep breath, walked over to the bar, put out her hand on Will's arm and said, "I'm your mother and reasonably sane." As he turned, her numbed mind asked her: what if he isn't your son? What if you imagined the conversation you just heard?

Will stood up so quickly that he startled people at the tables around by knocking over his bar stool. He blushed, then bent and picked it up with one athletic twist of his arm. "M...most embarrassing," he stuttered.

His companions sat immobile and stared at Fanny. She smiled at them in turn, and, as graciously as she knew how, put her hand forward to shake theirs, "Francis Rider, formerly Ardel-Rhys." The words came automatically, not at all expressing the hysteria that raced through her. It's my English training, she thought. The young men introduced themselves in turn. The dark-haired one as Roger Cormick and the sandy haired one with the loosened tie as "Bill McPherson, pleased to meet you."

Fanny nodded her head, "I think I used to know your mother, quite a tennis player. How is she?"

Bill had paled, but he answered with composure, "Very well. I'll tell her you remembered her."

"Please do." Fanny turned her attention to her son. "Is there somewhere we can talk quietly before the Meades get here?"

Will shrugged his shoulders, clearly dumbfounded. He looked over to his companions for help. They ignored him.

Fanny knew she'd seized the advantage. "No matter. They'll be here any minute." Tears rolled down her cheeks in spite of her need to be strong. She took Will's hand. "My darling boy, you're so tall. I don't know what I expected."

He grimaced. "You're younger than I expected. You don't look a bit unbalanced." He smiled. "Are you going to shatter all the myths of my childhood?"

Relief flooded Fanny and she concentrated on relaxing her tense muscles. He didn't seem to hate her, or even appear angry. He had survived anyway. He looked as overconfident as any other young man who has never known real difficulties. She allowed the question to gust through her: how different would he be if she had stayed? Would he have had that confidence? Would he have lived to be standing there? What could she tell him about it anyway? "I don't want to shatter anything. I want to get to know you."

He didn't answer and looked around to his friends for support. They were tactfully discussing restaurant choices with each other, no longer involving themselves in his affairs. He said to Fanny, "Could I buy you a drink?"

"I'd buy you one, but I'm not a member any more. Actually, I don't need a drink. I'd rather get to know you sober."

"Well, I need one," said Will and he ordered another San Mig, which he downed quickly. He pulled a package of Benson & Hedges out of his jacket pocket and offered one to his mother.

"I don't smoke," she said stifling the urge to say, and you shouldn't either, cigarettes aren't good for you. She didn't have that right yet. She mustn't make that kind of mistake with him.

Jean and Alan Meade appeared next to them. Jean spoke first, "So you've met. Was it as bad as either of you thought?"

"Worse," said Will.

"Better," said Fanny at the same moment.

They all laughed artificial, stilted laughs. Alan said, "We've a table waiting upstairs."

As he stubbed out his cigarette, Will invited his friends to join the party. Fanny was sorry that they had the good sense to overcome their curiosity and refuse. She thought that any diversion would be a good thing.

Alan, Jean, Will, and Fanny walked upstairs to a dining room that bore no resemblance to the old golf club. Fanny couldn't stop the tears pouring down her face. She needed a quiet place to sob. The others pretended not to notice, but Jean slipped her a packet of tissues. An efficient older man seated them at a small round table.

Will, who seemed to be Alan's student in these things, insisted that Alan help him choose wines. Much as she needed a drink, Fanny refused it. At least her tears had stopped. All she could think about was her son. She just wanted to stare at him. So much like Peter had been at his age. Not just confident and well spoken, but commanding, too. Once he regained his equilibrium, he didn't lose it. She couldn't decide whether she would have recognized him. His eyes were the same. She hated it that she couldn't remember him as a small child. She could only picture little Nigel, who was quite different, small-boned, quiet.

Fanny wasn't called upon to talk much during the dinner. Alan and Will ordered a Chinese meal that Fanny couldn't have described later. She knew she liked what she'd eaten: shrimp, chicken and grouper, spring onions, bok choy, peppers and sprouts, some noodles and rice; but it all melded together. Will, in his desire to impress and please, told stories of school and work. He explained his suit by saying that he had been working this very day, trying to close a deal that had fallen through at the last moment, for complicated reasons involving stock transfers, bribery, and Taiwan law. His conversation steered clear of the rest of the family. Fanny couldn't bring herself to ask, no matter how much she wanted to.

Towards the end of the meal, Will surprised Fanny by asking, "Are you going to invite me to America? Am I going to meet your new family?"

"Come anytime. I want you to meet them. It's your family, too," Fanny replied, though she didn't really believe it.

"Is it really?" He arched an eyebrow. Then he lit another cigarette and launched into a description of the last holiday he had taken in Indonesia, which had nothing whatsoever with the question he'd asked.

Will signed for the meal, and said he'd drive Fanny back

to the hotel. As Jean kissed Fanny goodbye, she said, "Isn't he simply gorgeous?"

Fanny nodded. Her head spun. Her anxieties were only slightly relieved and tiredness overwhelmed her.

Will retrieved his red BMW from the car park. The evening had become very cool. Fanny shivered. As he drove onto the street, Fanny said, "Is there anything you'd like to ask me?"

He said, "No, I don't think so…. Well, yes, there is. Why didn't your husband come with you?"

"Because I didn't want him to complicate things. Is that all you want to know?"

"Yes. That's all." He reached into a side pocket on the door and fished out a cigarette, which he lit.

Cigarette smoke in the car suffocated Fanny. She had lost a lucrative design client by refusing to travel around with him in a smoke-filled car. She pressed the button and opened her window. Cool air brushed her face. She spoke into the night loudly enough that he could hear her. "So what are you going to report back to Drew and Caroline?"

He turned to look at her, and the car swerved slightly. Before she thought better of it she said, "Keep your eyes on the road."

He snapped, " I don't take orders from you."

The lights on the hillside flashed by. Fanny couldn't read the speedometer, but knew he was driving too fast. She said, "Sorry." He reminded her so much of Peter. His control. He must be upset. His insides must be churning. He wouldn't have said that otherwise. She wondered if the girl that he eventually married would go mad and leave him.

He turned off the air-conditioning and opened his window. "No, I'm sorry. You asked me what I'm to say to Drew and Line? Well, I'll tell them what I think."

Fanny knew it was rash to ask, but couldn't resist. "What do you think?"

Will shrugged, and said very quickly, "That you are as sane as I am and I still have no idea why you left my father, who is, without a doubt, one of the greatest men to ever live, and left your children who loved you as much as small children can possibly do. Women who have children should be prepared to take care of them. You know, just because you decided that you didn't like my father, doesn't mean that you had to abandon the rest of us at the drop of a hat."

Fanny sighed; he'd spoken the words she dreaded. "Of course you feel that way. I'm glad that you are letting your anger out. Can you tell me more?"

"That psychiatrist of yours has worn off on you, but there's nothing doing. I have very few feelings on the subject, thank you very much. The ones that I have, I have just expressed for the first and last time." Will drove deliberately and silently through the Aberdeen tunnel. The lights on the hillside blacked out like the glimmer of friendship between them. She felt her tears returning.

Fanny didn't want to say anything, but knew she needed to. "It wasn't a sudden thing, leaving you. It was a long and painful decision. The truth is never simple. When you're ready, I'll tell you." She paused. "I'll try to tell you everything."

Fanny stared out of the window for a moment, then added, "Please, just drop me off at the Star Ferry. It's only a short walk to the hotel."

Will didn't answer. When they were at the Ferry and the car stopped, he turned off the engine and turned at the waist to face her. "Tomorrow is Easter. I presume that you don't have any plans that can't be broken?"

Against her better judgment, she shook her head no.

He continued. "I'll pick you up here tomorrow at noon. I'm having the family to lunch, and you must be there." Fanny opened her mouth to interrupt, but he anticipated her and put up his hand. He spoke so quickly. "Don't worry; it will all be quite civilized. I am taken with the idea of having both my parents eat Easter lunch at my flat with Ann as witness. Drew and Helga will be there. It's a crying shame that Line and good old Tony can't be there too, though we could probably manage someone from his family without too much effort. Perhaps Caroline's mother-in-law. She's quite a charmer. And of course, your Dr. Rider. Isn't this what extended families are all about?"

Fanny took a deep breath. This was a test. She wanted to take the next plane back to New York. It had been a mistake. She looked up to see if she could find the moon. Perhaps the answer would be written there at last. She only saw clouds. "I...I don't know. I'm not sure I could face your father."

He said, "You have to see Drew. Why did you come if you didn't want to see us?"

"I wanted to see you and Andrew, of course, but your father is another story."

"Stop worrying. I've never seen him bite."

Fanny thought how little he must remember. She made her decision. "All right. Noon then. Here. I'll look forward to seeing you tomorrow."

She decided not to attempt to kiss him. The limited space inside the car made it difficult. She stepped out of the car, onto, as she thought, dry land. He got out of the car too and came around to her side. She said formally, "Thanks for dinner. It was excellent."

He grinned, and as he gave her a kiss on the cheek, a strand of thick, straight blonde hair fell over his right eye.

Back at the hotel, Fanny kicked off her shoes and rang New York. Her need to talk to Rider and the children was overwhelming. They were her touchstone to the real world. They were her proof that she could be a good mother.

The phone was answered on the first ring. "Hi Mom, it's Nigel. How ya' doin'?" He sounded so happy and normal.

"Oh, Nigel. I'm so glad that you're there. I miss you. I'm doin' okay. How about you?"

"Mom, you'll never guess what. Our team stinks and Mr. Beeley yells at us all the time and we try but he doesn't tell us how to do any better, and, yesterday, he yelled at Michael Ferrari and Jeff Connoly and made them both cry and Michael never cries and Peter's dad yelled at Mrs. Riley because she said the other teams are better than we are which is true because we really stink, and Mrs. Riley got really mad and Mr. Riley came looking for Peter's dad but he'd left by then. Everyone's always yelling at everybody. I don't like baseball that much. Can I quit?"

Fanny laughed, "You've only just started and I haven't even seen a game yet this year." She thought, if he were Peter's son he'd never be allowed to give up a sport. Perhaps, if he were Peter's son, he'd never want to.

Nigel continued breathlessly, "But Mom, number one, it's hot on the field and Mr. Beeley doesn't let most of us go up to bat at practice only John Beeley and Brian Smaks. That's because Brian's good and John's Mr. Beeley's son. But that's playing favorites. That's no fair. Everyone should get a turn. He won't even let us go get drinks. Number two. How are we going to get better if we can't go up to bat? I'm not going to do baseball next year. It stinks. No one on our team likes it. We always lose and Mr. Beeley always yells at us. Dad says maybe this will teach me something but I don't think it will teach me anything except that I'm never going to sign up for baseball again. It's not fair that I get put on a team with all the worst players. You can't depend on any of these guys. When they are supposed to be watching for the ball they are messing around and then they miss the ball and Mr. Beeley yells at the whole team. And one time he yelled at me and it wasn't my fault. Chuck Ferguson was fooling around and he thought it was me. I wish you were here, Mom. When are you coming back? Anyway Sarah wants to talk to you. She says I'm talking too much."

"Hi, Mom." Cough, cough.

"Hi, Sarah. Sounds like Nigel is having a bad time."

"Yeah. I haven't been in school much. The nurse called Daddy and told him I'm disrupting class with all this coughing and I should stay out of school until it gets better. It's worst in Spanish because the room is so hot. Can you believe the heat is still on in school? Everyone's wearing shorts?" Cough, cough. "Oh by the way, do you remember where my denim cutoffs are, the ones I wore all last summer? I looked everywhere."

"I hate to tell you this, but I probably gave them away. You've grown so much, they'll never fit." She worried about the cough. Could Sarah really be sick?

"Then I need new ones when you get home. I really miss you. Dad says it costs humongous dollars to call Hong Kong. By the way, when are you coming home?"

"Pretty soon. Get that cough better."

"OK, bye. Dad wants to speak to you."

Fanny took a deep breath. "Sounds as though you have your hands full."

"I've never appreciated how much you do around here. The place is a mess and no matter what I do, it's not getting any better, which is a euphemism for saying that its rapidly getting worse."

"Who cares? Isn't Sarah going to school?"

"They're off for Easter now." He paused. Fanny had forgotten that they'd be home. What kind of mother forgets something like that? "She'll have a week to work on it. It's psychosomatic, of course. What have you been doing?"

Fanny gave a limited account of her visit to Water Music and a more detailed account of her dinner with Will. "I miss you. I'm lonely, but it's okay. Don't worry about me."

"What are you doing tomorrow? It will be Easter there, won't it?"

"It doesn't feel like Easter here, but Will has invited me for lunch. I'll see Andrew and his wife." She hesitated, then went on, "He's turned into such a yuppie—or what do they call twenty-somethings?"

"Generation X."

"He was wearing a double-breasted pinstriped suit, and carried a notebook computer. Quite a smile."

Rider laughed. "Doesn't sound as though he's frightened you—just one question, quick. What do you usually let Nigel eat when he gets home from school? I think I'm being taken advantage of."

And so it went. Everyday conversations with her Rider family. They were going to have Easter without her. What would they do? Where would they eat? They connected her with reality and the present. They helped her focus that all this in Hong Kong was temporary and past and just the reminder of a different motherhood. Though motherhood was the same both places. The giving up of the self for another, the making way, the loving, the sacrifice of time and money and energy.

The children she'd left thought she hadn't given them

enough, and they would be right. Nigel and Sarah had so much more. Nevertheless, Caroline, Will, and Drew didn't nearly know quite how much she'd given to them. Maybe no one knew. Are children always ungrateful?

Fanny lay back on the bed and pictured Nigel in his baseball uniform, serious and ready for play. It's not that she'd never leave Nigel, because, of course, she would. Why couldn't anyone but Rider understand? Because she hadn't died. Suicide, after all, would have been more acceptable than desertion and abandonment. Her crime was surviving. Perhaps it should be her goal to make Caroline, Drew, and Will understand. If she'd died, they would never have known her. Perhaps there still would be time.

What about children who never find their parents? Fanny knew she must find a way to put it in perspective for Caroline, Will, and Drew. They were lucky. She'd still be there for all her children. The trouble was that she'd let the rest of the world dictate terms and rules to her for too long. The anger, the accusing finger didn't matter a hoot.

Motherhood isn't only about nurturing and food and clothes and education. It's also about trust and a lifetime. The only thing wrong with what had happened with her Ardel-Rhys children was the gap. Time to make up.

Fanny was surprised and pleased with herself for thinking so rationally. If she kept thinking this way, with these priorities at the top of the pile, the next day wouldn't be so bad.

九

When the dust settled, and there was time to sit back and absorb the horror of Water Music's history, Fanny remembered that the servants had left on the night of the Harvest Moon Festival. That autumn, references to the moon were everywhere.

Was there a coincidence? She'd always loved the moon. As a small child in Lancashire, she'd watch the moon while clouds like so many cars on the highway streamed past. Her bedroom looked upon a field of cows and the moon danced its beams upon the animals as they slept. Wherever she was in the world, the moon had been with her. A huge harvest moon suspended in the sky, brightly lit, but not lighting the night.

The night before the servants left, Caroline had asked Fanny to read her the bedtime story about the man who sees the moon reflected in a pond and thinks he can pick it out of the water. The air felt cool and the atmosphere clear and unsullied. The sea strummed an unharnessed continuous rhythm underneath. A few sampans drifted. How are the tides connected to the moon? How could that be? Who believed all that stuff about the poles being magnetic? Jasmine and camphor perfumed the night.

The Easter after the servants left, Peter installed Fanny in the mental hospital.

She knew why he'd put her there: he hadn't known what else to do with her.

In the days when everything had been hopeless, when taking care of the children was an unfathomable burden, when Peter was too busy elsewhere, when Fanny's depression came on so badly she could barely spend ten minutes without crying, they had said to her, "We think you need a bit of a rest." It wasn't just Jean who used these words. Penelope used them. Dr. Greenwood used them. She dreaded hearing it. What she needed was months of sleep, deep Rip Van Winkle sleep, Sleeping Beauty sleep, Gulliver sleep.

Of course, Peter never said anything like that. Peter said, "If you can't pull yourself together and act like a rational human being, I'll have no alternative but to commit you." She knew he didn't mean it, but his patience had worn thin. He had no time for "nonsense" as he called it. Peter didn't want her to be sent to the hospital, because her illness would reflect on him. People would talk. When it became common knowledge that he had a crazy wife, it would affect his chances of reaching the heights he aspired to. Personal difficulties made a man appear to be less effective. He resisted it longer than he should have.

It was only when it became apparent that Fanny would be more of an embarrassment at home than if she were sent to the hospital that Peter agreed to send her.

The Easter egg incident had sealed her fate. The children had become more and more unkempt and unruly. Fanny wanted to give them a treat. Someone had lent her a pile of American magazines to read and one of them, *Good Housekeeping*, had an article on decorating Easter Eggs. Inspired by this, she bought several packets of dye from the Dairy Farm and ten dozen eggs. She dyed them in colorful swirling patterns. She made pastel tartans. She drew on them and painted a few silver and gold. One hundred and twenty eggs. She piled them up in the dining room in baskets and boxes. Peter stayed upstairs to sleep in. He'd come in very late, tipsy, the night before. The children skipped downstairs Easter morning and spied the eggs.

Drew was the first to crack one. He watched it drizzle down his arm over his pajamas. His initial alarm evaporated when he realized Fanny wasn't annoyed with him. He reached out for another egg and cracked it deliberately while she watched. Then Will took an egg and rolled it on the floor. When it rolled under the settee, he took another and dropped it on the floor. It broke. Caroline stood in the doorway and watched. Drew laughed in glee. Will took several eggs and smashed them onto the floor. Havoc erupted. Caroline joined in before long, her fastidious nature overcome by the prospect of anarchistic adventure.

Within half an hour, one hundred and twenty egg yolks and whites were smeared over the expensive carpet and furniture. When Peter came downstairs, foggy in hangover, he found Fanny lying, with the children, flat on her stomach on the parquet floor smearing the mess around, happier than she'd been in months. All four of them were infected with a giggling slimy glee.

Later, when they asked her, Fanny insisted that the article hadn't mentioned hard boiling the eggs before decorating them.

She hardly smiled any more and most things made her weep. She wept all the time. She wept while cooking. She wept while bathing the children. She wept salty tears over gin and ice. It didn't alarm the children. They were used to it. She stopped taking the pills Dr. Greenwood prescribed. She didn't believe in pills because they made her fuzzy headed. They certainly didn't improve the situation the way they were supposed to. She swallowed the pills for a month, then threw the rest away. Gin was far more effective but gin didn't arrest tears.

She made a serious effort to rise above her unhappiness. Sometimes she'd get energetic and start ill-conceived projects that she wouldn't finish, like cleaning out the cupboards. She'd pull everything out, see the hopelessness of the task and leave the tumbled contents strewn around the floor. She'd be unable to rouse herself to care enough to finish.

Once she decided to sew matching summer dresses for herself and Caroline. She bought a deep-blue, cotton gingham, scissored it out carefully and sewed the pieces together. When she held it up to herself it was lopsided, and she realized the folly of the enterprise. Without attempting to rectify the situation, she shredded the cloth into tiny squares, letting the pieces float out the window onto the rows of marigolds planted below.

Fanny didn't know how to stop her tears. She knew that Peter was right. Standards had dropped. She was indulging in self-pity and drinking far too much.

One sunny morning, a few days after that messy Easter Sunday, Penelope arrived. Fanny had already consumed her first few gins of the day and hadn't been expecting her.

She should have suspected underhand intentions, but she assumed it was a surprise visit. Then, Peter announced casually that he wasn't going to work that morning, he'd heard of a doctor newly arrived in Hong Kong who could help Fanny. Dr. Greenwood had suggested that he make an appointment and Peter had done so.

That was how Peter got Fanny to the mental hospital.

There was no new doctor after all. Dr. Greenwood met

them at the guard hut at the entrance to the hospital and took them to his hospital office. She'd only visited Dr. Greenwood before in Kowloon.

His office was bright with books everywhere. It smelled of pipe tobacco. She hardly heard what he said because she was concentrating on a wide-leafed plant growing in a big terra cotta pot in the corner. She'd never seen a plant like it with yellow and pink zigging and zagging up the leaves. She wondered if he talked to it to make it grow so well. She was sure that he would soon be talking to her and she hoped he didn't have her zigging and zagging around the place. She did hear him say that she needed a rest. He wanted no argument. He had decided to sedate her.

She didn't protest when he injected her upper arm with a fluid the color of beer. Fanny watched it disappear into her flesh. She wondered if it was a truth serum. She didn't think it would harm her.

Dr. Greenwood took her and Peter to a larger building through a locked metal door, down an empty long corridor with a gleaming, speckled, yellow tile floor. They finally stopped and Dr. Greenwood opened a door into a plain room with white walls, an iron bed with white sheets and a blue wool blanket. Fanny felt so dizzy from the injection, she let them guide her to an upholstered easy chair. They left her in a drugged stupor staring at a badly painted, unimaginative picture of a vase of flowers.

With a turn of a key in the lock of the door she realized they'd left her alone, imprisoned.

Those first moments she kept thinking, what about the children? What is Penelope going to do with them?

After Dr. Greenwood's and Peter's footsteps died away, the building was completely silent. She'd never been anywhere so quiet before. She smelled floor polish.

She almost succumbed to sleep. Would she ever see her children again?

What about the children? All these months she'd held onto her reason because the children needed her. Not once had she had so much to drink that she couldn't give them what they needed. Food. Sleep. Play. Not once had she fallen asleep while they were awake.

The same thoughts flashed through her mind over and over again. What will happen to the children? Who will take care of the children? Penelope hasn't a clue. How long are they going to leave me here? She'd promised Drew to make him fried rice and eggs as a treat, the way he liked it best. She and Caroline were in the middle of reading the story about twelve dancing princesses. Caroline would never know how it ended.

In spite of the injection, and in spite of her inertia, Fanny forced herself to stand on unsteady legs. Then with a determination that took every ounce of her willpower, she made her way to the door, and she pounded upon it.

She screamed. "Come back! Let me out! I need to see my children! What's going to happen to my children? Let me see my twins! I want Caroline!" She wanted a drink. She wanted to die. She wanted to kill Peter. She wanted to kill Dr. Greenwood. She wanted to drown. She needed a drink. She slumped onto the door.

She heard voices arguing and muffled footsteps running down the hall towards her. She heard a click in the lock, then a competent female voice ordering her away from the door. Fanny moved backwards and to the side, preparing herself to lunge and escape, although she probably couldn't have made it. The door surprised her by opening out into the corridor. Two well-built Chinese orderlies were expecting her. They restrained her in a tangle of muscle and white. The woman spoke a few words in Cantonese to the men and introduced herself in English to Fanny. "I'm Lily Chen, Matron. I'm in charge of this section of the hospital. I hoped that we'd have a more congenial meeting." The orderlies relaxed, but still held Fanny by the arms. Lily told them to assist her to the chair. Fanny collapsed into it.

Looking down, Lily shook her head and said in perfect American-accented English, "If you want to leave, that's the wrong way to go about it."

Fanny sobbed, "My children. They don't know I'm here. What are they doing about Will and Drew? It's Caroline's birthday on Friday. Remember Caroline's birthday. Peter doesn't know what to do. Not the first thing. He doesn't even know where I've hidden her presents. We were going to have a party. Penelope can't take care of them."

"Peter is your husband? Who is Penelope?"

Fanny wept and wept. Her body shook. Lily gave her another injection. She didn't remember anything else.

After that, the days melded into each other.

Her clothes miraculously appeared each morning, clean and pressed: a sleeveless cotton dress, underpants, a bra and her sandals. Day after day. They gave her injections and she slept. She craved drink. She swore at her captors. She ranted and raved. She couldn't concentrate to read, and, anyway the books lined up in the two bookcases in the patient dayroom were too religious to capture her interest.

From what Fanny could see, it wasn't nearly as bad as she'd thought an insane asylum would be. For the most part, as long as they behaved passively, patients were treated with compassion and patience. They let her sleep as much as she wanted to.

The hospital had been built in a single storey E-shape in the 1930s. There were several other buildings in the complex. Fanny was housed with the least extreme cases at the end of the top stroke of the E. The other wings were separated by a series of wrought iron gates and heavy metal doors. Lily told Fanny they were reserved for the seriously disturbed and the dangerously disturbed patients. She forbade Fanny from entering these areas.

Later on in her stay, Fanny defied Lily's order and took advantage of a series of open doors to satisfy her curiosity. She came face to face with angry, uncontrolled, wild-eyed individuals who leered at her threateningly.

There was great excitement one day when the rumor spread that a famous cleaver murderer had been brought in. No one ever got a glimpse of him.

Fanny yearned to see Peter and the children. The first week, Peter visited several times. By his third visit he became alarmed at her listlessness and demanded an appointment with Dr. Greenwood at once.

Peter refused to sit in the chair Dr. Greenwood offered him. He towered over the doctor. Fanny hadn't seen him so angry in a long time. She turned and stared at the strange plant in the corner of the office, relieved his fury wasn't directed at her. Peter raged at Dr. Greenwood, "I see no improvement in my wife's condition at all. In fact she looks a damn sight worse. She's drugged and ill and I won't stand for it. What are you playing at here? What are you intending to do with her?"

Fanny thought it wonderful that Peter was defending her. She hadn't known he liked her enough to do that.

Dr. Greenwood, taken by surprise, stuttered his way through an apology and explained that drugs were part of the treatment and some of the side effects were grogginess and the need to sleep. Peter took Fanny by the elbow and asked her gently. "Do you feel better, Fanny? Answer me, are the drugs making you feel better?"

Actually, they weren't. They took away her need for gin, but they made her head swim. "No, they make me worse. My head hurts all the time."

Peter turned back to the doctor. "From now on you are to stop administering them to her. From now on she receives nothing whatsoever without my explicit permission—in fact, my signature. Do you hear? It's bad enough having to keep her here without you making matters worse before my very eyes. Do you hear?"

Dr. Greenwood fought a little to maintain control but saw it was useless. Fanny wondered if he'd make Peter take her back home. He shrugged his shoulders and agreed to Peter's demand. "On your head be it. Her recovery will be a good deal slower if you leave things to chance."

After that Peter continued to visit, but less frequently. She never knew when to expect him until Nurse Chen appeared and told her to brush her teeth and smooth her hair before escorting her to a private sitting room. Later on she realized that on the days that Peter was expected, whoever chose her clothes took more trouble. They chose a newer dress and sandals with higher heels. It was confusing because sometimes she wore her better clothes and Peter didn't appear.

She made a great effort, when she saw Peter, to appear sane, but she couldn't stop her hands from trembling and the tears from tumbling down her face. She sensed that he was convinced she wasn't ever going to recover. She kept asking him to bring the children, but she knew he was so ashamed of her that he never would. It was clear to Fanny that he dreaded visiting her, he loathed the hospital and the weakness it represented, and he despised Dr. Greenwood. Yet sometimes he was tender and warm. He brought her books and magazines and cheered her out of her stupor with funny stories and memories of rag week at university. The day after her birthday, he even brought her two dozen perfect yellow roses. He rarely sat down, always paced, and never stayed long enough.

Fanny looked forward to seeing Lily every day. She liked Lily particularly. Dr. Greenwood met with her because he was paid to, Lily because she wanted to. Lily refused to let Fanny fall deeper into her sadness. Every day she stopped by, if only for a few moments and made her laugh.

They would argue a lot about Fanny's treatment. After Peter's directive, Fanny received no medicines or treatment. Lily told her she couldn't expect to get better unless she took the latest shock treatments and pills. Fanny, whose head was clearer now, told Lily that never did she want to take any of that stuff. If she couldn't have alcohol, she didn't want anything.

Lily told Fanny about herself. She said that she'd never married for many reasons, one of which being that no one meeting her very high standards had ever asked her. She had sisters and brothers who had married with varying degrees of success, but she'd never met a man who was as well educated and cultured and modern as she wished. Fanny recognized sadness in Lily, as well as reservoirs of self-control. She told Fanny that her biggest regret was not having children.

Lily was in charge of their small cadre of patients, but her main job was to act as liaison between the doctors, mostly of European extraction, and the staff, who were more often than not, Cantonese.

When Fanny met Sister Bentley, the prim, thin-lipped woman in charge of the more severe cases, she was grateful that she had no dealings with her. One of the other patients,

Christo, told stories of her cruelly restraining patients and torturing them which Fanny thought were probably made up, but she didn't want to find out.

Lily interceded for the patients. She made her own decisions about important matters like smoking cigarettes. She had an intuitive grasp of human nature. She told Fanny that she decided which patients could be cured. Sometimes she was wrong. Fanny hoped Lily was right when she said there was no doubt that Fanny would recover on her own, even if it would be faster with modern treatments.

Lily spent hours listening to Fanny talk about the children. She would tell Lily about how clever Caroline was, things they said, fights they'd had, Caroline's love for drawing, Drew's singing. Sometimes, if she was in a good mood and Fanny had some energy, she would let Fanny accompany her while she did her chores. They discussed Peter. As Lily listened to her, Fanny felt less splintered.

One day there was more time than usual. She had helped Lily count supplies that had been delivered to the wrong building. Afterwards Lily invited Fanny to have a cup of tea with her at a stone picnic table in the garden.

She thought that if she had a friend like Lily, she might not have fallen so sick. The hospital was quiet and dull. The routine had to be adhered to. Lily challenged Fanny to paint again. She assessed Fanny's interests. She convinced Dr. Greenwood to assign a vacant room for her to paint in. Lily procured paints, paper, oil pastels and an apron to protect her clothes. For her birthday, Lily had the woodworking group make a easel for Fanny.

Indulgently, Dr. Greenwood watched the relationship develop. He didn't altogether approve of his matron fraternizing so closely with a patient, but this time he made an exception, partly because Fanny was a special case. He wanted to see her cured and handed safely back to Peter. Peter intimidated him. Perhaps someday he would need Peter to help the hospital.

The two orderlies fascinated Fanny. Christo told her that in their off-hours they were hit men. She wasn't sure she believed him, so she asked Lily, who said it was possible. When Fanny asked why they bothered to work at the hospital at all, Christo explained that it suited their nefarious purposes. Killing people wasn't a steady business for them and they needed something to do during lean periods. Working at the hospital gave them an alibi in case overzealous police ever investigated their activities. The hospital gave them unrestricted access to medical supplies regularly required by their other profession.

The orderlies never spoke with Fanny at first, but she cooperated with them. Later she taught them useful English phrases like, "What are we having for dinner?" and "Pass the marmite, please." They were always courteous.

The patients' dayroom was the center of activity. It was here that meals were served and the small group of Western patients interacted. She was grouped with the women for therapy sessions: a silent Dutch woman they called Marta; Marisa, a Yugoslavian woman younger than Fanny; and Marianne, a missionary wife. For meals, they were joined by three men, an Irishman called Patrick Dempsey who had worked for the British Trade Commission, Portuguese Christo, whose family had committed him for life, and Dan, a bodybuilding Australian. These six moved aside to let Fanny into their lunatic circle. Except for Christo, they were all short-term patients waiting for their families to decide what to do with them.

Fanny questioned the nature of sanity when she was with these other patients. Hers didn't seem to be madness like theirs, except perhaps Dan. She still had her reason. She still knew

who she was and who she used to be, but being with them
gave her permission to act mad. No one blinked an eye if she
bit herself on the arm in the patient dayroom, or cried, or
took off her shoe and slammed it against the dinner table.
Some days she did it often. It was a new kind of freedom and
enticing.

Still, until Lily started her painting, Fanny chose to spend
most of her time alone in her room staring at the cardboard
print on the bare white walls. She couldn't sleep at night and
was weary all day. She wavered between absolute terror for
her children and caring about nothing. She thought about her
parents and her dead sister and she wept, she missed them all
so much.

She discovered the picture on her wall was cardboard
when she stood on the bed and pulled the frame apart. She
was in a paranoid mood. She'd thought that perhaps her new
existence was like a James Bond film and a camera was watching her from behind the picture. Peter and Dr. Greenwood
would be watching every movement. She couldn't believe that
they'd just leave her unattended like this in boredom and frustration. Did they really think that she'd come to her senses
here? Or was this merely punishment for past transgressions?

Fanny looked for solitude. She would try to sit in the
hospital dayroom when it was empty, first thing in the morning before the others wandered in for breakfast, or when the
others were being seen by doctors, at basket weaving, or woodworking. She moved a chintzy overstuffed armchair to the
airconditioner. It came to be known as her chair, even when
the room was crowded, and the others would leave it empty
for her. The airconditioner was old and weak and what little
cold air it pumped into the room warmed almost immediately.

If there was a day when someone had forgotten to pull
the bamboo blinds closed, Fanny couldn't usually be both-

ered to stand up and do it herself. She couldn't be bothered
to do much. She knew if she didn't close the blinds as the
morning progressed, the room would heat up like a furnace.
She would sit and watch the white-faced clock on the wall tick
the minutes away. It was the same kind of clock they'd had on
their classroom walls at school. Most of the time she no longer
cared about anything or anybody. They could all do what
they wanted as far as she was concerned. She was content just
to sit and watch the dust motes drift across the polished tile
floor.

In some ways the hospital was a relief to her; Dr. Greenwood and Peter had been right to deposit her there. She didn't
miss making decisions and never wanted to have to make one
again. She didn't have to decide how to dress that day, what
meals to prepare, how to make Peter want her. She liked meals
appearing on cue, even if she didn't much care for the meals
themselves. They were served soggy, bland, pale English food:
bread and butter, meat drenched in whitish gravy, potatoes
and puddings. Even the peas were gray-green. The only meal
where there was a choice was afternoon tea. Nurse Chen carried a square tin of biscuits into the patient's dayroom and she
let each patient pick two. Petty squabbles erupted as the tin
emptied and the choice became more limited. Fanny didn't
worry about her choice. She put in her hand and took out the
first two biscuits she felt.

Sitting in her chair, she let life drift on around her. Even
if she'd eaten breakfast, she wondered later what she'd had. It
was so hard to remember anything. The days dripped one
into another. Sometimes she heard voices in the distance. If
it was very hot because she hadn't closed the blinds, sweat
would run down her back. She could feel her dress sticking to
her. She would think again about standing up and closing the
blinds but then she'd think that she didn't want to shut out the

light. After sitting for a while, her legs would become heavy and immobile. She would wonder if the voices were talking about her. Then again, most people didn't even remember she existed. Sometimes she wondered if she really did. She'd watch a cricket who lived outside by the window pane. During the morning, he was quiet, resting, waiting until dusk to start his racket.

If she sat up tall, Fanny could see pine trees outside, and sometimes grass being cut by a very old man with a rickety lawn mower. She could see bits of string holding the grass catcher onto the front of it.

If she did pull the blind closed, the room would darken immediately. She'd stand in front of the air conditioner letting the freezing cold waves hit the wetness of her dress and the chill of her back.

She sometimes wondered why there were no Chinese in the group that she had been assigned to. There was a several large groups of Chinese in their wing of the building, grouped by gender. They kept to themselves. She would see them shuffling around together. They had their own dayrooms and kept together except for a very noisy woman who kept trying to break off and join Christo. When Fanny did the rounds with Lily, she saw that the Chinese patients had their own dining room near the kitchen with chopsticks and bowls. The smells were delicious. She asked Lily why she couldn't eat there. Lily said that the Chinese patients didn't want to mingle with mad foreigners. Things worked out better this way.

She could see a picture on the wall from where she sat in her favorite chair. It was an abstract painting, all browns, reds and blacks. She loathed it.

One morning she read in the newspaper that an American astronaut wearing a great, lumbering, plastic, silver outfit, walked on the moon. He planted the American flag there, presumably making the moon, hitherto belonging to all humankind, a territory to be governed by the U.S.A. She tore out the article. This man was up there, actually on the moon. A scientific achievement. Where was the mystery? The moon was just cold and rocky and he'd left his debris.

No one would discuss it with her at breakfast. Christo monopolized the scant listening audience by describing how prostitutes use mangos. Later Fanny tried to explain her concern to Lily. She worried that the moon would now belong to America. What would they do with it? What if they did atomic tests on it and blew it to pieces? If they shattered it, would it still guide the tides? Would the calendar change? Both Lily and Dr. Greenwood told her to worry about more immediate things. She didn't mention it to Peter when she next saw him, but she wanted to know what he thought about it.

She painted the moon over and over again with thick paint, then thin and watery, then bright, then light like the seasons, a dark sky and a round rocky moon, and ten hot red suns with ghostly faces.

Fanny was becoming convinced that she belonged with these lunatic people, and that she was probably as mad as they were, because she felt comfortable with them whereas normal people like Peter didn't.

✝

About four months after her arrival at the hospital, when the days had become routine, Fanny had a revelation. Dan had just been released into the care of a Chinese girlfriend who had come to fetch him in a flashy red MG. If Dan could be released, so could she. Fanny hadn't had a gin since she'd arrived and only half a bottle of whiskey that Dan's girlfriend had smuggled in and he'd shared. She craved drink less now, and she worried about her children. Peter had told her that Ann was taking care of them.

The revelation came during one of Dr. Greenwood's cozy little chats with her. He always said, "Let's have a little chat.... I'm pleased to see you taking an interest in something. Your paintings are quite fascinating." Then he zigged and zagged a bit, but then later on, when she asked what would entice him to release her, he said, "You have to appear to be sane."

So there it was, perfectly simple—pretend. Take up acting.

She made it a project. She decided to ignore her fellow inmates and concentrate on the bosses: Lily, Peter, the nurses, orderlies, and Dr. Greenwood. It would be like learning to walk. She would have to control herself. Speak in clear coherent sentences. Every day when she woke up, she went through in her mind what she was going to do and focused on getting back home to the children.

Perhaps, though, her biggest incentive to get well was William Rider. Lily introduced her to Rider one warm June afternoon a few days after the astronaut walked on the moon. Lily said to Fanny, "I'm going to bring someone to meet you. He's working with the addicts at Tai Lam Cheung. He's an American doctor." She gave one of her dazzling grins, "I think you'll like him."

Lily brought him to the hospital and gave him a tour. Fanny was sitting in her favorite chair close to the airconditioner, pretending to read a novel that Peter had brought her. She hadn't been able to concentrate on the book, but she used it as a ruse so people would leave her alone. She could just sit and stare at the pages and turn them every now and then. She tried to ignore Dan discussing women with Patrick, Marianne talking to God, Marisa showing her mosquito bites and Christo, even more animate than usual, telling a story to Marianne about stray dogs that saved a priest from succumbing to temptation. Fanny was beginning to notice that Christo, like all good storytellers, adapted his tales to the listener.

"...And ze biggest chow pulled ze priest's robe, ze only one, tearing to shreds ze hem of it...." Lily walked in with the stranger and Christo broke off mid-sentence and stared. Anyone new in the room was a novelty and all the patients showed some reaction, except Marta who never reacted to anything. Fanny suddenly wondered if Marta was deaf.

Lily said, "Our intermediate private patients. Recovering alcoholics, depression, that sort of thing." Rider wore wire-rimmed glasses then, and a trimmed reddish beard. His eyes were kind and smiled a lot. He kept his distance from the patients, but those whose eye he caught, he nodded to. Fanny liked the way he seemed to respect the patients. It wasn't the standoffish superior treatment she'd noticed from other visitors.

Lily noticed Fanny and led Dr. Rider over to her. "This is the patient that I was telling you about, Mrs. Ardel-Rhys. We call her Fanny." Then she turned to Fanny, "Fanny, this is Dr. Rider."

He turned to face Fanny and said in a deep soft voice, "Call me Rider." His gaze was thoughtful and considerate. He didn't cause her worry about her disheveled hair and trembling. He didn't make her want to cry the way everyone but Lily did. He possessed the same steady gentleness as Lily.

Fanny heard herself in amazement. Her voice held steady, she actually sounded flirtatious, "Charmed, I'm sure, and what brings you to us? Has Lily offered you one of her famous challenges?"

He laughed outright. "Well, yes. She did challenge me, she used that very word."

Lily blushed.

He continued, "I'm not working at this hospital. Lily just promised to show me around and introduce me to you."

Fanny responded, "Pity. You look like a distinct improvement over Greenwood and that lot. Can't you persuade them to give you a job?"

"I'm only in Hong Kong for a year. I work with addicts."

There didn't seem to be a response to this. All Fanny wanted to do was lie down and cry. She was an addict. She'd forgotten. She turned her back on them so they wouldn't see her tears. She opened her book.

Rider didn't walk away as she expected him to. He persisted. "Why are you here?"

She kept her back to him and pretended to be looking for her place in the book. "Depressed alcoholic...tell her to show you my records."

"May I?"

"I can't stop you."

"I'd like your permission, though." He paused then added, "May I ask you something?"

In spite of her determination not to, Fanny looked up at him.

"May I visit you on my afternoon off? Thursday?"

"Why would you want to?"

His answer sounded genuine, "To tell you the truth, I don't have much else to do. I don't know many people and your case interests me. I might be able to help you."

She liked his voice and she liked his answer. Lily fidgeted restlessly, anxious to continue the tour.

He said, "I must read your records if I'm to help you. May I ask Dr. Greenwood?"

Fanny surprised herself again. "Only if I can read it."

He sighed. "I can't promise you that. You see if they let patients read their own records doctors would be inhibited about what to write there. Reading their diagnosis might hinder the treatment. I'll tell you what it says."

"The truth?"

"The truth."

She believed him. She nodded. He shook her hand. Fanny watched Lily take him over and lead him away. He turned to glance back at her before he left. He waved.

Patrick Dempsey sidled over to Fanny. "The bugger's hard for you, my lovely. Be on the lookout. All he wants is to stick it in." He thrust his middle finger up and down. Fanny glanced towards Christo and Marianne. They hadn't noticed. Marianne was examining her foot.

Fanny's mouth was completely dry. She was thirsty. They boiled the drinking water and they prepared the food. They made the decision on what to make for dinner. She needed to search for drinking water. No one had put out a jug and glasses. Should she make a fuss about it or just wait until her body turned to desiccated leather? She sat in her chair clutching her novel wondering about it until the bell rang for dinner.

That Thursday, right after painting, he came to see her. Fanny had forgotten that he said he'd visit. She was cleaning the oil paint off the brushes with turpentine, slowly, carefully, immersed in the task, thinking about whether the colors she'd used were exactly right.

His voice startled her, "The record says you are a depressed alcoholic with marital difficulties and three children."

She looked up at him and tried to remember where she'd met him. She said, "That about sums it up." She was surprised they'd written marital difficulties. She hadn't discussed it at all with Dr. Greenwood. Peter must have told them that. She hated Peter sometimes—most of the time. "What did it say exactly about my marital difficulties?"

Rider jacked himself onto a tabletop and swung his legs. "Not much." She'd never seen a doctor act so informally. He asked, "Can I see your painting?"

Fanny brought in her canvas of the ten moons high in the sky above Tsing Ye Island.

He looked at the picture for a long time, careful not to smear the wet paint. He said, "You are very good. Lily didn't tell me that you're an artist. You've had training—this work isn't primitive. The colors are striking. Not colors I would associate with a depressed person."

Fanny looked down, "Oh, I'm not as depressed as I used

to be." She wanted him to believe her.

Rider said, "They are angry colors."

Fanny took the painting from him and put it back against the wall. "You said that you could help me. I want to go home."

He said, "Were your marital problems causing you to drink and get depressed, do you think?"

She couldn't help it. She started to shake. Her teeth chattered. She was freezing cold even though the room had seemed hot moments ago. She'd had no drugs or drink. It just happened.

Rider jumped down from the tabletop. He guided her down the hallway out into the sunshine. Even though Fanny knew it was hot, she couldn't feel it. She didn't want him to see her shaking like this. Would it never stop? Would she never recover?

Rider walked with her around the building. Around and around. Fanny could see curious stares from the barred windows. She smoked cigarette after cigarette. Crazed faces peered through the windows. Eventually Rider took Fanny back to her room where he left her sitting in her chair, no longer shaking, but very tired.

"I'll see you on Tuesday, Mrs. Ardel-Rhys."

She tried to smile but knew it didn't come out well. "Fanny."

"Okay Fanny. I'll see you then."

She knew he wouldn't come back. She'd ruined her chances. All hope of appearing normal was gone forever. She was a crazy lunatic and there was no more to be said or done about it.

She was wrong. Dr. Rider did come back, and she did begin to recover. He apologized to her the next time they met. He said that she had to expect upsetting episodes during her recovery.

Twice a week, on his afternoons off, Rider visited Fanny. When she was able they would walk outside or in the patient dayroom lost in conversation. He was easy to talk to. He questioned her about her life, her thoughts, everything. Sometimes she cried. Sometimes she shook, but he didn't seem to care. At one point he asked and received her permission to take notes. Although it wasn't official, and he never said so, he psychoanalyzed her. He delved into her history. She recounted her life in a detail that astonished even her. Things she hadn't thought about for years.

One afternoon she told him about her sister Sarah's death. Eight years old, she'd drowned in a cold, fast, deep river that ran not far from their house. Everyone knew she was a good swimmer. It was Fanny who couldn't swim then. No one knew why Sarah died. She was found after a frantic search under a stone bridge, face down among the rocks and weeds. Fanny was only five at the time. She knew that her parents secretly wished it had been Fanny who had drowned. She was the one they didn't want, the third unexpected child. Sarah had been the favorite. Everything a daughter should be. When Sarah died, Marjorie, their mother, wept for two sad years, and their father drank every night at the kitchen table, until he slept with his head heavy on his arms. John, her elder brother, spent more and more time with his friends. Fanny watched them all from a distance. That was what had probably convinced her to leave as soon as she could.

Rider made her tell him the story over and over again. Fanny covered the same ground until she admitted her greatest burden. Sarah had asked Fanny to play with her by the river the day she'd drowned, and Fanny had refused. Sarah had been angry and gone alone. Fanny had known all these years that if she'd gone with Sarah that day, she would have been able to save her. If she'd been with her, Sarah would have undoubtedly been playing somewhere safer. Adult reasoning said it wasn't so. Five-year-old Fanny would never have been able to save eight-year-old Sarah. Fanny knew she could have run for help or drowned in Sarah's place.

She was free to ramble on without Rider making her feel crazy. She told him about Peter. He pointed out that whenever she talked about her husband she twirled her wedding ring, which had become very loose.

"I don't know why I married him in the first place. I don't remember why I hated the house. I probably didn't. I love the house. All I can think is that I want to get back to it—to him even. Can't you help me get out of this place? I really got good at doing the housework. Sometimes I don't remember what my children look like any more. Why can't he bring them to see me? It wouldn't be hard. Does Ann sleep in my bed with him? I just want to go home and find out. It may not be my home any more. He acts so strangely when he visits. He grins and changes the subject when I ask him. I'm acting sane, I really am, don't you think so? But he still expects me to be mental. He hasn't noticed that I don't tremble much and that I haven't cried when he's visited the last three times. I want to show him my paintings.

"I've done a portrait of him in his uniform. He looks sober and aloof just like he does before he goes to work. It's a good likeness and I did it from memory. When he comes I memorize his face to paint it later. Dr. Greenwood said I shouldn't show the painting to Peter. He wouldn't like it. I know why, too. I made him look sly. Perhaps you'd like to see it. I think tomorrow I'll start on a new painting. I want to paint Christo. I wonder if they'll let him pose for me. I'm not sick like Christo. Dan wasn't mental— just a drunk. I was a drunk, too. Not anymore. Funny, but I don't miss it much now."

At first it didn't occur to Fanny that Rider might be interested in more than curing her. She didn't suspect a romantic interest; it had been so long since anyone had shown her this kind of attention. When he later asked the question lovers always do, "When did you first realize?" Fanny had difficulty pinpointing when. She might have suspected when Rider suggested that he take Fanny on an outing away from the hospital for the afternoon. He didn't treat her as though she were depressed and she didn't act that way. It was as though they'd let her out of school for a few hours. They walked around Lion Rock, not noticing the hot summer afternoon. They refreshed themselves later with a cold soft drink at the Shatin Heights Hotel. She spent most of the afternoon laughing. He drove her back to the hospital as though taking her to her home. She wasn't as tired that night the days when she'd done nothing.

Rider suspected she returned his interest when Fanny shyly gave him a miniature portrait she'd secretly painted of him.

They enjoyed each other's company. Fanny worried that Rider would realize that she was really crazy and lose interest in her. She feigned sanity when with him. She worried that he would remember she was married to Peter and stop coming to see her, but he kept his promises.

Dr. Greenwood was the first to notice a change in her. He mentioned that she might like to go home with Peter for a day. She couldn't admit that she dreaded it more than anything. She was filled with doubts. What if the children rejected her? Peter would be horrible; he liked her in the hospital. She worried that she'd appear to be crazy and be unable to cope. Dr. Greenwood convinced her to try. "Give it your best, my girl. It won't be as bad as you think."

Peter arrived one steamy Saturday morning and escorted her to the car. Tension sung in the air. They drove the few miles home in silence. Fanny couldn't think of anything to say to Peter. She hadn't noticed before the gray hairs that had appeared in his sideburns. His face was creased in worry.

Water Music looked solid and welcoming in the shimmering heat—exactly as she'd imagined it. As she opened the car door, she listened for the children but heard nothing but crickets. When they were in the house she asked Peter where they were.

He said, "Ann thought it best to take the children out until you've settled in. They're quite noisy and you're not used to it. She'll be back with them in an hour or so. Come into the sitting room, have a gin."

Fanny frowned. Dr. Greenwood had forbidden her to drink. He had specifically told Peter not to offer her anything. "I can't," she said. "Is there any pineapple juice?" It was disconcerting to be a visitor in her own house. She noticed subtle changes in the room. One of the antique card table chairs was missing. A gladioli-filled earthenware vase she had never seen before had a place of honor on the coffee table. "Has anyone been asking about me? Any of my friends?"

Peter was pouring himself his second whisky. The first he had downed in one gulp. "Have a gin. Don't be such a bloody fool." He handed her a glass. Still standing, she politely took it and put it on the table beside her. She noticed that the piano was closed up and her music, normally scattered on the top had been piled up on the bench. She was glad no one had played while she was gone. She sat down in the nearest chair, an overpriced uncomfortable Chippendale reproduction Penelope had convinced her to buy in their early days. She crossed her legs and then uncrossed them again. It annoyed her that she was trying to look sophisticated for him.

He finished his second whiskey in another gulp. "I daresay there have been a few polite enquiries, but could anyone care less?" He spoke louder now. "Is that the question?"

Fanny looked down.

"The answer is that no one cares less. You can jump off a cliff or blow out your brains for all they care. You can have all the little tantrums you want. No one will raise an eyebrow. You have to make your own way in this world."

The front door slammed and she heard the children running down the hallway. Then she saw them. The twins ran right into her and wrapped themselves around her knees tightly, competitively. Caroline held back, curious and tentative. Fanny bent down and scooped up the twins as only she knew how, both together. She loved the wriggling mass of them. They felt so familiar and comforting, the warmth and the way they fit right into her body. "I've missed my little fellas." She looked over to Caroline. "Come here, darling. I want to give you a big hug." To her relief, Caroline walked towards her and took her hand. Her expression was serious. "Mummy, don't go away again."

Only after she had put all three children down again did she look up and see Ann watching her. Their eyes met. Ann said stiffly, "Welcome home, Mrs. Ardel-Rhys."

"Hello, Ann." Fanny walked over to the table where Ann was standing. She intended to kiss her and thank her for taking care of the children.

Ann moved quickly away as if towards Drew.

Fanny shrugged and said, "It looks as though you've done a marvelous job with the children."

Caroline took her hand, "Mummy, don't go back tonight. We can look after you here. I've done some drawings. Come see my drawings."

Fanny didn't miss Ann and Peter exchanging glances over

her head as she bent to look at the pictures Caroline held up for her. She told Caroline they were good. "I've been painting pictures, too. I wish I could show them to you."

Peter poured himself his fourth whiskey and turned towards Ann. "What's for lunch?"

Ann looked as though she was ready to burst into tears. "We're having cold beef and rice, actually. Come into the dining room." She walked out of the room. Caroline asked, "What's the matter with Ann, Mummy?"

"Not a thing, darling."

That first lunch, Fanny didn't say much. She ate a little of the roast beef, more out of curiosity than hunger. She was thinner than Ann now, which gave her a perverse pleasure. She watched the interaction between Peter, Ann, and the children. They behaved as a family should. Peter clearly depended on Ann to run the household and, in doing so, she appeared proficient. The children looked to Ann to fill their plates and their cups, and it was she who took the twins for their naps. Peter complimented her on the meal and asked her about a car repair. Fanny had been replaced by a much more competent housekeeper. She didn't wonder if Peter and Ann were lovers because it was obvious.

While Ann put the twins to bed, Fanny did not attempt to clear the meal off the table. Instead she persuaded Caroline to walk outside with her show her the goldfish. Caroline told her about a new friend of hers in a high piping voice. "...And she has heaps of dolls and things. Her dad is always going somewhere and when he comes back he always brings her a present." She looked up at Fanny expectantly.

An answer was required. "I'm sorry darling. There are no presents to buy in the hospital where I live. It doesn't mean I don't think about you every single day."

"Every single minute?"

"Just about."

Caroline seemed satisfied.

At four o'clock it was time for Peter to drive Fanny back. She kissed the children and ignored Ann. Caroline begged her not to go. Ann tried to subdue her by promising her an ice-lolly.

"I don't want an ice-lolly. I want Mummy."

Ann hustled her into the house.

During the short ride Peter said, "You were very rude to Ann. She's taken such good care of the children for me." When Fanny didn't respond he continued, "She cooked you a lovely meal."

Fanny answered softly, "I don't like Ann as much as you do." Buses filled with beach goers clogged the road. A ten-minute journey was going to take an hour. She couldn't wait to get back to her refuge at the hospital to look at her paintings. The atmosphere was thick with the approaching storm. A flash of lightning streaked the sky.

"You could at least show her some common courtesy."

Fanny looked down. "Sorry, tell her I'm sorry." Thunder rumbled.

Fanny closed her eyes and didn't open them until she felt the car take the sharp turn into the hospital grounds. She didn't want Peter to talk to her any more. She ached for her children. Tears backed up behind her eyelids and she tried to hide them.

When the car stopped, Fanny got out, slammed the car door and ran towards the hospital. Thunder and lightening exploded all around her. The first heavy strikes of rain stained her blouse. She didn't turn back and wave. She didn't care if she never saw him again. There was a hole in her stomach where her children had come from.

On Monday morning, the corridors were deceivingly quiet.
During the many months Fanny had lived in the hospital, except for the night she'd arrived, it had never seemed so completely silent. The sun shone through the barred window
making uneven squares on the tiled floor. She knew it was
late.

Something had happened.

She looked for her clothes but they hadn't been readied
for her. Normally if she slept this late, someone would have
woken her by now and hustled her to the patients' dayroom
for breakfast. Her stomach rumbled. She pushed at the door
with all her strength, but it stood firm. They said they locked
it for her protection, not to keep her imprisoned. She tried to
peer through the window in the door into the hallway beyond,
but could only make out the white wall ahead.

Fanny slumped back down on the bed. She peered at her
watch. Wearing it was one of the privileges of her near recovery. Half past nine. She lay back and let her imagination
wander. Perhaps China had invaded. Perhaps she'd been forgotten. If so, she wouldn't be discovered for a while. Then
what?

She thought she heard shuffling in the corridor and
jumped up to the door to listen. Nothing. She lay back down
on the bed and eventually drifted off to sleep again.

She was woken by Lily, "Fanny, Fanny are you going to
sleep all day?"

Fanny sat up. "It's late. What happened to breakfast?
Where are my clothes?"

"So you woke up earlier?" Lily pointed to Fanny's clothes
set out neatly on a chair by the window. "Did you hear any-

thing?"

Fanny shook her head, no.

"A very sad thing has happened. Very bad for us at the hospital." Fanny noticed how pale Lily's face was and that she had been crying.

"What is it?"

"Marianne died in the night. We thought she was recovering." She helped Fanny up. "There will be an official inquiry."

Fanny noticed how still the world seemed and how tired she felt. "How did she do it?" Lily hadn't said it, but Marianne had been trying to kill herself for so long.

Lily closed her eyes and drew her fingers across her forehead. "I think she stole medicines. She took a lot of pills. Not all of them hers. It was not a pleasant sight. She choked on vomit." She smoothed the sheet of Fanny's bed and said more to herself than Fanny, "Where did she get them? Where did she get the pills to take?"

A flush of guilt washed over Fanny. She'd known Marianne hadn't been taking her pills, had been saving them in her sock, pretending. She'd thought that Marianne had tired of the medicines and just didn't want to take them anymore. She herself was so passive she wasn't capable of making a serious plan like that. She thought about all the trouble Marianne must have taken to pretend to swallow the pills and find a good hiding place.

In the dayroom that afternoon, it was as though nothing had happened. No one mentioned Marianne. Fanny couldn't stop thinking about her. Wanting to die. Being that determined. Making that much effort. Caring enough.

On Tuesday, Dr. Greenwood asked Fanny if the visit to see Peter and the children had been a success. It seemed long ago to Fanny, before Marianne had died. But she said "No" and forced herself to concentrate.

He sighed. "Francis, it's time to start reentering the world. You can't stay here forever."

"Why not?"

"Because you know, and I know, that you are a lot better. You could get along now with living at home and coming to see me in the office, or even here, a few times a week."

Fanny shot him a look of fury.

"You're ready. I'm going to ask your husband to let you stay the night this next weekend and we will take it from there. I want no arguments."

Fanny didn't respond. She concentrated on her foot. She needed new flip-flops. The rubber was going to snap one of these days. She wanted blue ones next time.

"Francis, don't you want to be with your children?"

"Of course."

She played her trump card. "He keeps trying to make me drink. He poured me gin after gin. He told me that you're a bloody fool."

Dr. Greenwood took out his pipe, filled it with tobacco and sucked on the stem energetically without lighting it. "I see. I don't know what he wants us to do with you, if we can't pull out our bag of tricks and treat you."

Fanny wanted to go back to her room. "Can I go now?"

"Yes." He looked towards the window. "We need to meet later this week and talk."

Dr. Greenwood did nothing. Fanny didn't think he could have spoken to Peter because when she was back at the house the next weekend, Peter pressed another gin into her hand. "Take it—it'll do you good—relaxation and all that."

She said, "When are the children going to be home?"

"Fanny?" Peter's voice didn't sound like him. It was low and uncertain. She recognized the voice. He sounded guilty. He was going to say something he didn't want to say. "Fanny, it's time we decided what to do. Do you want to go back to England? Perhaps go live with your parents?"

"My parents? God, no." She thought of her mother and father in their tidy little house. They wouldn't want her anymore than she wanted to go back to them. She continued. "I'm getting better now. I'll be able to come home soon."

He said, "You're not going to be able to take care of the children. You'll just be a burden. There will be no one to take care of you. It's just not on."

She laughed, surprised that his rejection hadn't hurt her. She spoke steadily, without trembling or tears. "You're wrong. I can come back and I will. You are my husband and I love you. They are my children and I love them. I know how to take care of them best. I'm able to come back now." She believed it now. Dr. Greenwood would be proud of her. "I have to try."

The children came running in. The twins climbed up onto her lap. Caroline stood next to her. "You're here for the whole weekend—two whole days."

Fanny directed her answer as much to Peter and Ann as to Caroline, "No, love, I'm back for good. I'm not going back to the hospital." It was time to reclaim the house.

Ann gasped. Peter looked over to Ann and nodded as though to reassure her, then he turned to Fanny. "Does Dr. Greenwood know about this?"

"Dr. Greenwood has nothing to do with it. He knows I'm ready and told me so. He said it was up to me. I think it's time we were together as a family again."

Caroline asked, "Does that mean that Ann is going to

leave?"

Fanny hugged her. "Ann was taking care of you while I was gone. Now I'm back, she can probably leave when she's ready."

Ann walked out of the room and Peter stood up abruptly to follow her. "This is one hell of a surprise." He looked in Ann's direction then turned back to Fanny. "I hope you're satisfied."

Fanny looked him in the eye. "Quite, thank you."

As Peter left the room, Caroline said, "Oh dear, oh dear."

The twins echoed, "Oh dear, oh dear."

The four of them huddled together, listening. Caroline broke their concentration, "I daresay Daddy and Ann have to sort things out."

Fanny answered, "I daresay, darling."

That night while Peter drove Ann back home to her parent's house, Fanny rang the hospital to tell Lily she wasn't coming back and to pack up her things. She'd collect them when she visited Dr. Greenwood. "Be careful with my paintings. You can choose one to keep, if you'd like it. Any one you like."

Lily laughed, "Thanks, I'm so glad you've gone home, but I'll miss you."

Fanny answered, "Wish me luck, Lil. It's going to be even harder than I thought."

That night, Fanny waited until eleven for Peter to get back. Although she was tired, she sat in Peter's study for a while and then walked out to the piano. She found some Scarlatti and without thinking about it, watched her fingers find their places and play the music as though she'd been practicing for months. It was good to be there. Good to be playing to the sleeping children. The spirits were welcoming her—they made her safe. Eventually she went up to bed and slept.

The next morning Fanny woke up first, surprised to be in her old bed with Peter snoring next to her. The sun warmed her where she lay. She watched specks of dust dancing in the sunlight. She heard whispering in the hallway outside. She sat up and climbed out of bed. Two faces appeared through a crack in the door. Caroline and Will, their grins joyful and friendly. Energy suffused her. She took their hands and danced downstairs with them still wearing her nightgown. She made them pancakes for breakfast, then remembered that Peter better not catch her in her nightgown in the kitchen. He'd be sure she was still crazy and take her back. She raced upstairs and pulled on a dress before he woke up.

"That was a close shave," she told Caroline.

Fanny hadn't spent all that time in the hospital in vain. She had planned what she would cook, what she would clean, and what games she would play with the children. She would have dinner parties and she would seduce Peter.

The small amount of social contact she had enjoyed before her hospitalization had evaporated. Even Jean seemed to have changed. Fanny rarely saw her. Jean never sought her out, but at least acted friendly when Fanny called on her. Until the summer ended, she took the children to the beach every afternoon. Women who she knew superficially, who had been come once or twice for dinner, or who had invited her and Peter to their houses, viewed her curiously through their sunglasses, sometimes even nodded to her, but otherwise made no overtures of friendship. One or two even shunned her rudely. She suspected they didn't know what to say to her. Maybe they knew Ann.

She couldn't afford to waste her energy hating or forgiving them. She ignored them. It hurt her feelings, but she thought that maybe it was a good thing. If she sat with them she would be tempted to share their gin. She'd promised Rider she wouldn't.

She missed him.

Occasionally, Ann would appear at the door bringing presents for the children. They welcomed her warmly so Fanny made an effort to be polite. She would invite Ann in for coffee or tea. They had very little to say to each other.

At first Peter came home from work early. He was concerned about leaving Fanny alone too long. He would linger over coffee with her in the morning. He worried about the children. They would eat dinner as a family, and put the children to bed together. Sometimes they made love. Fanny thought that maybe it was all worthwhile. Maybe he had changed and she had changed and things were put right.

Then, the old pattern reemerged. Peter would accept the occasional invitation and then every invitation. He was too tired and drunk when he came home to touch Fanny, and spoke with her little. She had no idea how to seduce him. She didn't dare shout or cause a scene, because she was afraid he would call Dr. Greenwood.

Fanny knew she shouldn't, but she asked Caroline if Ann had slept there. "Of course," said Caroline.

"Where?"

"Different places," answered Caroline.

"In my bed?"

"Yes." Caroline hung her head. She knew it was a terrible admission even if she didn't really understand what it meant. She clung to her mother. "Don't leave again, Mummy."

"I have no intention of leaving," said Fanny.

In spite of Peter, Fanny slept well every night. She awoke in the morning having no memory of her sleep, no dreams, no feelings that she'd been somewhere, talked to someone important, had erotic encounters. Her sleep came on her quickly and when she awoke, she only had the brass clock's testimony that she had slept at all. Why, she wondered, if I sleep like this every night, am I so afraid of dying? Why do I crave it so much? Death would be just like this.

Except that if she died, she wouldn't wake up. Is that bad? Nothingness isn't peace. What is there to fear? It's saying goodbye to all the good things. The children. To be afraid of death maybe there needs to be more good than bad in life. To crave death is to crave sleep.

She told these thoughts to no one.

Fanny tried hard to stay busy. She had more time than she'd had before. While Fanny was away, Peter had arranged for an industrious, but silent, woman from a nearby village to clean the house twice a week. Her name was Ah Bin. She wouldn't live at Water Music and balked at cleaning the study, but on the whole, she did a good job.

When Caroline was in school and the twins were at their nursery school, Fanny visited the hospital three times a week to see Dr. Greenwood officially, and Rider unofficially. If he could get away, Rider visited her the other days. Sometimes they met at a prearranged place and they walked together. Once in a while, he came in the afternoon when the children were home and when he did, he never stayed long. The twins were wary of him. Caroline showed him outright hostility. Fanny always worried when he came to the house, but he ignored her concern, "I've just come to reassure myself. I want to keep you my success story."

Fanny would laugh and try to make the best of it. She'd invite him in to tea. They tried to involve the children, but at some point, they would become immersed in each other. The children would be left out. It didn't work.

Fanny hadn't been so happy for years. No one but the children witnessed their visits. It became her secret, harbored in her heart. She had no idea where it would end, but she knew it had to. She knew Rider would be going back to America and she'd be abandoned. Every moment with him was important. She knew she'd have to remember it forever.

The longing became unbearable. She needed him.

To make the days between visits go faster, Fanny painted. Peter encouraged her and had supplies freighted from England. She painted the children, the house, abstract geometric patterns, goldfish, and the view. Every time she painted one of the children, it burned the child's face into her memory. She knew the exact arch of Caroline's eyebrow, how Drew's hair grew in lopsided tufts in one direction and Will's the other direction. She sketched them while they ate and slept because they couldn't sit still for her.

Peter liked the abstract paintings the best and had them framed and hung them on the hall landing. Fanny thought it telling that Peter gravitated towards the canvases Rider called her angry paintings: huge blotches of vermilion, green and yellow ochre overcut with a chicken wire pattern in cobalt blue.

One morning at the end of October, Fanny and Rider were walking on one of their favorite water catchment paths up on the hill behind the house. There had been an almost imperceptible change of seasons. Their hands locked tightly together. Rider spoke to her about the future. "My time's up in December. I'm supposed to be home for Christmas."

Fanny counted the weeks. The nights were getting cooler. She'd started to think about what to buy for the children for

Christmas.

"I don't know how I can leave you here." He kicked a stone and a fine cloud of dust powdered his brown suede shoes. "I don't think I can. I don't know what to do. I'm looking for a job here, but there isn't one for me. Howard suspects about us. He wants me gone. He thinks I'm bad for you. He says there is a fine line that I'm walking. I'm interfering with your progress, which he takes full credit for, by the way."

Howard was Dr. Greenwood. Fanny never could call him that. She growled, "He doesn't know anything…." The thought of Rider leaving crushed her. "I'd die without you." People say it all the time, but when Fanny said it, they both knew it was literal. She meant it. She'd be dead with Marianne or back in the hospital before you could say Jack Robinson. She began to shake for the first time in a month. "Oh God. Oh God. You can't leave."

He put his arm around her and didn't discuss leaving again, but it was between them, hanging in the air. She knew she wanted him more than she had ever wanted anything. She hoped he was concocting a plan. He couldn't just leave her high and dry.

In October, Fanny had two unexpected visitors. Very early one morning, just after Peter had been driven to work and before the twins were awake, Fanny heard a knock at the door. She was wearing her dressing gown and slippers, sitting at the kitchen table drinking tea and reading the paper. A tingle of fear raced through her for several reasons. She hadn't heard a car on the gravel driveway, there was a perfectly good bell by the door, and she was alone and not expecting anyone. With the quick thought that if it was a murderer, all her troubles would be over, she went to the door and opened it.

The sight of Julia Wo pacing the front steps made her smile. She hadn't seen Julia since the wedding. In an instant the women sized each other up. Julia scrutinized Fanny's disheveled dress and tired, un-madeup eyes. Julia was elegantly dressed in a turquoise, brocade cheongsam. She handed Fanny the gifts she had brought: oranges and a healthy philodendron in a red octagonal pot.

Julia, who had never been inside the house before, walked straight to the settee in the main room and sat upon it.

Fanny placed the gifts on the hall table and said in broken Cantonese. "How can I help you?"

Julia examined the room before she replied in English. "Ask Mr. Ardel-Rhys. Have done many thing for he. Many time. Now no help me. You woman, you understand. Must have job. Must go from husband. No good. No have baby."

To Fanny, in her permanently lethargic condition, Julia's fire and energy overwhelmed her much as a typhoon would. Julia could now speak English better than she could speak Cantonese. She wanted to help—she admired Julia so much— but the thought of it was so exhausting. Julia wasn't happy and would do anything to change the situation. It was quite inspiring, really. She nodded and tried in Cantonese again, "I understand. I'll put in a word with my husband for you. Would you like some tea?"

After dinner, Fanny interrupted Peter in his study. As she sat on the arm of the easy chair, she told him about Julia's visit. She had planned the argument that would appeal to him the most. "Darling, I know it's sticky, but, think of it this way. Julia has been very useful in the past. She could be just as useful in the future. If you do this for her she'll be eternally grateful. If you got her a job on the Hong Kong side...what I mean is this...." She paused for a moment, "Wouldn't you like to have a spy in Government House?"

Peter sighed, but Fanny wouldn't let him argue.

She continued, "Besides which, she has no children and I'm sure her mother-in-law would welcome a face-saving way of getting rid of her. All you really have to do is handle Jimmy."

Peter sighed again. "I don't have a chance against both of you women." His demeanor changed. Fanny knew he was deciding. "Leave it to me and I'll try to think of something."

A week later, he told Fanny that he had given Jimmy a promotion and transfer to a much more important office. Jimmy was going to divorce Julia because of her barrenness. There was a suitable secretarial opening on the island after all.

Fanny had just returned home with Caroline and the twins from nursery school one day when a gleaming white Ford Escort pulled into the driveway behind her car. She didn't recognize the man who emerged. He said he was John Carr. He reminded her they'd met at Tai Lam Chung and she'd asked him about the house. Caroline was the first to remember. She liked him. "You said you had twin brothers. Where are they? Have you come for lunch?"

He laughed, "Oh no. You're going to think I always appear at mealtimes. Actually, I've had my morning constitutional and was driving by as I often do, and I thought, why, in God's name, not? She seems such a nice girl." He said to Fanny, "You very kindly gave me your ham sandwich, do you remember?"

She nodded. "Come on in, then."

He produced colorful Chinese kites for the children with

long tails and faces on them, proving his visit was not the impulsive gesture he'd said. He excused himself by saying, "I bought them weeks ago thinking I'd be bound to bump into you all one of these days."

The children paraded around the drawing room trailing the kites behind them. Fanny pushed open the swinging kitchen door, "If you'd have let me know you were coming, I would have put on something special. I was planning a can of soup and toasted cheese but I've got a section of Brie here and some apples we can supplement it with."

"Marvelous house. Glorious view. Magnificent. You must be very happy here."

"We are." Fanny realized that he had no idea about her madness. He didn't know she had a lover and her husband didn't like her any more. He didn't know she had no idea what she was going to do. Her first thought was to practice on him. See if he thought her sane. So far he hadn't noticed anything amiss.

She asked him, "Would you like a gin and tonic?"

"Marvelous."

For the first time since she left the hospital, she went over to the drinks tray with the ice bucket, a silver sphere embossed with penguins. She took two glasses and poured. She stirred and handed him his glass. "Cheers."

He took it from her, "Cheers."

They drank. It tasted good. Cold with blasting potency.

Over lunch, Fanny drank two more glasses of gin. Her head spun with the relief of it.

John said, "You have no servants?"

"Just Ah Bin who comes to clean every now and then. The others left because of the ghosts."

Fanny told him about the spirits and the exorcism. He

was fascinated when she told him her theory of the Kempati. "I think you're close. I'll look into it. Give me something useful to do."

He left soon after. Fanny never saw him again.

There were still two hours before Fanny had to be on the Hong Kong side of the Star Ferry for Will. She couldn't relax. She'd telephoned New York. She'd taken a walk, showered, eaten, and dressed.

How ironic it was that Caroline was the one to have contacted her. The only one who really wanted to see her again, and she would see Caroline after the others. She thought that this would be just one more thing for Caroline to hold against her.

With escape in mind, she telephoned the airport to ask about planes to New York that day. There was room on a United flight leaving that afternoon. They told her that her airline ticket held a large penalty for an early return. She told them she'd think about it.

Although escape was tempting, she knew that it would be cowardly to leave now. She'd never get another opportunity like this one, and never be forgiven. She argued to herself that she'd never be forgiven anyway. She forced herself to admit that she half wanted to see Peter again, and desperately wanted to see Drew and Will together.

A pile of English-language newspapers, carefully hoarded

since her arrival, were stacked on a side table. Fanny decided to tackle them and look for mention of Peter. Jean had said he made the news regularly. It would give her something to talk to him about. She tried to focus on the task at hand but found nothing. It was all old news, a few international items and social items, but nothing to talk to Peter about. Then her attention became riveted on a photograph and its caption.

> *Easter zealot… Belgian Godelieve*
> *Rombaut, 54, hangs on a wooden cross*
> *in the Philippines to mark Good Friday.*
> *Ten-centimeter spikes have been driven*
> *through her palms by Filipinos dressed*
> *as Roman soldiers.*

The article describing the event was worse.

> *SAN PEDRO CUTUD. A former novice nun*
> *from Belgium, a Filipino thief and at*
> *least 12 other Filipinos were nailed to*
> *crosses while hundreds flogged*
> *themselves with whips in bloody Easter*
> *rites yesterday.*
> *…Hundreds of local and foreign tourists*
> *surged forward to see the re-enactment*
> *of Christ's crucifixion….*
> *"It's something I have to do. It's a*
> *duty," the insurance agent from Flanders*
> *said before she was impaled on the cross*
> *amid circus-like scenes in San Pedro*
> *Cutud, a dusty farming village 75*
> *kilometers north of Manila.*
> *Garbed in a white robe and with flowing*
> *wavy tresses, Ms Rombaut stayed on the*
> *raised cross for about five minutes.*
> *She collapsed after she was brought down.*
> *Fernando Macapagal, 38, who has had*

himself crucified for 10 straight years,
hung in agony on the cross for 15
minutes. He said he was doing it to ask
for good health for his family.

Fanny read it through twice and then again. The thief's motives made perfect sense. Why not turn crime into martyrdom? Fanny understood the value of publicity like that.

But the Belgian woman. What on earth did she hope to achieve? If she was so religious, wasn't she being presumptions asking for the same torture as her God? Besides which, Godelieve (what kind of name was that anyway?) knew they wouldn't let her die up there.

The article helped put the day's luncheon into perspective. She smiled. Some people are even more self-destructive than I am, she thought.

She thought over the ordeal ahead. Since arriving in Hong Kong, she'd been careful but she'd had a lot to drink that night with Jean. Would she be able to resist today? Why not get a head start now? They would better recognize her if she'd had a drink or two. Unless he'd completely changed, Peter would certainly have started drinking early.

The minibar at the other end of the room was a constant temptation, with the rows of miniature bottles, the packages of chocolate and peanuts, the Coke and ginger ale, frosted cold. Something could be found in there to give her the courage she lacked. She wondered if she could ask the hotel to remove the minibar.

She noticed a small smudge near the hem of her dress, the same cream linen sheath she had worn to Water Music that first time. She stood up and unzipped it. She could have worn it into the dirty house for all the good it was going to do her now. She stepped out of it, threw it on the bed and went back to the closet. What to wear? She had to look good.

She didn't feel good. Her hair was a mess and nothing would make it right. What about her turquoise pants? Too flashy. Too out of place. Their sort of people didn't wear turquoise pants to Easter lunch. The tan skirt and navy jacket, too severe. She wished she'd brought a black dress. There were several in her closet at home. She'd worn the navy blue dress to the golf club. She had nothing whatsoever to wear, nor any time to buy anything had there been any decent shops open on Easter Sunday anyway.

She carried the cream dress to the bathroom and soaped the smudge. She couldn't tell if she was making it worse or better as the fabric darkened to the exact color of the stain as soon as it got wet. She noticed another bit of dirt so she wet and wiped that. The dress was becoming badly creased.

She laid the dress back on the bed and returned to the closet. The digital clock by the bed shone 11:15. Time to go and she had nothing to wear. How about jeans and a blouse? That would tip them all off guard. That would show them how American she'd become.

She couldn't.

Looking in the mirror she noticed how bloodshot her eyes were. She went into the bathroom and doused them with Visene. When she opened them again, the hot tiredness had gone but her makeup had run. She wiped the damage away with a tissue. She told herself that in five hours it would all be over. In five hours *it will all be over.* That's all she seemed to be saying these days.

Taking a deep breath, she smoothed the cream dress out and slipped it over her head again, reapplied lipstick, picked up her handbag, and with a loud sigh and several obscene curses she had never used before, closed the door behind her.

Will was leaning on the side of his BMW reading the

paper. He looked up when the surge of passengers from the ferry passed around him. Fanny caught his eye. He grinned and took the handle of the passenger door. "I'm very impressed. I wondered if you'd really come," he said.

Fanny shrugged. She decided not to kiss him.

Will continued, "Before you get in, I just want to say that I know how hard this is going to be. If you don't want to go through with it...."

Fanny hadn't expected him to be much bothered about how she felt. "Let's get on with it, shall we?"

He opened the door for her and waited to close it until she had settled. Fanny thought she'd been prepared to weather this test, but her determination withered fast. Could he really be on her side?

Neither of them said anything as he negotiated the traffic, quieter than usual, but still congested. "They've just renovated the Hilton and now they're going to tear it down. They say more money can be made if it's an office block. Historic building or not."

"It wasn't that remarkable. 1960's boring," Fanny responded. "Have you been back to Water Music recently?"

"No. Don't even remember it that well. We moved soon after you left."

"That's an historic building now." She waited a moment, and then decided to risk it. "Was Ann a good stepmother to you?"

He stiffened and didn't answer for a long time. "She wasn't you and we didn't want her and we still don't."

"I used to think that you liked her more than you liked me." She knew she shouldn't have said it, but it just popped out. "Poor Ann. She can't have had an easy time." Fanny was thinking about Ann putting up with Peter and children who weren't even hers.

"She's had a perfectly smashing time, I can assure you. Packed us away to school as soon as it was humanly possible, then she was rid of us for most of the time."

Fanny wanted to turn back. Panic rose in her like vomit, uncontrollable and vile. He didn't notice because he continued, "You probably should know that she had miscarriages. Didn't endear us to her."

"No, probably not." Poor Ann. Fanny struggled to regain control. Deep breaths. She looked at her son while he spoke. His face was serious, and incredibly square and blonde.

He said, "I'm glad you've come back to us, really I am, but I'm sorry about today. It was foolish to force you and Dad together this way."

"I'm trying not to think about it." She could think of nothing else. She feared the most that Peter would glibly discuss terrible things that she wanted to remain buried forever. What would she do if he started talking about it? With every mile, terror gripped her harder.

Will had driven them out Pok Fu Lam way. Built up now. Unrecognizable. He parked below a tall narrow block of flats, one of many. They went up in the lift together, neither speaking. During the slow ascent, smells of meals being cooked, sounds of excited children and family parties wafted around them. When they reached the top, Fanny groaned, "I'd rather be going to the dentist to have a tooth out than this. I can't do it. Take me back."

Will laughed and pulled out his key. "We're only your family. It'll be all right." He took her arm. "I promise." It was something Peter would have said years ago.

Fanny trusted him suddenly. Perhaps he would protect her. "Oh God!" she said. "I haven't brought anything. I meant to buy a bottle of wine or something. I'm so nervous, I completely forgot."

WATER MUSIC 203

Will said, "That's the least of our worries. Here we are."
The door slid open. "This is Pam," he said.
Will's girlfriend, Pam kneeled in the hallway, she was
searching through the bottom drawer of a bureau. She wore
a tight mini-dress, long straight hair and a contagious grin.
She swiveled herself to a standing position. "I'm trying to
find the bloody napkins." Fanny liked her immediately. She
reminded her of her young self, anxious to please.
    Then she saw Peter walking towards her, drink in hand.
How tall he was. How old. He looked different, but she
would have known him anywhere. His hair had turned all
gray, his face was longer than she remembered, but his body
was still lean and powerful.
    His eyes were the giveaway and he didn't know it. When
Fanny saw his eyes, she almost forgave him. They glittered
dangerously and his cheek twitched. She recognized the signs.
He was more afraid of seeing her than she of seeing him. In
spite of all his success, he remembered the hurt and rejection.
He expected recriminations and was waiting for them, more
on the defensive than the attack.
    Relief flooded her. What an amazing thing, that after all
these years, he was afraid of her. Fanny reached up and pecked
him on the cheek. "Good to see you again. You look wonderful," she said. "Should I curtsey or something, Sir Peter?" He
smelled good, but not the same. Something expensive.
    He hadn't relaxed, but his diplomatic training stood him
in good stead. "No, Madame, you should not." He recovered
himself completely and became the host, "And how are you?
Come on in and let me get you a drink."
    "I'm quite well," she answered. It had a false sound to it.
Good to see you. How are you? I'm quite well. Inanities.
They must have more to say than that, but then again, honesty
was too terrifying to contemplate.

She stopped. On the wall behind Will, she saw her favorite painting from her time at the hospital, of Tsing Ye and the hanging red moons. She wondered if Will knew its history. Peter said, "Will always liked it. I gave it to him when he moved in here." He sniffed, "God knows, he's had little enough of his mother."

Her hurt was immediate and expected. She considered grinding her high heel into the arch of Peter's shoe. How could she have thought herself, just a few minutes ago, still in love with him? She was determined not to let him get the better of her. "Did you like the painting?" Fanny asked and then regretted it. Was she still looking for his approval or waiting for his insults?

"I liked some of your others better."

They advanced to the large, light main room. Fanny scanned quickly and saw only three other people. Ann was engrossed in conversation with a tall, stunning blonde creature. Could only be a Helga, Fanny thought. Drew stood by the terrace, drink in hand, watching Fanny in concentration. Delicious smells wafted from the kitchen. Ann, wearing an impeccable white suit, her hair drawn severely back from her face and secured with a heavy gold band, her neck encased in a heavy gold necklace, her wrist encircled with a heavy gold bangle, smiled up at Fanny. "Francis, it's been a very long time. Let me introduce Helga, Drew's wife."

"Helga, this is Drew's mother."

Fanny had, of course, thought about Ann often. She had disliked her when she had become infatuated with Peter. Ann, she calculated quickly, must be forty-four —not a girl any more. I'm glad I didn't wear black, she thought.

Fanny smiled, took Helga's hand and said, "How do you do?" She was pleased to notice that Will had a grand piano, not her old one.

Ann said, "I was just saying that Helga's getting two mothers-in-law for the price of one. Quite common these days. Heaven knows, it was bad enough with one, don't you think?"

Fanny sensed that all ears in the room were waiting for her to deride Penelope, but she couldn't. It was too soon. She gave a little nod and smiled.

She walked over to Drew who surprised her by wrapping his arms around her in a suffocating hug. When he released her he held her at arm's length and then hugged her again. His eyes glistened. She whispered, "Andrew."

Their greeting must have embarrassed the others because several conversations behind them started at once. He said, "I'm so glad you've come back. I've waited so long." Then he hugged her a third time.

She said, "Andrew, Andrew. I've missed you...." Tears were streaming down her face. At least he towered over her. She didn't want Peter to see. She didn't want Ann and Helga to see. She didn't care if Will saw. Her makeup was running down her face. She felt so tired. He must have been sympathetic, he blocked her from the others.

She sobbed, "You look like him, of course, but you're not like your brother, are you?"

"More than you'd think," he laughed.

Fanny's voice wavered. "Are you two are still in competition?" She bought time by looking out the sliding glass doors at the spectacular view. She missed Hong Kong. She missed England. She'd missed watching these children grow up. They were men now.

Peter thrust a glass in her hand. "Gin, I presume?"

"Thanks." She wanted to say, no, I would like a small glass of white wine with lots of ice in it, or even better, tonic without the gin, but she was too weak. She didn't turn to face him. She wiped her cheek with the palm of her hand. Drew and Peter stood on either side of her.

The telephone rang. A young Filipino woman entered, "The telephone for you, Mrs. Ardel-Rhys."

Fanny turned too quickly, then realized that she wasn't Mrs. Ardel-Rhys any more. She hoped no one had noticed. Ann responded.

Drew said, "Lorenza never calls her Madame or Lady Ann, which as you can imagine irritates the good lady beyond endurance. She keeps telling Will to give her the sack." Fanny wrapped her arm through Drew's and sipped her gin. She took note of a cemetery with stone-marked graves lined up on a hillside, Llama Island and the glimmering green South China Sea. The new airport was out of sight.

Fanny said to no one in particular, "It's very difficult, isn't it?"

Peter answered, "There's nothing difficult here that you haven't created yourself."

Fanny cringed.

Drew tried again. "Hong Kong must have changed a lot since you were last here."

"Yes," Fanny said. She took a deep breath. "It has. Where do you and Helga live?"

"Clearwater Bay. By tunnel and motorway, doesn't take us long to get here. You'll have to come out and see us. Have you been back to Water Music?"

"Of course." Fanny placed her gin on a table, one of the antiques Peter had brought from his grandmother's house. This flat was full of remembrances. Fanny thought she couldn't count the number of times she'd put a gin down onto this very table. She couldn't stop herself glancing up at Peter. He was watching her. Their eyes locked. She'd thought of him so often, and here he was, judgmental and arrogant as ever.

He remembers it as I do, Fanny thought. He hasn't healed any more than I have, less probably. Good.

Ann joined them. She broke the trance. "The girls have gone to see to dinner. These Filipino servants are wonderful. They do most of the cooking."

Fanny nodded and asked Peter, "Did you ever find out about the house? I mean about the hauntings? What had happened there?" She half-expected Peter to say, what hauntings? What are you talking about?

He answered, "The supposed ghosts were Chinese and Japanese. Do you remember that old fellow, John Carr?"

Fanny nodded.

"After you left he turned it into a project. Fancied himself as a bit of a historian. Not much else to do, I suppose." He told her that it happened during the war, while the Kempati occupied the house. It seems that there had been a power struggle between the Japanese and a local triad. The Japanese had been using the servants' quarters as torture chambers. A popular local landowner was killed in a case of mistaken identity. They accused him of helping the British. He'd been innocent. It was the last straw. The landowner's wife led a group of Chinese into the house at the dead of night and they massacred as many sleeping Japanese as they could find. The repercussions were ferocious. Whole families wiped out.

"Quite a complicated and depressing affair. Only natural the servants should hear about it sooner or later. In fact, the very day they heard about it was the day they bolted. Some local fellow from the village was around stirring things up. What a lot of superstition. I doubt that all the priests in China could rid the house of its reputation. The place should really have been torn down after the war, but anything still standing was pronounced good as new." He poured himself another gin. "Very disappointed that you left, was old Carr."

Fanny nodded, "He was a sweet old man. Is he still around?"

Ann interrupted, "I daresay. We lost track of him when we moved."

Peter ignored her. "He died a few years ago, still in Hong Kong. Not many people at his funeral, poor old chap."

Ann shot him an angry look, "You went?"

He nodded, "Of course."

So, Fanny thought, all is not well! Hah! They don't talk to each other. Good.

The phone rang again, this time for Sir Peter. Lorenza apparently had no trouble remembering his title.

Will called them to dinner, saving Peter's place at the head of the table. Pam and Helga sat on either side of him. Fanny sat opposite Ann. Will opened the wine. Two Filipina women served the meal. Peter returned in time for the starter of cold prawns.

While the plates were cleared and a salad was served, the doorbell rang. Pam called Peter away to sign papers for a serious young Chinese associate with an official-looking leather briefcase. Ann said to Fanny, "It's always like this. He's terribly important."

When Peter finished his signing, they ate the main course of New Zealand lamb, new potatoes, peas and mint sauce.

Fanny couldn't remember a meal that took so long. She looked from face to face and played with her food. The atmosphere was thick and stilted, the conversation light and superficial. Will and Drew tried hard. They discussed their various jobs, tennis, rugby, and they drank a lot of wine. Fanny calculated that they had at least a bottle each. Ann occasionally joined the conversation and she, too, drank seriously. Fanny couldn't contribute. The things she would normally talk about, her family, her work could all be misconstrued. She'd exhausted

her remarks about how much Hong Kong had changed. She
wanted to ask, what have you been doing for twenty years?
Practical things: What did you do with my piano? My other
paintings? Impractical things: Did you miss me? Were you
sorry when I left?

Peter flirted with Helga and Pam, and the young women
rebuffed him in a practiced, fond way. Fanny was so glad for
his sake that Rider had been spared this meal, though she would
have liked to discuss it with him later. He always had interesting insights.

Peter held up his wine glass and said, "A toast to Caroline.
A damn shame she can't be here."

Drew said, "To Line and Tony."

Most of the diners echoed Drew, "Caroline and Tony,"
but Peter said again, "To Caroline" and emptied his glass. Pam
refilled it.

Pam and Helga served the coffee, tea, cheese, and past-
ries. Pam explained, "The Filipinas are going to have their
own Easter lunch now. They've taken the rest of the food
away upstairs to a flat upstairs; the family has gone to Bali for
Easter. We've offered to clean up."

Will excused himself. He walked out to the terrace and
lit a cigarette. Drew joined him, then Ann. Fanny watched
them through the glass doors. Helga and Pam began to clear
off the dishes into the kitchen. Fanny, tired and saddened
with the banality of it, all took some coffee cups into the
kitchen. Helping with the dishes would give her time to get to
know Helga and Pam, women's time in the kitchen. But Pam
shooed her out. "Thanks, but I'm afraid not. What would you
think of us?"

"I'd feel welcome. I've been sitting around. I'd love to
help."

Pam was firm. "No, I can't let you. Not the first meal

you ever have with us. Talk to the boys."

Fanny didn't want to beg, but she felt like it. What now? Peter had joined the other three on the terrace. Fanny stood in the living room and watched them through the glass. The tall sons, so like their father. Were they like her at all?

She wanted to leave. Just pick up her handbag and walk to the front door. She could take a taxi to the ferry but it would require too much energy.

She flopped down in a low, deep armchair covered in heavy yellow-striped cotton. Forget the hotel, she was ready to go back to New York now, to Nigel, Sarah and Rider. Even to Caroline.

Fanny looked up with a start. Peter was in the room staring at her. She hadn't heard him re-enter.

He said, "We have a lot to talk about."

She said, "For instance? I think it was all said years ago."

Peter said, "You have nerve turning up like this. I wouldn't have thought you'd ever come back." He shrugged and looked outside. He added in a very low voice, "I thought I was rid of you."

Fanny asked, "And you're not?"

He looked directly at her, "No, I'm not." He stopped for a moment before he asked, "May I visit you at your hotel?"

Fanny asked, "Is that a proposition?"

He shrugged, "If that's what it leads to, why not? It was rather fun, I recall."

She knew of no way to extricate herself gracefully from the deep chair she sat in. Was this just what she had been afraid would happen? Or was it what she'd been hoping? "That was a very long time ago, I'm afraid. It wouldn't be a good idea."

"Why not? You're my wife."

"You divorced me."

"That didn't change anything, did it? You'll always be my wife."

Why didn't someone come into the room and save her. Where was Ann? Where were Drew and Will? She could see them on the terrace through the glass doors, their backs turned to her. "You are married to Ann now, or doesn't that mean anything to you?"

Peter smiled, "Merely a marriage of convenience, my dear. Not love, the way ours was."

"Was ours love? Was it love the way you treated me?"

"I treated you quite well, I recall. Yes, it was love."

She spat, "What about Eleanor and Genevieve, etcetera, etcetera? What about them?"

He laughed, "I remember Eleanor and Genevieve but not etcetera or etcetera. What did they look like?"

Fanny sputtered, "Bastard."

Peter shrugged. "Sorry. I know it all upset you, but they didn't mean anything to me, as you well know. What did you have to go and run off with that dreadful psychiatrist for? You could have done a lot better."

"Your feelings weren't a consideration at the time."

This is what I've been waiting for, Fanny thought, a real conversation.

"No, I don't suppose they were." He sat on the arm of her chair. His leg brushed her arm. Fanny could smell him. "You're still beautiful."

In spite of herself, Fanny blushed. She pushed at his back ineffectively. "Go away and stop bothering me."

He leaned over towards her. His voice was low. "You blushed. I'll stop around tomorrow to see you."

It was so public. At any moment, any of the others could have seen them. "I'm going shopping with Jean. I have a life, you know."

He sat up straight again. "I'm glad to hear it. The whole problem before was that you didn't. I hear you're in advertising. Just the sort of thing you'd be suited for."

"I won't be patronized, Peter. I'm happily married to Rider and I'm going to stay that way."

"By all means, don't get hysterical." His hand squeezed her shoulder. "I wouldn't want to break up a happy marriage. Actually, I pride myself on the fact that I've never broken up a marriage."

"You broke ours to pieces." She brushed his hand away. "This is getting tedious."

"You're quibbling. You left. I would have been happy with you forever. It wasn't my fault that you couldn't live with me. God, you're stunning."

Fanny didn't care any longer whether she got out of the chair gracefully or not. With a awkward twist, she forced herself up and out to the terrace where the others were.

He'd nearly seduced her. So easily. With the twins on the terrace. With Ann right there. With Pam and Helga clanging around in the kitchen behind them. How dare he? Not only that, but she had to admit to herself that she'd been pleased. A little flattery and she'd fallen for it. He still wanted her. He still found her attractive. Her anger with herself was founded in shame. Did she really want him again? What did he mean when he said his marriage to Ann was one of convenience? Perhaps for Peter, but Ann had surely never felt that way.

She needed another drink. She needed to be sick. She wanted to go back to the hotel.

Will interrupted her thoughts. "Do you still play the piano and paint?"

She forced herself into the present. "I haven't painted

in years, but my job gives a similar sort of satisfaction. I do play the piano, though. Did any of you turn out to be artists?"

Will said, "Drew and Line both. I get frustrated. I can never get it to look as good as I want it to and give up easily. Drew is the best, but he'll never use it. Would you like to see some of Line's drawings? I've a box of them. She left them here because she was afraid her mother-in-law would throw them out."

Ann overheard, "No, don't get those out. Caroline would kill you. Let her show them herself if she wants to."

Fanny said, "Are you all going to stay here after 1997?"

No one answered her. She looked at Will. He seemed lost in thought. Drew said, "It's a continual source of speculation. None of us are quite sure what we are going to do. Probably stay until it doesn't make sense to do so any more. We all have contingencies." He touched Fanny's arm, "We have so much time to make up. I want to take you to Lantau to see the new Buddha. It's very impressive. I'm due a day off from work. What day can you go?"

They settled on Tuesday. One more day that Fanny wouldn't be in the hotel if Peter showed up.

十二

Easter Monday, even though an official holiday, made hardly a difference in Hong Kong. Fanny followed Jean from factory shop to factory shop, up dingy ill-lighted staircases, to rummage through poorly organized shelves and tabletops for clothing that would be many times more expensive in New York. Still she could not muster enthusiasm for the task. Jean tried to coax her. To please Jean, she bought a denim shirt for Rider. Then, remembering that she had to bring presents for the children, bought a Karate sword for Nigel and a peacock-blue silk kimono for Sarah and stainless-steel ying-yang balls in brocade boxes for both of them. "I dunno, Jean. I'm just not inspired. I never was much of a shopper."

Jean waited until the day was almost over before she popped the question. They had just walked into a furniture shop on Saigon Street. She wanted to know all about Easter. "Come on, I can't wait all day."

Fanny found herself speechless. She needed months to think about it. The superficial description she had prepared for Jean had long since dissipated. "Ask me something specific, and maybe I can answer it."

"Where do I start? What was meeting Peter like? What

did you think?" Jean pretended to be examining a pretty Korean chest.

"Well. Just the same. Come on, Jean. You see him all the time. You know what he's like—he's just the same as he always was."

Jean glanced at Fanny sideways and winked. "Meaning? You said he's just the same, twice. Are you still in love with him?"

Fanny blushed and said no. Jean smiled. She changed the subject, "Helga—quite a looker—isn't she."

"Yes, wish I'd been born with legs like that," said Fanny. "I really liked Pam." Fanny's loyalties were split and her position tenuous. The strain was beginning to wear on her. Time to get back home. These were her sons' women they were talking about. It was so complicated. Jean knew them better than she did. They couldn't discuss them the way they had strangers in the old days. What if Jean told Will and Drew, even inadvertently, what she'd said about them?

"I was so uptight and...I can't think straight."

Jean looked crushed. "Do you remember Julia Yau?"

"No."

"Oh! You knew her several incarnations ago, but I can't for the life of me remember what her name was then. She's a Chinese girl. Worked for Peter. There was a big fuss about a divorce. Don't you remember?"

Fanny racked her brain. Yes, she remembered. "Julia Wo?" Lingling. She nodded.

Jean said, "Yes, that's it. Well, I bumped into her yesterday at the Jockey Club in Happy Valley. They really fixed it up after they moved the horse racing out to the New Territories. Anyway, Alan and I have dinner there quite often. I told her you were here for a few more days. She's quite the woman about town these days. She does go on a bit. Desperate to see you. Married to a doddering old billionaire."

"A billionaire, huh? I'd like to see her again."

Sure enough, back at the hotel, there was a message from Julia Yau. Fanny dumped her packages on the bed, kicked off her shoes and was about to dial the number when she glanced over at the desk in corner of her room. There by the stack of newspapers, she saw a beautifully arranged bouquet of long-stemmed lemon-yellow roses in a cut glass vase.

She walked over and counted two dozen. No note and no identification. But what identification could she possibly need? Only one person had ever sent her yellow roses. The fragrance was exquisite. Also his trademark. He would never buy scentless roses. How dare he violate her room? The arrogance of the man. She knew what this was about. He wanted to seduce her. He couldn't bear it that she'd left him. Her wedding bouquet had been yellow roses; she wondered if Ann's had been, too.

She wasn't too badly shaken to walk back to the phone and, with her back to the roses, ring Julia. A servant answered in Chinese, "Wei?"

Fanny hesitantly asked for Julia Yau. The voice at the other end let out a loud stream of Cantonese, there was a pause, a clicking on the line and then Julia came on the line talking very fast, "Fanny? I think of you for six years. I think that we meet again. I know it soon. Why you didn't tell me you were coming? You make me very mad."

"How are you, Julia? Jean tells me that you have a new husband."

"Yes, but not new. Old husband. He wants me for nurse and sex-thing. I want to meet you for lunch tomorrow. Tai tai lunch. Okay?"

" I'm free on Wednesday or Thursday, then I go home."

"Not meet tomorrow?"

"No."

"Why not tomorrow? Why you can't meet me? Who you see tomorrow? Where you go tomorrow?"

Fanny sighed. "To see the Buddha on Lantau with Drew and Will."

"Big handsome sons, two for one. Very lucky woman. You crazy if you go tomorrow. Buddha not worth trouble."

"Why?" Fanny felt the beginnings of exasperation.

"Ching Ming Festival. One million people and their relations go to Lantau on Ching Ming."

The Ching Ming Festival is the day Chinese pay their respects to their ancestors and honor the dead, sweep away dirt from the graves, have picnics and leave offerings. There are many huge cemeteries on Lantau. "That's the only day they can both take. So taitai lunch on Wednesday or Thursday?"

"Stubborn girl. O.K. Wednesday. I meet you at Grand Café, Hong Kong side. In Grand Hyatt at twelve o'clock. O.K.?" She continued with barely a pause, "Everybody very mad when you leave. Big trouble for Peter and children. I think he lose very much face. I think everybody still very mad with you. Why you come back?"

"I will tell you all about it on Wednesday."

"See you."

"See you."

When Julia left Jimmy Wo, Peter found her a job at Government House on Hong Kong side. Julia knew that she owed her name (which by now she considered lucky) and her job to Fanny. By the time Fanny left Hong Kong, just a few months later, Julia was well established. She was sufficiently bilingual by this time.

When Fanny knew she was leaving Hong Kong, she had a problem. She and Rider had decided that the easiest way to leave was by tourist visa. She would have to visit the American Embassy on the Hong Kong side several times to procure one, and might be seen by any number of people Peter knew doing so. She had passport photographs taken in Tsuen Wan and asked for Julia's help. She knew that Julia would never tell Peter. It is Chinese way to pay back debts and although Julia owed a debt to Peter, she owed one to Fanny, too. She obtained the visa for Fanny efficiently. It was a secret they shared. Other than Rider, a ticketing agent and the American Embassy, no one else in the world was privy to Fanny's plan.

Fanny took the roses out into the hallway and placed them on the floor before she rang Rider and the children. It would be seven a.m. in New York.

Sarah answered coughing and sputtering. "Hi, Mom. What's up? The sore throat has gone away but I think I have an ear infection. Good thing it's vacation. Nigel is still asleep, but Dad's awake. He's making coffee downstairs. Wanna talk to him? By the way, when do you come home? I still can't believe you were gone for Easter."

"I'll be home on Friday. Sound good? What are your plans for today?"

"I'm going over Kelly's house. She has a new dog, a spotty kinda sausage-dog. Wish we could have a dog. Why does Dad have to be allergic? Dad's taking Nigel to the office today. D - a - a - a- d." She let out an ear-piercing shriek, "D - a - a - a - d."

"Fan, what happened?"

"What do you mean?"

"I've been calling you all night. You haven't been there."

"It was daytime here, remember? I went shopping with Jean. I bought you a present."

"You tell me that you are going to have lunch with Peter, Ann, William, Andrew and all the rest of them and you
don't call. I can't sleep. I can't eat. I'm booking the flight
already."

Fanny laughed. Rider loved her. She loved him. Those
roses could bloom somewhere else. "Don't worry about me.
I survived, believe it or not."

"What do you mean, you survived. What the hell happened?"

"Nothing. I went to lunch with them. Peter is just the
same, but old. Ann is just the same, but old. The twins are
men and beyond my mothering. Nothing happened."

"You were so worried." Rider waited a moment. "I was
so worried."

"No problem. How's Nigel?"

"He's fine. Hates baseball. Getting good grades at school
though. He's very smart if he'd just apply himself. Fanny?"

Fanny held her breath. She knew what was coming and
she couldn't lie to him. "Yes?"

"Do you still have intense unresolved feelings about Peter?"

"Yes."

"Are they passionate feelings?"

"No, I'd say more submerged than that. Just a fascina-
tion. An interest. It's history. Don't worry, I'm not intending
to have sex with him."

"I know you're not *intending* to have sex with him. What
are his feelings about you?"

"Are you sure that you want to have this conversation?"
A loud knocking on the door brought Fanny back to reality.
"Do you hear that? Someone's knocking on the door. Hang
on."

A uniformed woman from the housekeeping staff stood

outside her door holding the flowers. She spoke loudly, "For you. Very pretty." She smiled and held them out.

Fanny took them from her. "Thanks."

She carried the flowers to the desk and placed them by the newspapers again, then returned to the phone. "O.K. Where were we?"

"What was all that about?"

"Nothing."

"Francis. I hate it when you say nothing in that tone of voice. You sound distinctly guilty. What was that all about?"

Fanny remembered a television show where someone in a hotel room had to answer the same question. "The maid wanting to turn down the beds. I presume that's okay by you?"

"What's going on there?"

"Nothing, I promise. I told her to go away. Look, I'll be home on Friday for once and for all. This is my schedule between then and now." She told him about Lantau and the Ching Ming Festival, and her taitai lunch with Julia.

"I distinctly heard someone say 'These are for you. Very pretty.' What's pretty?"

She took a deep breath. "Peter has sent me some roses. He always sends roses to everyone. It's nothing. Stop worrying."

"He's sending you roses and I should stop worrying? What were they, yellow roses?"

"How did you know?" Was he ever there when Peter had sent her flowers? Maybe at the hospital.

"Some things stick in the memory banks like a shred of meat in the teeth."

"Oh Rider, I love you."

"I have a neurotic hatred for the man. I'm having a testosterone rush. I want to beat him to a pulp. I want to kill him with knives. I want to slit his belly open. Get those fucking roses out of your room now."

"Who is the one who sounds crazy?"

"Get those fucking roses out of your room. I want you on the next fucking plane home."

"Calm down, don't be ridiculous. I'll get rid of the roses. Lighten up. I'm cool."

"If that fucking asshole shows up at your door, get the management to show him out. Whatever you do, don't let him in. Why didn't you tell me about the roses?"

"It's not as bad as you think. I just didn't want to upset you. In fact I put them outside my door to get rid of them, if you must know, and they've just given them right back to me."

"How many fucking roses did he send you?"

"Two dozen, twenty-four."

"I should have dealt with him when I had the chance."

"I like you jealous. I've never heard you like this before."

His voice softened. "Come home where you belong. You know, Clara really needs to hear from you. There are big problems in your office. Meanwhile you're going to lose the Bresso account if you don't put some effort into keeping it. I can't believe he's sending you fucking roses."

"They aren't fucking roses."

"Yes, they are fucking roses. He wants to fuck you. That's what the fucking roses are about. Sometimes women can be so fucking stupid. He thinks you're stupid enough to fall for his fucking bag of tricks, but I got news for him. You might have been that stupid once, but you're not that stupid now."

Fanny laughed. She couldn't stop. He sounded like the hero in a bad Bruce Willis movie. "I'll give him the news personally."

"No, I'll give him the fucking news."

"Are the children in the kitchen with you? Please don't speak that way."

"I want you to call me in the morning. I want you to call me three times a day until this is over. I can't believe it. Fucking yellow roses all over again. Tell him that yellow is the color of cowards."

"Jeez. Let up on the guy. He's a little mixed up, that's all."

"See, that's another one of his dirty little tricks. You're falling for it already. He makes pathetic so you feel so sorry for him that all you want to do is love him. Give me a fucking break."

"My dearest man, calm down. Take three deep breaths. You're likely to give yourself a heart attack if you carry on at this rate. I love you and it's okay."

"It won't be okay until it's over. Until the fat lady sings. Don't you kid yourself, until he is fucking dead."

"Take it easy. Don't you have to get Nigel up? Don't you have to go to work today? You are going to be more loony than your clients today."

"Isn't it the truth? Sweetheart, get rid of those fucking roses and call me in the morning. Sweet dreams."

"I will. Good night, and calm down."

Fanny decided to dial Clara before she forgot. She was amazed at herself. It was as though the studio didn't exist at all any more. It all seemed so distant. Within two minutes of speaking with Clara, the full familiar load of aggravation struck her. From everyday logistical problems like the copier not working, to design decisions, to Bresso needing more attention.

" ...And not only that, the $10,000 check we were waiting on from Littors still hasn't appeared...." Fanny made decisions and boosted her with some compliments and a promise to be there next week. Then she hung up. She decided that she really needed to bring Clara back a present.

A headache had already taken hold. She tried to ignore it and put her shoes back on. She peered out of the door to see if the hotel housekeeper was prowling. When she saw the coast clear, she carried the glass vase of roses down the hallway and up six floors in the elevator. The doors opened onto a floor that looked identical. The same Chinese vases turned into lamps, the same elegant Chinese rosewood furniture and almost the same Bonsai tree in a blue pot, but with any luck a different housekeeper who couldn't identify the owner of the vase. Fanny walked over to one of the tables and plunked the vase of flowers on it. She took the elevator back to her floor, walked back to her room and succumbed to the headache, which now shone blindingly white and throbbed. She turned out the lights, lay down and slept, fully clothed.

Meeting the twins in the crush before the ferry ride to Lantau was just as frenetic as Julia predicted. Luckily Drew and Will were a head taller than most of the crowd and could be easily seen. "First class is sold out. I'm afraid we're going to have to go steerage," Will said.

Fanny hadn't seen them in casual clothes before. In oversized polo shirts and baggy jeans and tennis shoes, they looked younger and very alike. She could see a glimmer of the little boys they had been.

They jostled their way through the gray concrete pilings onto the lowest deck of the three-decker ferry which was packed to bursting with humanity. The few flimsy seats were taken and most of the floor taken also, so they found a place to stand by the stern of the vessel. All around them, card players, feasters, readers and conversationalists settled down. The smells of the food and the diesel exhaust mingled with the salty sea air filled Fanny with nostalgia for years ago when they would cross the harbor by vehicular ferry from Jordan Road.

They rode in a luxury coach from Mui Wo to Ngong Ping. The spectacular, rolling, green, treeless hill outside the bus windows flashed by almost unnoticed because the twins were such interesting, well-read companions. Nothing had prepared her for the pleasure she would get from her adult children. Nor did she feel she deserved it. Yet there it was.

The day became warm, clouds came and went. They climbed the steps from the Po Lin Monastery to the gleaming, placid new Buddha. In spite of the other people there, Fanny felt alone with the boys and forgiven by them. She tried to see their likeness to Peter, and found their charm and looks comparable, but, otherwise, they were different. These boys were not natural politicians like their father, nor did they want to talk about the past. If Fanny tried to talk about it, they changed the subject quickly and skillfully.

The crowds had interspersed to the graves on the hillsides. They were alone waiting for a ferry back. They decided they had enough time before it arrived to walk along the beach at Silvermine Bay. A group of Filipina maids were hymn singing before their picnic. It wasn't important to talk, but to be together.

On the ferry back to Central, Drew and Will argued about where to take Fanny for late lunch. "Anywhere will do, really."

They settled on a small hole-in-the-wall where they ate a huge lunch of prawns, squid, scallions and bean curd tossed in a chili sauce. Fanny was so thirsty that she drank four bottles of water.

They were seated at a rickety table on a worn linoleum floor. Fanny tried one last time, "I want to tell you about it. I want you to understand."

Drew said, "We do understand. You can tell us whatever

you want. We will listen, if you need us to, but I speak for both of us when I say it's not necessary. We've discussed it more than once. We know you loved us. We missed you. You've come back to us now for five minutes. But you're not going to live here, you're not going to be much of a factor in our lives, no matter how much you would like to be. Perhaps before you leave, we can see each other again."

"You can come see me in New York."

Will answered, "We could, I suppose, but what about your husband and children? It's better this way. You can come see us every now and then. Whenever you want to."

"Your attitudes sound terribly mature. It seems that there it is all cut and dried and packaged. You really don't want to know what it was like and why I left."

The boys sighed in unison, identical again. They started to speak at once, "You're right."

Then Will withdrew and his brother continued, "You see, you left our father for another man. It's clear as day. You left us and then you had other children. It's clear as day. Clear as day."

Fanny said in a low, unsteady voice, "Your father left me, long before I left him."

"No," they said in unison. Drew continued again, he seemed to be the spokesman, "He didn't leave you, that's the point. You were living together in the same house and sleeping in the same bed until you left him for another man."

Fanny stood. They continued to sit. Will stared into his glass of tea, Drew looked at the wall.

She said, "I enjoyed today. I had no idea that adult children could be such wonderful companions. I am sorry a thousand times over for what happened and what I did to you. You are right, of course. I did leave your father for another man. I also left you and your sister. It was the hardest thing

I've ever had to do in my life and it can't be undone. You are also right that there are no excuses." She picked up her hand-bag. "Can I take you to dinner on Thursday night? It's my last night here."

"We'll give you a ring at the hotel," Drew said. He stood and kissed her on the cheek. Fanny bent and kissed Will, then left the restaurant.

She walked and walked trying to hold back tears that she knew would be uncontrollable. She was exhausted. She hated her sons and she loved her sons. She didn't even know her sons. She'd waited too long and really, they were lost to her. They had none of the shared parent-child history. Fanny realized how much of it is memories of when the cat died, or when the dining room table collapsed. It was the everyday stuff. The time passing that couldn't be made up. It was silly to want to turn it into one big happy family.

She found herself on dirty, crowded Hollywood Road. Antique shops cluttered with dusty furniture. Elegant and spare shops displaying ceramics, silver, rugs, and chests. She stopped at a newer shop she didn't remember with ornate woodcarvings in the window and purchased a burl wood box for Clara.

Fanny stepped out of the taxi in front of the Grand Hyatt. She still hadn't recovered from her trip with the twins the day before. The hurt was still raw. Then when she'd returned to her hotel room, another delivery of yellow roses, this time small rosebuds arranged in an exquisite but simple cream Ting bowl, had surprised her. Again, no note had been attached. She knew the bowl well. She and Peter had bought it together when they were learning about ancient Chinese porcelain. It was actually a copy of a Ting vase attributed to the Ming Dy-

nasty. This time she threw the roses in the wastebasket and wrapped the bowl carefully in a T-shirt and put it in her suitcase. No one would ever guess its worth. She'd loved the delicacy of the bowl. It glowed like the moon.
She tried to think about the lunch ahead, but couldn't. Sorry she'd accepted, she wasn't at all in the mood to face an interrogation from Julia Wo or whatever her name now was. Nor would she be able to talk about Drew and Will and whether they'd ever accept her or give her a chance to explain. She desperately needed someone to talk to.

From Julia's impatient stance it was clear to Fanny that she wasn't used to waiting for anyone. Her foot in a black high-heeled suede pump with a gold bow tapped against the floor. To Fanny, Julia looked a lot older, but then she'd been expecting the sweet young girl she'd named years ago. Her clothes looked too expensive to label her a tart, but the flash and style were unmistakably come-hither.
"I tell you meet me at twelve o'clock."
"It is only five past. I'm sorry."
"Five minutes more and table gone." Julia spoke quickly in Cantonese to a passing waiter who took them immediately to the only empty table with a full and magnificent view of the harbor. She recovered herself when they were seated. Her smile was charming. "Have good lunch. Wine, too. Remember you like to drink."
Fanny shook her head. "Not any more."
"You like to eat, very much."
Fanny laughed, "Yes, I like to eat, but today not very hungry. Hong Kong has very good food. This restaurant is rather fancy to be a coffee shop." She gestured to a large plaster Greek God, "The columns, the statue, it wasn't what I was

expecting at all."

Julia nodded. "Good for our discussion."

So, Fanny thought, this is a business lunch. Julia is cashing her chips in. Good grief.

Julia studied the wine list. Fanny marveled at how far Julia had come under her own steam from the naive young daughter of a New Territories pig farmer.

Julia ordered a bottle of Piper-Heidsieck champagne. "You still speak some Cantonese?"

Fanny shook her head, "I never was very good and I fear most of it is gone."

Julia nodded, "Very happy to see you. Think that we long friends."

"Yes," said Fanny, "we are."

Julia interrogated, and Fanny answered, questions about Rider and the children. Julia was especially interested in the design studio. "How you learn to do this?"

"Art is my subject. I worked in a studio. It's what I know how to do."

"You make a lot of money? You get very rich?"

"No, definitely not."

"Why you do?"

How could she explain to Julia that money wasn't everything? That she needed something that was hers. That a lot of the time it was fun. That eking out a living this way made her independent and stronger. "Surely you're not interested in money. You must have enough. Your husband is wealthy."

"Never too much money. Fanny, Fanny, sometimes you very stupid."

They ordered. Fanny chose fresh salmon salad with avocado and pesto sauce. Julia, the lobster and prawn salad. "Good with champagne." The champagne arrived, was poured, and Julia lifted her glass. "See you in New York."

Fanny lifted her glass and smiled. She'd guessed and she'd been right. This wasn't going to be a free meal, far from it. She emptied her glass. The champagne tasted dry and metallic.

"So," she said, "when are you coming to New York?"

"Need favor from you." Julia smiled sweetly. "Live with you in New York. Short time only. Buy house. Get citizen. Help me? Hong Kong no good for Hong Kong Chinese. Have got good lawyer from San Francisco."

"Buy house?"

"Help buy house. Get good price. Make very much money. How much good house cost in New York?"

The waiter refilled Fanny's glass. How could she refuse? What would she be refusing anyway? So far, the request wasn't at all clear.

The meal arrived. Fanny drank her second glass as she answered Julia's barrage of questions on real estate. She glanced at her watch. It was almost one. Julia changed the subject long enough to let drop that she'd been married once between Jimmy and the billionaire. "Michael So, very good man. He die."

"Died of what?"

"Heart attack. Bing, bang, dead. Very sad. Have newspaper. Now Henry Yau have newspaper."

"I think I get it." She knifed a piece of avocado.

"When you leave Hong Kong, Peter very mad."

Fanny nodded, "Of course."

"He very sad, too. I think he like you very much."

"Really?"

Julia nodded. She poked at her lobster buried among intricately carved vegetables.

"Then he move Hong Kong side. Marry Ann. Very English. No good for him."

You have no argument on that score, Fanny thought. "Did you see my children?"

"Sometimes see children. Grow up very fast. England school. Think very good children. Like very much. You very lucky."

"Do you see Peter now?"

"Sir Peter, very important. See him sometime at party. I think he very sad they do not make him Governor. Must have big-shot from England. Peter like Hong Kong better than England. It very bad."

Fanny drank her third glass of champagne. She wanted to put her head onto the table and sleep. She'd had enough. She forced herself to continue the conversation. "Where do you live now?"

"Penthouse Flat in Happy Valley. Henry has many building."

Eventually Fanny found an opportunity to ask, "Do you remember our house in New Territories?"

Julia nodded.

Fanny asked, "Who owns it now?"

Julia shook her head. "Everybody buy, sell, buy sell. All the time."

The lunch had been a bust. Fanny had learned nothing and now Julia was going to come live with them.

As Julia signed for the lunch, Fanny drank her fourth glass of champagne. The room was becoming fuzzy. Who would put a statue of a Greek God in a Hong Kong coffee shop anyway? She wondered how she would get back to the hotel. She wished she were back on the plane to New York. Only one more day and she would be. But she should go back to Water Music one last time.

After she and Julia had kissed goodbye, slightly tipsy, she'd wandered around Wanchai and Causeway Bay until she was too tired to go further.

By half past five, Fanny was walking through the arcade below her hotel past the tourist shops, her exhaustion worse for the champagne at lunch. Every window was brightly lit and most were crowded with gold bracelets, chains, necklaces, rings and earrings. There was an Indian tailor and a flower shop. Fanny gasped. She saw Peter's back in the flower shop behind a spray of orchids. He was paying with a credit card and chatting to the saleswoman. Her heart did a double turn, and although her first instinct was to run like the wind, there was still enough champagne in her system to lessen her anxieties. She strolled past the bank of elevators and stood half hidden, pretending to absorb herself in the gaudy display of a jeweler's window. She wondered what arrangement he had purchased to be delivered upstairs for her today. It would be difficult to match the value of yesterday's offering.

After a long moment he appeared. Except it wasn't Peter. It wasn't anyone she knew. She had mistaken someone else for him. A young man from the shop whose doorway she was standing in asked her to step inside. She stared at him in confusion. She'd completely forgotten where she was. Her disappointment and embarrassment irritated her and she took it out on him. "No, thank you very much."

"Oh, Missie. Can make for you. You want? We make. Custom. Ring. Necklace. What you want? Very reasonable."

"Nothing.."

She stomped off towards the lifts and took one to her floor. She had one day left here and then she was leaving. Neither of the twins had telephoned since the fiasco yesterday. No one had asked her to dinner. It was too late to ring Jean. She wanted to go home tomorrow. She hadn't hit the mini-bar so far, but tonight was the night. She didn't care what happened. Rider wanted her to ring, but she wasn't in the mood. Her head hurt again. This whole trip had been a terrible idea from start to finish. And at the end of it she'd have to mop up a mess at the studio and pay the bill. Still waters inside of her had been churned up without a chance they'd settle again.

She placed the plastic door card into a slot by the door to turn the lights on in the room, then hooked the PLEASE DO NOT DISTURB marker on the door knob. The phone was ringing and she didn't move to answer it. She scanned the room for a flower arrangement and saw none. She sat on the bed by the telephone and felt sorry for herself. Peter was playing games with her. Roses for two days, then none. Typical. He wanted her to expect them, look forward to them, like the attention, and then he'd withdraw it. Wasn't that always his game? How could she have fallen for such tripe? What did he expect her to do, call and thank him? The nerve of the man was overwhelming. The telephone had stopped ringing. She waited for the light to appear so she could call to find out who it was. No light appeared.

She went over to the mini-bar and got out a small bottle of vodka. She emptied an ice tray into a glass from the tray above and poured the vodka in. It tasted bitter. She kicked off her shoes and went into the bathroom to run a hot bubble bath. She'd open a bottle of wine and sip it in the bathtub.

She turned on the hot tap and poured a thick stream of lavender oil into the tub. It foamed comfortingly. The phone rang again. She let it ring. She didn't want to speak to anyone. She undressed, throwing her clothes onto the bed. By the time she was completely naked the phone had stopped ringing. She leaned over the bath and turned the water off. Steam had filled the bathroom. The water felt too hot, but she lowered herself into it slowly after pouring the contents of a half bottle of California chardonnay into a couple of glasses. All the grime and frustration of the day seeped from her. Her feet, which had become numb while she was walking, were recovering their feeling. The lavender scent reminded her of England, of her parents, of her grandparents. All that was so long ago.

She had finished both glasses of wine and almost dozed off when the phone rang again. She thought it might be Rider, angry she hadn't rung him. Perhaps it was one of the twins. Maybe Jean was trying to get in touch with her, or Clara. She didn't allow herself to think that it might be Peter or that she cared at all. Pulling herself drowsily from the bath, Fanny quietly thanked whoever was trying to get in touch with her. She could have easily drowned in there. Not such a bad way to go all things considered. She toweled herself dry and opened the bathroom door. The freezing cold air-conditioning hit her in a blast.

A loud knock frightened her. She looked over to reassure herself that she'd chained and double locked the door. She shivered and pulled on her sweat pants and sweatshirt. She looked a terrible mess. She couldn't even let the maid see her in this condition. She lay down on the bed. Her head swam.

The knocking went away. About five minutes later, the phone woke her up. This time muttering to herself that if she was going to get any peace she'd better talk to someone she picked up the receiver, "Yes?"

"Overseas call. Is Mrs. Rider there please?"

"Who wants to know?"

There was a click and a conversation she couldn't hear. If they didn't want her to know, to hell with them, she thought. She replaced the receiver, and dialed the front desk. "This is Francis Rider in room 625. I'm very tired. Please hold all my messages and phone calls until the morning."

A very young female voice responded, "Yes, Mrs. Rider, we will take care of it. Sleep well."

Fanny pulled the sheet and blanket over her. Loneliness overwhelmed her. She missed Rider. She wanted to curl her body around his and fall asleep against his safe, warm back. She didn't like sleeping alone anymore. When she'd lived in Water Music, she hadn't known the kind of comfort and consistency Rider gave her. She would lie in bed and wait for Peter to get home. She'd listen to his progress crashing drunk through the house. When he finally got to bed, sometimes he'd be amorous and she'd have to fight him off. Mostly though, he'd be snoring within a few moments. She'd be too disappointed to reach over and touch him. She'd wiggle away from him, as far away as she could sleep from him without falling out of the bed, and feel the hurt eating away at her.

She looked at the clock. Rider would be driving into the city now. She'd have to wait an hour or so if she wanted to talk to him. She turned off the light and fell into a sleep as deep as the ocean.

十三

The last day started badly. The phone rang and rang. She'd asked the girl at the switchboard to stop her calls. She'd been dreaming about messages all urgent, all impossible to answer. The phone woke her up and she didn't want to hear from anybody. She'd slept a long time. Her head throbbed; her mouth had dried to powder. She wondered if it was the wine that made her feel so groggy. What did they all want?

Pieces of white paper had been pushed under the door of the room. It couldn't have all been dreams. She bent and gathered them up. She prioritized them in a patchwork on the desk.

Call Mr. Rider in New York, URGENT: You know the number.

Telephone Message from the Office of Mr. Andrew Ardel-Rhys with a number.

Telephone message from Jean Meade with a number, Ring NOW.

Telephone message from Imelda of the Double Sunshine Travel Service.

Clara Kidosky from Rider Design Studio, you know the number.

A package has been delivered and is waiting at the front desk, must be signed for.

Tours of the New Territories available for visitors, stop by at the desk in the lobby.

Nothing from Peter at all, unless the package was from him, but of course it wouldn't be. He'd never sent her a package in his life. He was busy. What was she looking for anyway?

Her rational mind knew that she was wading in dangerous swamps. She loved Rider. She loved Sarah and Nigel. Her life in New York was fulfilling and interesting. What was she thinking of?

She tackled the messages one at a time. Rider needed reassuring: she'd promised to call and hadn't. She was able to tell him truthfully that roses weren't being delivered anymore and she missed him. She reminded him that she would be home tomorrow. She told him what Drew and Will had said about Rider, Sarah, and Nigel not wanting them to visit. He said, "You're going to have to think about telling Sarah and Nigel. They're curious. It's time."

Andrew was in an important meeting, but a perky secretary relayed the message. Could she please meet them at the Hong Kong Club at 6:30 p.m. for dinner? Fanny accepted, disappointed not to be speaking with him directly.

"Jean's gone to get her hair done," Alan said. "She wants you to come for dinner tonight."

She told him she was meeting the boys.

Imelda Chang wanted to confirm the time to take her to the airport the next day. "Wait for you to say you want my brother to drive you. Why you no call?"

Clara had been trying to ring her all night from the studio. She had good news and bad news. The good news was really big news. Neil & Greer had decided to use them to redesign packages for their luxury line of soaps, talcum powders, creams, and colognes. It had been a long time coming. She'd been pitted against a mammoth Madison Avenue advertising company and, though she knew she could beat them on price, their pitch was more polished.

"Can you believe it? We've done it. And won't it be fun? The bad news is that the check still hasn't come from Littors. They say another week. I don't think we can pay anyone this week. Good thing you're coming back."

That was the reality. A victory and no money. Problems. At least there was good news. She'd have to think carefully about the theme and the colors.

The messages were taken care of. This was the last day. The last chance to ever see Water Music. She pulled on her clothes, jeans and sneakers, brushed her hair out, grabbed her wallet, and without makeup or a glance in the mirror, rushed downstairs.

On the MTR to Tsuen Wan, Fanny remembered that she had forgotten to ask at the desk for the package. She started to think more clearly. She needed a flashlight and a picnic. She'd have to buy them in Tsuen Wan. There so many things that she'd meant to do. She'd wanted to go to the monastery above Tsuen Wan. For that matter, she'd thought to revisit the Taoist monastery, Ching Chung Koon, which was near the hospital. She hadn't been close to the eastern part of the New Territories. The Meades had told her that Sai Kung hadn't been ruined in the least. That it had been turned into a country park, with trails for hikers. At least everything hadn't been ruined.

By the time Fanny had wandered around the town, and bought a flashlight, a pomelo, biscuits and bottled water, by the time she'd explored Tung Uk, the Hakka compound turned into museum, it was past two. She sat for a while in one of the bare, cool ancient rooms and tried to imagine the lives that had been lived there. She especially concentrated to see if she could feel spirits like those at Water Music. She couldn't.

She made her way to the bus stop and formulated a plan. She decided to get off the bus above Hoi Mei Wan, the beach by the house. She walked halfway down the concrete steps. It was a humid day. Not hot yet, but uncomfortable. She took a left turn and stopped at one of the elaborate concrete shelters built for beach parties by weekend visitors. She sat in the shade of a sandy but deserted terrace and peeled her pomelo. She could see the beach below without a footprint on the sand. Debris, from the construction just across the water, had washed up onto the shore, wood, metal, food packages. The sound of the beating of waves on the rocks had been drowned out by the noise from the pilings being driven into the channel and the engines of the tugs and barges and hovercraft.

Above, to the right on the jut of the peninsula, Fanny could see Water Music, imperial, grand and white. From this angle, it didn't look deserted. The bamboo grove partially obscured the downstairs windows. There was no evidence of the Chinese family who lived on the grounds now.

The acidic tang and sweetness of the pomelo reminded her of eating just such a fruit years ago. Perhaps she shouldn't go back into the house again. She should go on past the San Miguel brewery, through Castle Peak. Alan and Jean had said that Castle Peak had changed beyond recognition. It was now known as the gold coast and the bay had been filled in to make room for the huge new town, Tuen Mun. It didn't sound inviting. Alan and Jean hadn't known whether the Dragon Inn was still standing.

The Dragon Inn had been a favorite with the children. Five monkeys were chained to pole by a metal band around their necks and did tricks when fed peanuts. The children didn't notice the scabs on the backs of the animals, the matted fur, or the partial blindness of the largest of them. The children didn't notice the red paint peeling from the columns of the pagodas or sticky black flies hovering over the tables. They liked the colorful birds in cages, however unmotivated the birds were to fly. She constantly worried that one of the monkeys would bite the children and give them rabies, or that they would pick up some rare undiagnosable tropical disease from an insect bite. Peter laughed at her fears. "They are more likely to pick up an immunity that will serve them well. You can't wrap them in cotton wool, you know."

Caroline had insisted Fanny take her to the Dragon Inn to make up for missing her seventh birthday. They'd had an ice cream and a 7-Up at a dirty concrete and green-tiled table and Fanny bought peanuts to feed to the monkeys. It was during the worst time. She hadn't known that she had the option of leaving. She knew she had to do something, but she'd no idea what. The Dragon Inn was so depressing it only made it worse.

Later when she and Rider had met secretly, she'd told him about the visit. He'd said that she was identifying too strongly with the monkeys. He'd been right. She could feel their chains and their wounds. She shuddered at their boredom and frustration.

Fanny hid the pomelo peels under a bush, which looked as though it needed biodegradable boost, and trudged back up the steps to the road. At least the steps hadn't changed, and with her back to the view, it still felt like the same place, the same sandy soil and same spindly shrubs.

She glanced towards Water Music. Three expensive cars were parked on the side of the road. As she walked closer she saw a Mercedes, a Jaguar, and a Porsche. They all looked shiny new. Her first instinct was to turn tail and run. If only she had dressed as well as she had the first day. She'd been prepared to clamber up hillsides, armed with a flashlight and sneakers, and looked a total mess, but she'd come this far, maybe she could meet the new owners. She touched her mouth; she hadn't even remembered lipstick.

She pushed her way though the overgrowth towards the house. The front door was wide open, but no one was in sight. She heard a dog barking and faint voices some distance away. She walked into the house tentatively. Light streamed in through the open door and she saw details she hadn't seen in the gloom last time. She saw the old brass hinges on the door, and a new crack in the wooden parquet. She had a change of heart. Instead of walking to the back of the house to face the new owners, she raced up the stairs two at a time, to the bedrooms, avoiding piles of plaster. She crept into the master bedroom, listening carefully for voices and footsteps. The house was empty. The voices were outside.

She leaned against the bedroom wall, catching her breath, listening to her heart pound. Footprints laced the dusty floor, and not just those she had made a few days ago, but new. She forced herself to relax, one limb at a time. The room was so silent. She wondered what the penalties would be if the fancy car owners caught her there. She didn't care. How dare these total strangers invade her house on the one day in twenty years she was there?

She heard voices directly below her. The house, even though empty and echoing, had been too well built for her to identify the speakers or even the language she spoke. She listened carefully. They were men's voices, but she could have deduced that from looking at the cars. The voices moved towards the front of the house and out the front door. It closed with a thud.

After a moment, Fanny crept out to the hall landing. She

waited for the jingle of a key or the turn of a bolt. She inched into the room that used to be Caroline's at the front of the house. She stood by the window but saw no one. She thought she heard the sound of cars revving up and being driven away, but it could have been her imagination. Her ears strained against the silence. She heard children shouting in Cantonese below her but she couldn't see them either.

She waited a few moments and walked downstairs slowly, a step at a time, prepared to run back and hide, if she heard the slightest sound. She was alone. She wasn't flooded with memories the way she had been during her last visit.

Just as she got to the bottom step, the front door opened without warning and a stream of late afternoon sunshine illuminated her like a spotlight. Well, she thought, I'm either going to laugh about this as one of life's most embarrassing moments, or I'm going to jail.

The men at the door were silhouetted, and, because her eyes were so unaccustomed to bright light, she was temporarily blinded. One came forward. He spoke with an American-Chinese accent. "Who are you? What are you doing here?"

Fanny thought the questions unoriginal and wanted to say so, but didn't. She couldn't think what to answer. He probably didn't have a sense of humor.

The other figure came to her rescue. "It's all right, David. I know this woman; she was my wife once. Her name is Francis...something or other...I've forgotten." He turned to Fanny, "I wondered if we'd find you here today."

David, turned to Peter, "Wife number one?" and laughed.

Peter laughed too and said to Fanny, "Private joke."

"At my expense," Fanny said.

"If you will come creeping around other people's houses, you will discover that people do make jokes at your expense. I'm afraid the jokes have hardly started, my dear."

Fanny couldn't think of a clever reply and decided to keep quiet.

David said to Peter as though Fanny wasn't present, "Did you invite her?"

Peter laughed again. "In a manner of speaking. Francis, this is David Lei."

"Charmed," said Fanny.

Both men wore expensively cut business suits and silk ties. Fanny said, "Am I to presume that you own this house now?"

"An investment," Peter said.

"It's worth less than it used to be. That bridge being built is unconscionable. How could you have let the airport go through?"

"I couldn't very well object on the grounds that it would blot the view of an investment house, could I? Besides it is the price of progress. The airport is badly needed."

Alan had called it progress, too. "What are you planning to do with the house?"

David spoke first. "Flats will be built here by this time next year. It will be nice. Very nice." He stepped back towards the door. "This is very pleasant, but I have to get back to the office." He turned to Peter. "So we are agreed then?"

Peter nodded, "Negotiate a little, then give in. I don't have to tell you."

David nodded. He said, "My best wishes to Lady Ann. Pleased to have met you Mrs…?"

"Rider," Fanny said. "Glad to have met you."

David turned and walked out the door, closing it behind him.

Peter said, "Alone at last." He walked towards her. "America has done nothing for your dress sense. Even off the peg would be better than that."

"I was dressed to break and enter, not to impress you and your friends."

"If you were still my wife, you'd have to dress for me. Lady Francis. Doesn't that sound grand?"

"Yes, but I'm not, am I?" Fanny frowned.

Peter held out his hand. "Come, let me show you something." He took her arm. They walked into the lounge over to the French doors. Light streamed into the room. Boards, which a few days ago had covered the glass, had been removed.

"Do you remember how it was to be as young and naive as we once were?" He watched her closely.

Fanny said, "Of course."

Peter looked away, "It doesn't seem that long ago. I've often thought about how you became ill. You know, it would have happened wherever we lived."

Fanny shuddered. Seeds of fond reminiscence faded into irritation. "Whatever it was has been discussed *ad nauseam*. I'm better now and intend to stay that way. Living here certainly didn't help and being married to you made it far worse."

"And I suppose your psychiatrist chappie is better for you in all respects. How bloody boring." He smiled, "Do you remember the tiger heads and orandas?"

Fanny had to think a moment. "The goldfish. What did you do with them?"

"Sold 'em to a Kowloon restaurant."

She should have known. He wouldn't let expensive fish languish and die. "Tell me about Caroline. What's she like?"

He turned to look outside the doors, "You'll find out for yourself soon enough; she's determined to resurrect bygones."

Two barefooted boys ran within view of the window. One crouched down at look at something in the grass. Fanny pointed to the boys, "Who are these people?"

"Squatters. We've turned a blind eye to them, though

the place doesn't really need watching what with the ghosts. They are going to have to go now. The wreckers will turf them out."

Just as he shrugged, a telephone rang in his upper pocket. He retrieved it, pulled out the antenna and answered it in monosyllables. When he finished he glanced at Fanny and said, "I'm turning it off."

"Oh, don't mind me. Keep talking for all I care."

He turned to face her again, "Why, Fanny are you so hostile? You exasperate me. I didn't leave you. The rest of the world is begging favors from me of one kind or another. Most women would be delighted to be my lover."

Fanny snorted, "You flatter yourself. I was your lover once, remember? Look what came of it."

He leaned close to her and put his arm over her shoulder. "Come upstairs with me, like we used to."

She shrugged him off, "You seem to have invented yourself some memories. We rarely used to go upstairs together. You were too busy shagging everything else in sight and drinking yourself blind the rest of the time."

"Did I have time to do any work?"

"Occasionally, in your spare time. Seeing's how we are here and don't have anything else to do, would you consider unlocking the door to the room that used to be your study? It's the only room I haven't seen."

"I wouldn't mind in the least." He grinned.

She was sorry she asked because he seemed so pleased.

They walked together to his study by the front door. She found herself wondering about the cars parked outside. Which was Peter's? The jag, too British, too obvious. The Mercedes, more likely to belong to a Chinese. Of course Peter would have a Porsche.

He pulled out a key and opened the study door. "I wanted

to bring you here, in any case." His old leather-topped desk had been replaced by a cheap metal version. A few books still stood upright on the shelves. A leather settee against the right wall had replaced the two easy chairs that Fanny used to sit in and read.

She walked to the settee. "Well, well, isn't this cozy? Peter's lair. Are you carrying on the tradition started by the previous owners? Do you torture people here?" She sat down.

"Not precisely." He sat next to her. "It's astonishing how middle-aged women can get by wearing this sort of garment." He touched Fanny's jeans. "Take them off."

"Here?"

"Have you a better place in mind?"

"I didn't mean here. I meant no. No. No." She jumped up, walked over to the desk and leafed through some papers lying there. "These are official looking. Have you been working here?"

"Yes, for the last few days. When I saw the footprints upstairs, I knew you'd come back sooner or later."

"Do you feel the spirits when you are here alone?"

"Absolute nonsense, always was. This is a quiet place to work on new ideas. Far from the public, far from telephones and faxes."

"You aren't exactly out of the reach of telephones, I've noticed."

"Come here, woman. Sit next to me."

Fanny looked at her watch. Four-thirty. In two hours she had to be at the Hong Kong Club. "I have to leave."

He stood up, closed the door, locked it and put his arms around her. "Where are you going?"

She smelled the vaguely familiar alcoholic breeze from his breath. She stood very still, feeling his body press against hers. Her body responded with a tingle and warmth. She couldn't pull away. It was as though she was watching someone else. This is interesting, she thought. I'm tempted. No one need ever know. I could deny it to the hilt. It's not as though we've never been lovers.

He pushed back her hair and looked into her eyes, "I always liked you better without makeup. You are so pale and English."

She tensed immediately. He had compared her with the dark ones, Ann with her olive skin, his Chinese lovers. She pulled away.

His gaze didn't waver. He was too practiced a diplomat to let his emotions show. Rider believed in emotions on the surface. He'd think Peter unhealthy.

His body pushed against hers. She could feel him eager for her.

She was weakening. He leaned back a little and unsnapped her jacket.

If she didn't, would she always wish she had? If she did, would she always be sorry? If they made love…. But what was she thinking of? There wasn't time. She had to get back to the hotel and to dinner.

Peter slipped the jacket from her shoulders. Still she stood pressed against him, her body needy, desperate almost, her mind reluctant and afraid.

He undid the top button of her denim shirt and then the next button. Her breast was partially exposed. He used to kiss her there. Rider never did.

Both his hands were exploring her breasts. He said, "Better than ever."

She hadn't resisted. She was letting him seduce her. Had she come here for this? Is this what she'd been hoping for? This would put a wall between her and Rider, even if he didn't find out about it. She wondered if he'd know anyway. Would

he think she had, even if she hadn't? Then she'd have the
blame without the experience. Good grief, she thought, just
go for it. What does it matter? If it weren't for betraying Rider
what would it matter? If she still loved him completely, was
she really betraying him? What about Nigel and Sarah? Her
nipple responded like magic to his kneading. His other hand
had unbuttoned and unzipped her jeans.

He whispered, "Relax." Her panic subsided and passion
took over. He kissed her gently. She kissed him back, roughly.

Then as she succumbed to him, she became aware of
the other things. The spirits in the room, watching, quiet now.

Peter pivoted her towards the leather pillows and laid
her there. He stood, and with his eyes fixed into hers, took
off his suit jacket, laying the telephone, his wallet, his watch
and keys carefully on the desk behind him.

As she watched him undress for her, she thought how
practiced at this he was, the male predator. He had done this
for so many other women. She thought about AIDS.

As though reading her thoughts, Peter produced a con-
dom. He ripped the black package open and palmed the contents.

Her reaction was extreme and immediate.

He thinks he'll get a disease from me! From me!

She sat up, pulled down her bra and buttoned up her
shirt. "Forget it, pal." She hoped she sounded tough.

"I won't use it, if you don't want me to. I thought it
would make you feel safer. It's for you, not for me."

All she could think about were the blackest days when
she wanted to die and he just didn't care. "Never in your life
have you thought of anyone but yourself." She didn't want
him any more. Her body had retreated. She zipped up her
jeans. "I have to go now."

He was naked and she was dressed. She took the keys

and unlocked the door. He grabbed her and slammed her against the wall. "Where do you think you're going?"

"Home," she said, "to New York. Get dressed."

Surprisingly, he did, and quickly. She recognized his anger from his choppy movements. She had won and he had lost. Again. He shook out his trousers before he put them on, just the way he used to. Funny the things you remember about a person, Fanny thought.

His anger-fuse was long, but she'd seen it ignited several times and it terrified her. Never before had she seen it directed at her.

"Peter, forget it. There are a thousand women out there waiting for you."

His voice turned nasty, "I could lock you in here and leave you. No one would find you for a month."

Fanny thought how ludicrous the threat was. She could smash the window and leave and still be at the Hong Kong Club on time, but then she saw the wire mesh in the glass. "I'm expected to dinner in an hour, and my husband is expecting a telephone call in half an hour. Get real. Just give me a ride back to the hotel and let's call it quits, like adults."

He wrapped one end of his tie over the other. His vacant expression, she knew, covered a multitude of violent emotions. She thought that this time he wanted to kill her, but he wouldn't.

She took his hand, "I loved you, but we aren't good for each other."

He snatched his hand away and hit her on the side of her head, and then hit her again on the rebound. She reeled back and fell against the couch, hitting her head on the arm. She curled herself up, and closed her eyes to protect herself from other blows, but heard and felt nothing.

He had never hit her before.

She sat in the same position for a long time. Her head throbbed. She tasted blood. She heard a door slam and the turning of a bolt.

When she opened her eyes, the room spun. Her vision was blurred. She stood shakily. The desk that had been covered with papers was clear. The spirits were there.

She picked up her bag. Her vision started to clear. The door was open. He hadn't locked her in the room, at least. She walked through the lounge and let herself out by the French doors. Her face smarted. She tried not to think about how she must look. She pulled her hair forward over her face.

Walking along the road, she considered reporting Peter to the police. It would take a great deal of time and explanation and she couldn't think what she'd gain by it. She waved down a passing pak pai, gave the driver five dollars and stood towards the back. People stared at her, quite openly. A conversation between an old lady and a young man started up. The woman pointed at Fanny's face and laughed.

The ride was short enough that it didn't matter. Fanny walked to the MTR. It was rush hour. She paid her money and once on the train, stood with her back to the other passengers as best she could, staring out into the blackness of the tunnel. Her reflection in the window looked truly awful, her face swollen, almost deformed. She pulled her jacket tightly around her. Just half an hour ago, Peter had been unsnapping it.

With her head bowed, she walked into the hotel and up to her room. It was six thirty and she was supposed to be at the club.

She turned on the light in the bathroom. Her face was red, swollen on both sides and there was a lump on her forehead. It throbbed and she felt so tired. She had to pack for her journey the next day.

The light on the telephone wasn't blinking. No one had tried to find her. She looked up the number of the club and dialed it.

"This is Mrs. Francis Rider. There is a party waiting for me..." and she gave the information. No matter how badly she felt, no matter how dreadful she looked, cancellation just wasn't an option. "Please tell them I have been unavoidably detained, but will be there within an hour. Apologize for me. Tell them to wait."

"Yes, Madam."

At eight o'clock, Fanny walked into the brightly lit bar where the foursome were waiting sitting around a low table on which rested a plate with several hors d'oeuvres and four half-empty wine glasses. Will saw her first and jumped up, "Good God! What happened to you?"

She was prepared. "I fell."

"Have you seen a doctor?" Drew asked.

Fanny laughed, "Of course not. It's just a bump. Don't worry"

Then something happened that she wasn't prepared for.

The four of them exchanged glances that excluded her. They didn't believe her, but even worse. They were sharing the kinds of looks that she remembered from years ago. People looked like that, a little afraid, quite a bit superior, when they were in the presence of a mad person. Perhaps they thought the injury self-inflicted. They probably wouldn't believe her even if she told them that Peter had done this to her.

She tried to suppress her panic.

She sat down.

"Look," she said, "I'm perfectly sane. I've just had a really rotten day. This is what happens when a middle-aged woman wanders around the countryside in a foreign country alone. We are all hungry. It's my last night. Let's make the most of it. I'd rather not talk about this. Keep my mind off it."

Will seemed really concerned. "I really think we should take you to a doctor. Are you in a great deal of pain?"

"Of course not. Mostly hungry. Just find us a quiet table where we can eat."

The pain was getting worse. Through the meal her head throbbed. A red heat burned her cheeks and temples. She thought she had a toothache, too. It was difficult to smile or talk.

They sat in an elegant room overlooking the old courthouses. The accouterments were perfect. Quite by coincidence, a yellow rose had been placed in the center of the table.

Later, lying back in bed in the hotel room, Fanny wondered how she had got there and survived the meal with her sons and the two beautiful girls. She'd had some wine and eaten a little. Pam found an ice pack. Drew and Helga had driven her back to the hotel. Drew had asked her why she'd come.

She said to him, "How could I cancel? I've let you down so much in your life. I can't ever let you down again."

He'd hugged her and offered to stay with her for the night, get her settled, find a doctor. She'd refused but promised to telephone him the next day before she left. "I'll be much better in the morning."

Fanny stood outside the hotel with her bags waiting for Imelda. Her face had become a mottled black-and-blue that no makeup could conceal. One of her eyes had almost swollen shut.

Sunglasses and a scarf hid most of her face. She thought she must look like the invisible man.

A minivan drove up and Imelda jumped out and walked right past Fanny.

"Imelda." Fanny waved her down.

"Oh. Mrs. Rider. Your face?"

"Yes. An accident, I'm afraid." She had assumed the lies and identity of battered women everywhere.

Imelda beckoned for the driver to load her bags.

A desk clerk ran out of the hotel, "Mrs. Rider! Mrs. Rider?"

Fanny turned to him and he handed her a brown paper package. She hadn't claimed it. She stuffed it into her hand baggage and didn't open it until she was on the plane. It contained a piece of formal embossed card, "With the Compliments of Lady Ann Ardel-Rhys." There was a photograph album with snapshots of the children growing up. All the times she'd missed: birthday parties, Christmases, the twins dressed identically, the children at the beach, school plays, at Water Music, in Thailand, in Singapore, in Burma, and older in Venice, Caroline playing the piano, the twins playing football. Many photographs included Ann and Peter. She stared a long time at a photograph of Caroline with her grandparents outside the house in Lancashire.

Rider and the children met Fanny at Kennedy. They hardly recognized her. Fanny thought that she had never been so happy to see anyone. She couldn't stop the tears, but it was so painful to cry. She just wanted to collapse in a heap.

Sarah forgot all her own troubles and mothered her. Nigel was bursting with two weeks worth of talking. Spring had arrived while she'd been gone. They'd had Easter and Passover vacation. He had two book reports to do for school and he still hated baseball. Rider shepherded them and didn't question Fanny until the children were in bed.

She lay on the bed, bathed and relaxed, but exhausted from the trip and her pain. She wore her old flannel nightgown. He lay down next to her. She curled up next to him. This was where she had longed to be. The house at night was chilly. "Have you turned the heat off?"

"No. It's still on, but way down. It only kicks in when it's below freezing outside. O.K. Fanny, cut the bullshit, I need to know."

She didn't want to tell. "I know you do. I'm in pain."

"I know you are, but is it just physical?"

"Yes."

"It doesn't matter." He sounded very matter-of-fact. "I'm going to kill that asshole. I should have done it years ago. When did he do this to you?"

"It's over. I'll never see him again. Forget it."

"Fanny, I need to know."

She told him about it. Not about the part where she had almost succumbed to his seduction, but everything else. She didn't leave out her confusion. She felt him calm down. He was always relieved when she talked to him, and once she started, it tumbled out. She'd kept it all inside for so long.

He let her talk herself out, then they lay in silence for a while. She wondered if he guessed what she hadn't told him. Rider turned towards her and traced his finger across her forehead. "Sleep now. It's been a long day."

十四

The crocuses had withered and the daffodils were past their best. A few late blooming tulips speckled the shrubbery. The lilac in full blossom scented the air. Fanny had never appreciated being anywhere more or felt more peaceful and happy. Everything had been working out since she'd been back. Her face had almost completely healed. The yellow and grey tinges of old black and blue were fading daily. She'd visited Littors, and firmly demanded a check for $10,000 and received it with apologies. Why Clara couldn't have done the same thing, she couldn't imagine. She'd been at her creative best working on the Neil & Greer designs. She'd decided to position the products as environmentally responsible, use soy inks and unbleached, post-consumer, recycled paper.

Caroline was expected the following week. Fanny couldn't put off telling the children any longer. She opened the kitchen door and walked into the house.

As usual, at ten o'clock on a Saturday morning, Nigel sat in his pajamas eating a late breakfast of cold pizza and apple juice. Sarah, her hair damp from the shower, was writing to her pen pal in the Antipodes. As Rider had predicted, her cough had miraculously disappeared the day after Fanny returned.

Nigel, his mouth full of pizza, said, "Hey, Mom, I forgot to tell you, Stephen barfed in science yesterday. Mr. Bradley was grossed out."

Fanny sat down at the kitchen table. "Poor Stephen." She took a deep breath. "I have something important to talk to you both about."

Sarah looked up, "Something good?"

Fanny said,. "Before I married your father, I was married before, when I lived in Hong Kong…." Nigel munched his pizza as though he hadn't heard her, but Sarah stared. "You have a much older half-sister and twin half-brothers. Your sister Caroline is coming to stay."

Sarah said, "What happened to your husband before Dad? Did he die?"

"We divorced."

Sarah asked, "Why?"

"Because we didn't get along together, and because I got sick. Daddy helped me get better."

"Is that why you went away? To see them?"

"Yes. They are grown-ups now. They were very young when I left. Much younger than you are."

Nigel scraped back his chair, but didn't leave. He said, "Did you wash my blue sweatshirt?"

Sarah said, "What's the matter with you? Aren't you interested?"

Nigel grunted.

Sarah interrogated. Are you and Daddy going to get divorced, too? Who did she like better, her other children or them, Sarah and Nigel? Had she missed her other children? What did they look like? When were they going to come to New York? What was her old husband like? What do they think about us? She concluded, "I bet they hate Dad."

Nigel sat silent. He didn't look at Sarah or Fanny. Rider

would have coaxed him to talk, but Fanny understood. She wanted to know what he was thinking, but it would come later. For now, he needed to think about it. Fit it into his scheme of things.

Fanny brought out the pictures to show them. She told them how sad she had been to leave her other children, and that they were still angry that she had.

A week later the three of them went to Kennedy to meet Caroline. Fanny took the children because she needed their moral support. Sarah had warmed to the idea of having a sister. She was determined that Caroline should like her. She wanted Caroline to share her room.

As Caroline walked out of the swinging doors into the Arrivals Hall, Sarah said, "That must be her. She looks like you, Mom." As much as a pregnant twenty-nine-year-old can look like a fifty-two-year-old, Fanny thought. Lately she'd been looking in the mirror, and, in spite of the lingering bruises, seeing her own mother's face staring back.

Sarah said, "Look at what she's wearing." Caroline wore knee-high boots and a tight black mini-dress that clung to her very swollen belly.

Fanny said, "In Europe, maternity clothes are designed to accentuate being pregnant."

Sarah said, "It's so embarrassing."

Caroline stood still for a moment scanning the crowd, her face serious. Nigel had slipped behind Fanny, Sarah had taken her hand. Fanny watched her in a kind of a trance. More than anything in the world she wanted to take this very pregnant, beautiful, young woman and hug her close and tell her how sorry she was and how much she wanted to make up for all the unhappiness she'd caused.

Fanny rushed forward, thinking now or never. "Welcome, Caroline. I'm so glad you've come."

Caroline pulled back. "Are you? There's no need to be a hypocrite."

Fanny blinked back her tears. She'd intended to be stronger. "I am truly glad. I'm not being a hypocrite by saying so." They stood still for a moment. Check. Then Fanny turned, "This is Sarah and this is Nigel. Come let's get to the car."

Caroline bent to pick up her grip. "It's bloody awful traveling when you're eight months gone."

Sarah said, "Eight months gone?"

"Pregnant." Fanny said as she took the bag from Caroline and dropped it on a cart. "Let's go."

Caroline and Sarah hit it off immediately. Sarah chattered and Caroline responded. They agreed that they'd always wanted to have a sister. Nigel, wary of women in general and pregnant women in particular, kept his distance.

The first few days of Caroline's visit, tempers were congenial, if a little strained. Fanny avoided real talk by substituting frantic activity. They shopped for food, they prepared meals, they cleaned the house. They all drove to Manhattan, showing Caroline the sights. Fifth Avenue, up the Empire State Building, around Rockefeller Center, 42nd Street, the village, SOHO, down to the Battery, to Chinatown for dinner.

Unavoidably, by Monday night, Caroline found Fanny alone in the kitchen, tidying up after the evening meal. She poured herself a glass of wine, "I've been very good. Haven't been drinking since I knew I was pregnant. They say a glass or two at the end won't do any harm."

She eased herself onto an old Windsor chair, her legs stretched in front. "You know, I'd always thought it was Dad who'd refused to let you see us. I thought he took away your letters to us. I hated him and I blamed him. I rebelled against him for other reasons, too. I hated it that he drank so much. He never liked my boyfriends. I was smoking dope. When I was fourteen, and home for the summer, I overheard him talking to Ann. I remember his exact words. Isn't it extraordinary that she's never even tried to contact the children? I'd expected barrages of interference. But none. Not a twit. Not a twit." She raised her voice. "Not a bloody twit. Why didn't you ever try to contact us? Why?"

Fanny shook her head. She got herself a wineglass and filled it. She sat down on the opposite side of the table. "I couldn't. I wanted you too much. I was so afraid of the madness. I was so guilty. I had done such terrible things. I was afraid Rider wouldn't want me any more. I loved you so much. I thought Peter and Ann would take better care of you than I ever could. I was a terrible mother, the worst in the world. I would close my eyes and see your little faces looking up at me and my insides would shrivel and I'd want to die. I'd let you down. I'd want to die every day. I forced myself to put it aside. I told myself that you'd forget me better if I didn't force myself on you. I thought I did it because I loved you."

"Then how could you have had other children, if you thought you were such a bad mother?" Her face grimaced, merciless.

Fanny laid her head in her arms. "Rider wanted them. I thought I'd lose him too, if we didn't have children."

"That's bloody marvelous, isn't it?" Caroline went to the refrigerator and poured herself some juice. "I'm tired. I'm going to bed." Without saying good night, she took the juice and walked up the stairs.

Fanny thought that having Caroline in the house was like

living with a splinter. Painful, but you know it will be gone eventually. She sat alone in the kitchen a long time. Wasn't it extraordinary that Rider had wanted her to have his children after everything that had happened? It had been the ultimate declaration of faith in her.

The next morning, Sarah, dressed for school in baggy jeans and a gray sweatshirt, pouring milk on her cereal said, "Mom? Is Caroline, like going to have her baby here? I mean, in three weeks it's supposed to be born. Like, what if it comes early? Shouldn't you make arrangements or something?"

Fanny had been thinking the same thing herself. "You're right, but don't worry too much. Babies do give a little notice. They don't arrive, just like that."

Everything that Sarah said these days sounded like a question. "On television there was this show? Where a baby just came unexpectedly? Plunk? The woman thought like the baby was getting ready to be born? And like ten minutes later? Zap? She's screaming? And like the baby comes out?"

Nigel, sleepy-eyed and morose, said, "Bay Watch. That's disgusting. Get her outta here, Mom."

Sarah continued, "It's not that bad? You like babies? We'll have to figure out what to do? I'll get a book outta the library. Like, you boil water? Whatta you want it to be? A boy or a girl?"

Nigel's eyes flashed. "Get her outta here, or I'm going to live at Eddie's house until it's over."

Rider, sleepier than Nigel, shuffled into the kitchen and poured himself a cup of coffee.

Sarah said, "Dad? Haven't you thought about it?"

Fanny took charge. "You're right. I'll call Dr. Metra and take Caroline to see her. Good grief. I suppose we will have to dig up the baby stuff, just in case. We need a plan."

After the children left, Fanny cleaned up the kitchen. She had to be at work early today and get the Neil & Greer designs finished. She didn't have time to have a baby, even vicariously. But Sarah was right, it was unavoidable. She would be amazingly lucky if this baby wasn't born on her watch.

She showered and dressed for work and Caroline still hadn't appeared. She knocked gently on the guest room door.

"Come in?"

She entered. A disheveled Caroline sat in the armchair by the window reading. "Can't sleep at all. Can't get comfortable. Have to piss. Baby kicks. Have to piss. Baby turns over. Have to piss."

Fanny sat down on the edge of the bed. "Do you want to have the baby here?"

Caroline sighed. "Here or England. God knows. I had to hide myself in a bloody great coat getting onto the plane. I've heard they won't let you travel if you're too pregnant. Getting back should be a laugh. Wearing the coat, pissing every five minutes. How I'll ever fit into an airline seat, I don't know. I'm getting enormous."

Fanny said, "If you're going to have the baby here, you need to see a doctor. We need to let the hospital know. Don't you have a doctor in England?"

"No, only Honkers, and Tony doesn't want the baby born there because of nationality problems. English mother, Chinese father, what have you. Will you let me have it here?"

Fanny sat still for a moment too long.

Caroline stood up, "I can take a hint, and I'm packing my bags. I can see when I'm not welcome."

Fanny pushed her back down. She looked so vulnerable. "Stop it. Of course you're welcome. I was thinking about Tony. Wouldn't he want to be here? Why don't you call him?

Ask him to come."

"He's too busy. He'd come after the baby is born if he's invited. You know, I didn't plan this. It's your fault. If you'd let me come when I first wrote to you, we wouldn't be in this predicament. But no, you have to run off to Honkers, so by the time I get here, look at me."

Fanny kissed the top of her head. "I'm glad."

Caroline said, "Won't it be terribly expensive? How much will it cost?" Then she seemed to reconsider, "Doesn't matter. Tony's got tons of money."

Fanny made an appointment for Caroline to meet Dr. Metra. She had to cancel the presentation she was making to Neil & Greer to take her there. She tried not to resent it. After all, it was a small price to pay for all the years she'd missed.

Dr. Metra, although barely taller than four-foot-six and almost as round as she was tall, frightened Fanny. She always spoke her mind. "What's all this about? No prenatal care? And you expect me to be her obstetrician? This isn't the way I like to do things. My plate is full. No new patients, especially in their late third trimester. I don't need this kind of aggravation. I have enough problems."

Shining tears streamed down Caroline's face. "They won't let me back on the plane. What am I going to do?"

"You are a very silly girl." Dr. Metra regarded her with a serious stare. "Where is your husband?"

Fanny interceded, "In Hong Kong. Please help her. I've told her that you are the best doctor in New York. There's no one as good as delivering babies."

"I suppose it won't do any harm if I take a look at you." Dr. Metra gave Fanny a wink. "Wait outside."

Fanny scoured the piles of women's magazines in the

waiting room for Neil & Greer competitive products. She'd rescheduled her presentation for the next week. She ripped out pages, hoping that no one would see her. Her mind kept wandering back to Caroline. She wanted to meet Tony. Why wasn't he here with her?

She read the pamphlets displayed in little plastic boxes on the wall. She read about everything from vasectomies to hysterectomies and the importance of a healthy diet. Women came through in every stage of pregnancy. Two hours later, Caroline reappeared, "Come in, Mum."

She hadn't called Fanny "Mum" before.

Dr. Metra said, "Looks healthy enough. Big vigorous baby, strong heartbeat, heading down the canal. Won't be long now."

"So you'll deliver the baby?"

"I've had a talk with the young lady. Taken blood, urine, done an ultrasound and a sonogram. If you can get the hospital to admit her without insurance, I'll do the same. I presume that you will guarantee the bill?"

"Of course."

"Isn't it time for you to come in for a mammogram and pap smear? How long has it been?"

Fanny shrugged, "Let's get this over with first. O.K.?"

Dr. Metra patted Caroline's arm. "Don't forget to take those vitamins that I gave you. It's too late for Lamaze. Call me if you feel anything unusual, otherwise come back in a week."

When the evening dinner rush had dissipated and the house was quiet again, Rider offered to take Caroline down to the basement to look at the baby clothes and furniture they'd packed away. Caroline refused. "I'm too tired."

The next night, Rider asked again and Caroline refused again. Fanny asked why. Caroline said "I want to go shopping. I don't want my baby sleeping on sheets paid for by him. I'll buy my own, thank you very much."

Rider never took this kind of thing personally, but Fanny flared. "And who do you think is going to pay your doctor's bills? Who do you think is going to pay for the hospital? We are."

Caroline sputtered, "No, I am, you stupid cow. Leave me alone. I'm going to ring Tony." She stomped upstairs.

It was on the tip of Fanny's tongue to scream after her, "You're sleeping on sheets he paid for, living in his house, you just ate a meal that he provided."

Rider laughed. "I wondered when her animosity would surface. She's held it in well. She still doesn't like me, after all this time."

"I'm sorry." Fanny rubbed his back.

She waited an hour hoping her anger would diffuse, but it didn't. With heavy steps, she walked upstairs. She knocked on the door. Caroline answered it. Fanny pushed her way in and sat on the perpetually unmade bed. "Rider saved your life, my girl, and don't you ever forget it."

"What the hell are you talking about?"

"You heard me the first time. Rider saved your life. He is the reason that you are alive today. Do I have to spell it out for you?"

Caroline gazed at her.

"He is the reason you can stand there and insult him."

Caroline said, "He never saved my life."

"You don't remember. It's probably a good thing." Fanny sighed and stood up. "There are a lot of things that you don't remember." She paced the room while she spoke. "I hadn't wanted to tell you, but you might as well know. Perhaps it will help you see me as I was." She looked Caroline.

"I'm agreeable. It's what I've come here for."

"Then let's go out to the porch. It's a lovely warm night. In fact it almost feels like summer. Take your pillow and a blanket, if that would make you more comfortable."

They went downstairs and out into the night. Caroline stretched out on the porch swing and Fanny in an old wicker rocking chair. She glanced up to see her old friend the moon, retreating behind a cloud.

"It's a long story." Fanny had promised Caroline that she would tell, but wasn't sure that she could really do it. How could she make it understandable? Tell it so Caroline would empathize and not blame? Caroline might not be ready to hear it yet, but she had opened the floodgates. Fanny had wondered if she'd ever tell the whole story.

First, she asked Caroline about Water Music and how much she recollected.

"I'm hazy on it, actually. I remember the house, of course. I even took Tony there last summer. I scared him with ghost stories. He's quite superstitious."

"Was your father shattered when I left?"

"I was. As I remember, my father took it quite in stride. It upset him, of course, but he called Ann in and she took over, and that was that. There was bugger all we could do about it. I was so angry with her. I wanted you. I wanted my mother. You'd gone and you didn't like me enough to take me with you. I wanted to go anywhere you went. Why didn't you take me too?" Caroline's body folded in two. Her knees jerked up to as close to a fetal position as anyone with that big a stomach could. "You could have given him the boys. He wouldn't have minded if you'd taken me. We were friends."

Fanny wondered if it would be possible to tell.

She walked over to Caroline and touched the top of her

head. "Yes, we were friends. Can we be again?"

"I don't know."

"I know you don't." She stroked Caroline's head. "I loved you. I've loved you always. I couldn't have taken you. Your father is too vindictive. Think about Penelope, your grandmother. They would have made me give you back to them."

Caroline loosened up. Fanny could fell the tension melting. "I remember that you were so beautiful. I remember silk dresses and your stockings and your jewelry and your golden hair piled up. You looked like a princess and I loved you so." She looked up. "I'm ready. I want to know what happened. Why?"

Fanny walked back to her chair and rocked. She stared at the indigo trunk of the old maple tree. A sliver of moon had reappeared from behind the cloud.

She talked about their first years at Water Music and the ghosts and the exorcism. She described her breakdown and the hospital. The night became darker. Neither of them stirred. The house behind them stood silently. Rider had turned off the television. A night bird sang a trill. Caroline sat in a kind of a trance When Fanny reached the apex of her story, she paused.

It was, she knew, within her power to change it. To keep the worst buried. To submerge it forever wrapped around a rock in the ocean of her subconscious. Only Rider really knew about that night and she'd never told him everything. Caroline snapped her into the present. "Was it that night that Rider saved my life? You haven't got to that part yet"

Fanny looked at Caroline still visible through the gloom and worried about her daughter's unhappiness. Would this make it better or worse? It was the truth. Shouldn't the truth be told?

The night that she had made her decision was extremely hot and humid. Fanny hadn't slept more than a few hours for three nights. It wasn't as though anything was keeping her awake except her enormously overwhelming melancholy. It sat in her as a huge weight, keeping her heart beating a little faster and her appetite suppressed. She couldn't sleep until Peter got home and then when he was sleeping next to her smelling of beer and perfume, Fanny would imagine terrible punishments for him.

She dozed lightly, only to wake, to hear a child calling in his sleep, or a clock downstairs chiming the hour. Sometimes she'd wake and feel the spirits churning the air around her, not threatening her, but oppressing her in their vaporous misery. After three nights of wakefulness and more days of loneliness, no visits to the hospital or doctors, no contact with Rider, Jean or even her mother-in-law, and only superficial contact with Peter, the oppressive depression settled on her.

She robotically fed, played with and bathed the children and put them to bed. Will wasn't feeling well that day and wanted her to stay with him while he fell asleep.

While she sat with him, the idea, just a kernel at first, grew as fast as an avalanche. It would be so peaceful to be dead. But what about Will, Drew, and Caroline? They would sleep so much better if they died. If they died as children, what pain and suffering they would be spared. If all four of them died, Peter wouldn't really care. It would probably be a relief. He'd play the bereaved widower with grace and a stiff upper lip but he'd be free to romance the hoards of sympathetic women who'd come to comfort him and he'd be able to march ahead of his rivals for power and prestige, unencumbered by family responsibilities. It would really be a perfect solution.

As she gazed at Drew and Will, their breaths in unison, their small heads dreaming, she knew they were happier asleep than at any time during the day. She stood and walked to Caroline's room. She, too, lay in a position of comfort and rest. Breathing clearly and strongly.

This would need planning.

She thought of smothering them. Then she decided that it would be best if they all died the same way. If they all drank something before they went to sleep, then died in their beds or if she were able to give them an injection of something.... She considered dissolving sleeping pills, aspirins and other medicines in juice, but thought it might not be enough for all of them. She thought of carrying them one by one to the water's edge and pushing them down over the rocks into the sea, and then throwing herself off after them.

So on the fourth night, she prepared it. She told the children that they were all going to sleep outside. She took their mosquito nets and made tents over each lounge chair. She brought sheets and a pillow for each of them. She told them they would be watching stars. They participated enthusiastically in the adventure. Caroline brought her stuffed rabbit. The four of them lay out in the garden under the night sky. Fanny was so convinced it was right that she hadn't wavered all day.

She'd decided that Caroline should be first. When Caroline and the boys were fast asleep, she pulled herself out from under the net. She was ready to do what needed to be done and then die.

She lifted the net over Caroline and lifted her. She carried Caroline, nestled comfortably in her arms, steadily to the cliff edge.

The night was calm, cloudless and moonlit. There hadn't been much rain. The waterfall had been reduced to a trickle, the waves below lapped at the rocks gently and invitingly. She kissed Caroline who snuggled closer. She could taste the hibiscus. She felt the relief.

Suddenly she was whirled around and face down in the grass struggling with someone. Caroline whimpered, half awake on the grass next to her. She thought it must be a burglar or one of the servants, until she remembered that no one would come near the house. She heard him swear, "God dammit. What the fuck are you doing?" It was Rider and he was angry. "You could have both been killed."

"Yes," said Fanny, "Go away. Let me get on with it."

Rider loomed over her like a giant. "Where is everyone?"

"Who?"

"Where's Peter?"

"God knows. At a party, with a woman, how do I know? Why would I know?" She didn't even recognize herself speaking. It all seemed so far away.

She saw him clearly. He leaned over closely and pulled her to him. She didn't shake or cry. She knew that she wanted him there. Why had he interfered with her plan? Caroline whimpered. The twins still slept under their mosquito net canopies.

Caroline said, "I want to go to bed now, Mummy. Can I go upstairs now?"

Rider knew what to do. He said. "Francis, take Caroline by the hand and take her up to bed. I will be behind you with the twins."

He looked deep into her eyes hypnotically. She dropped herself completely into his control.

Perhaps they had died and Rider was taking them to meet God. She had better go.

She took Caroline by the hand and walked to the French doors where they waited for the others. Caroline didn't speak. Her hand, warm and dry, clutched Fanny's tightly. The crickets had stopped their racket. The only sound was the water, slapping on the rocks below.

In a moment Rider was next to her holding a sleeping twin on each shoulder. His arm brushed Fanny's. He knew what to do and no one else did.

He commanded to her to go to Caroline's room and she did. She and Caroline, side by side. Step by step. Through the sitting room, into the hallway, down the hallway to the stairs, up the stairs one by one, making a right, step by step to Caroline room. Caroline ran from her and jumped into bed.

"Goodnight Mummy, sleep tight."

She turned over and in a few moments she slept rhythmically.

Later Rider told her that the children hadn't been traumatized at all. Fanny had been so calm, deliberate and desperate.

Rider wanted to put the twins in their beds, "Which one goes where?" he asked Fanny. He knew so much she thought, how could he not know this? But he doesn't.

His voice was strong, though. "Which bed, Fanny? Which boy? Just point."

She pointed. Drew by the window and Will against the wall. Sleeping still. Maybe they had died and he was putting their little bodies to rest.

She stood watching the twins just as she had the night before and last night and the night before that and the night before that and the night before that back into eternity. This is where she always watched them.

Rider put his arm around her shoulder and led her out of the boys' room to the bedroom, to her bed. He made her sit, and he sat next to her, his arm around her waist. He said nothing. Fanny stared ahead. Glad he was there. Needing to rest. Needing sleep. The heaviness of the night overwhelmed her. She lay back and drifted, clutching his arm, still. If she could only hold it forever....

Then the room was filled with the brightest of light and anger and fighting. Not her fighting. Two men were roaring. She opened her eyes and tried to focus. The blackness still enveloped her, the heaving and the deepest of grief. The tight weight in her center was spreading out towards the room. She heard their voices. What did it mean? Dr. Rider and Peter in rage and fury. Peter drunk, smelling of whiskey, Rider smelling clean. The two smells fighting—a battle of the smells. The good and the bad. They were fighting for her and she wanted to belong to them both and couldn't make a decision. Then they'd gone. The room was dark and Fanny slept again.

It may have been the next morning and it may have been three days later when she woke. Nothing had changed except that she'd slept. She didn't feel less tired. She propped herself up on her elbow. She heard noises from downstairs, the children's voices calling to each other and the clattering of dishes. She could almost have been a child again in her parents' house, sleeping late, listening to her mother in the kitchen and her little cousins playing below. But this was the room at Water Music. No doubt about it.

She smelled Rider again. Rider, urine and her own sweat. It was going to be another hot day. The sunbeams piercing the blinds pinpointing their pattern on the blue Chinese carpet, bleaching it.

She heard a creak and she turned. He sat in a chair watching the sunbeams, too. He didn't seem to know she was awake.

For a moment, she forgot that he had sabotaged her escape. She studied his pale face, fine hair and almost lashless, kind, intelligent eyes, a square jaw and perfectly defined lips. He had a worried expression. She wanted to draw him as he sat there. She needed to keep a copy of his face when he went away.

She pulled out her legs and stood. The floor was solid under her bare feet. She noticed that she still wore her old white shorts and they were damp and soiled. She heard her voice speak quite independently. She hadn't asked it to. "How long have I been asleep?"

Rider turned to look at her and smiled. "A long time."

She realized that she must have been ill, but all she wanted was to draw his face and take a shower. She unzipped her shorts. He stood. "I'm sure you'd rather I left? Nurse Chang is here from the hospital to help you. I'll send her in."

"But I want to draw you. I don't want it to be over. I don't want you to go. I want you to stay with me forever."

He smiled again, a sardonic lip twisting as though he was smiling in spite of himself. "Yes, of course you do, but for all the wrong reasons."

He stood up stiffly, stretching his long legs. "I'll be outside. Get cleaned up. You'll be all right, Fanny."

She noticed a purple and red welt on the side of his face. "I need to draw you."

"This afternoon, perhaps." As he walked towards the door to open it, the heat and the huge weight, the gut-eating, shaking distress welled up inside her and she cried. The tears stung her face. Nurse Chang, dressed in white, took her hand and let her to the bathroom. She undressed Fanny, she gently soaped her, washed her hair and wrapped her in a towel like a child.

Fanny asked, "I'm really sick?"

Nurse Chang answered, "Really sick."

After she was dressed, they forced her to eat scrambled eggs, toast, and milky tea. Rider had made it for her. He fed it to her slowly at first, but she discovered she was hungry.

As she ate, Fanny watched her children playing outside the glass doors with Ann Graham, she of the long legs and the crush on Peter.

When Nurse Chang went into the kitchen, Fanny asked Rider about the bruise on his face. Rider rolled his eyes. "Your husband discovered me with you in his bedroom."

Fanny couldn't imagine Peter caring enough to punch Rider over something like that. "Well, I hope you gave him a few in return."

"A few and then we sobered up and talked sense." He gauged her ability to hear more, "He only believed me when he saw the note you'd left for him, and the chairs outside."

Fanny saw Nurse Chang out of the corner of her eye watching and listening as she always had at the hospital. She said quietly, "I didn't want him to feel blameless or think it was an accident."

"It wouldn't have been seen as an accident."

"You know, you should have let me do it. I was prepared. The children wouldn't have to live through this horribly revolting existence. It was only a little pain to be spared so much. It's only fair that I who let them grow in my body, should give them back to God. I want to die, too."

Rider sighed. "For someone who wants to die, you've eaten a lot of breakfast. Come into the garden."

But she didn't want to. She didn't want to see the children.

"What has happened to me, Rider? Am I going to be put back into the hospital? Who knows about this? Where is Dr. Greenwood?" Then exhausted, she leaned back and said,

"I don't care. I want to go to sleep. I'm so tired. I'm always so tired."

"Come into the sitting room, Fanny. Do you want to draw?"

Fanny nodded. She took her sketchpad and pencils from a drawer in the sideboard where she kept them next to the silver. She sat Rider in a chair by the window. He went meekly. He sat with his face turned to the light.

十 五

Caroline asked, "Did they put you back in the hospital?"
"Of course, but I didn't mind. It was safe there. I couldn't
hurt you or your brothers. I could see Rider every day."
"And Dad?"
"Your father didn't come to see me. I hoped he would
come. He was badly shaken about what I had done, and I
suspect that he was enormously guilty about having left me
alone with you children like that. Anyway, after a couple of
weeks, they let me out and I went back home. My mother
flew out from England to stay with us. She wanted to convince me to bring you home and live with them for a while."
"I remember when Gran came. I remember you let us
wait up until she arrived. She is so old now. Why haven't you
ever been to see her to try to straighten everything out? Lots
of people get divorced now."
"I wrote to her after I left. She basically told me never to
darken her door again. I'd embarrassed her thoroughly, first
by being the mad woman, and then by leaving Peter. It was a
nasty letter in her writing that my father signed, too. I didn't
get out of bed for weeks after receiving it."
"Gran did rather think that you'd let the side down. She's

very fond of Dad, though. You know, it's hard to think of you
as mad now. I mean, it's impossible to think that I would want
to kill my baby."

"Yes, I know, but when you know life to be nothing but
torment, death doesn't seem like such a terrible option."

Caroline sat quietly for a long time. "Gran never understood.
She is the only one who really turned against you, and she is
your own mother. Dad and Ann would answer our questions
about you, but Gran never did. She pretended that you were
dead."

Fanny asked her, "How much did you see my parents?"

Caroline fiddled with the chain that hung around her neck,
"At first, quite a lot. The twins were only ten and I was eleven.
It was when we went to school. We started off at a disadvan-
tage."

"I wouldn't have thought so, why?"

"Well, the twins hadn't gone to prep school. It was quite
late for them to start boarding school, and we'd lived in
Honkers, which is completely different. We didn't know the
lingo."

"For instance?"

"We didn't know what an anorak or a pash was. We didn't
have proper prayer books. Penelope did her best to help us fit
in. It worked better for the twins. But, anyway, Gran was no
use at all. She'd not been to public school, but was quite proud
that we were going. They'd show up for Speech Day in their
Ford Capri thinking they were doing all right and everyone
else would have dusted off the Rolls. We couldn't take anyone there for half-term."

"Never mind. I'm sure Penelope did you proud."

"Oh yes. She dressed the part. Thank God for Penelope

and Alistair. We could always tote them out when all else failed. Wish they hadn't sold the Norfolk house. That would have gone over well with the girls at school."

Fanny couldn't help saying it. "So you learned at school how to be a snob?"

Caroline laughed. "Actually, it wasn't school. I was a bit of a snob from the start, but then Penelope got me early, and Dad is the most extreme example of a snob I've ever seen."

They laughed together. The black night crept around them. Nocturnal animals rustled in the hollow of the giant maple tree that shaded the porch. Fanny shivered, but didn't want to move. She didn't want this evening to end.

Caroline wrapped the blanket around herself. "I always defended you. I was so angry with you, but I defended you all the time. I wouldn't let Ann say anything against you. I always told her that you were a better mother. I tried her patience, I'm afraid. Ann could never live up to you. She hated your painting in the hallway. They still have it up, you know. Drew and Will liked her, but I never did."

Fanny said, "Are you going back to Tony?"

Caroline shifted, "We've had a terrible row. How did you guess?"

Fanny wanted to say, mother's instinct, but knew that would be going too far. She decided not to answer. "Your father doesn't like him, does he?"

"Dad didn't want me marrying Tony one bit, but he likes his family well enough. I'm the opposite. Like Tony, hate his family. We'll see after the baby is born if things change. Tony is always so busy. I never see him. I am such a small part of his existence and he is everything to me. He won't or can't take me with him when he goes to China. Actually, he did once. What a dustbin of a place. Now with the baby I wouldn't be able to go anyway. I hoped he'd miss me, but I don't know that he has."

"Of course he has. It was every bit as difficult for him to marry you, as you to marry him. Everyone has fights. Most people just don't have the means to take them international. Has he asked you to come home?"

"Of course, but he's proud."

"He must come here when the baby is born."

Fanny felt better to have said it out loud, but after that evening, their relationship changed. Fanny stopped trying so hard to win Caroline's love and Caroline withdrew a little. She became less rebellious and more considerate, helping with meals, tidying up after herself, but she also seemed more distant, as though her mind was elsewhere. More like a guest than a recalcitrant member of the family.

Fanny drove Rider to the train. Traffic was slow. They were stopped at an interminable red light. She said, "I've been meaning to ask you, why did you come that night? The night...."

"I know what night. I hadn't been able to get over to see you for a few days and I needed to see you. I knew that Peter would let me in for a drink. I wanted to see you and Peter together. I wanted to see how things really were between you."

"You found that out." The light changed, and Fanny eased her way into the stream of vehicles.

"Yes, I did."

"You always say that if I have something to say, to get it off my chest, even if it's unreasonable?"

The morning wasn't Rider's best time. He leaned back and closed his eyes. "Yes?"

"I'm angry. You kept me from them. You made no attempt to reconcile me to my children."

Rider didn't seem surprised, nor did he open his eyes. "Fanny, Fanny, Fanny, do you remember what you said to me early on about taking responsibility for yourself?"

"No." She swerved to avoid a pothole. She glanced over. His eyes were open wide. He'd turned to see what she'd nearly hit.

"You said that you didn't want or need psychiatric intervention. I remember you said intrusion. I thought it was particularly appropriate. You said that you want it this way. And haven't you healed? I remember...."

"Yes, I know. You're right. It isn't your fault, but I'm still annoyed with you. My children haven't existed in our lives and you accepted that. Be honest. You wanted me to yourself without those ghastly complications. It's not as simple as you make it out to be. Admit it, you hate Caroline being here."

"I don't hate it, but I'll admit she's projecting a hell of a lot of aggression."

They arrived at the station, but Rider made no move to leave the car. Fanny turned off the engine. "See what I mean? You can't breathe without some kind of psychoanalytic intrusion. Everything is always reasonable. Every form of expression is healthy. Leaving my fucking children wasn't healthy."

"You forget your state of mind at the time. You killed your children, metaphorically speaking, so you could live but you also sacrificed yourself for your children so they could live. I'd say they're thriving."

"Yes, but mothers are supposed to fight for their young, even metaphorically—to protect them. I left them defenseless and alone."

"You knew they'd be well taken care of. You knew Ann would step in and Peter would be forced to notice them. You knew they'd survive and..." He stopped.

Fanny finished his sentence for him, "...they might not

have otherwise? In other words, I'm a mother who eats her young, metaphorically speaking, of course?"

"Of course. No, you are a mother who had an opportunity to make a better life for her children at great cost to herself. Stop beating yourself up over this, Fanny. It's time. You have them back. I'm going to miss my train if I don't get out now."

She leaned over and opened his door for him. "Go, but I'm still mad at you."

He kissed her on the cheek, "We can continue with this tonight. I won't even charge you." He reached into the back for his jacket and left her alone in the car.

Two weeks into Caroline's visit it rained heavily for three days. The river rose and roads flooded.. On the second day of the rain, Fanny had an appointment to present the final work to Neil & Greer at eleven. She'd canceled the last one to take Caroline to the doctor, but it turned out for the best. She'd added some good stuff. She'd prepared slides, photographs, drawings and samples of the packaging, advertising and storyboards for television. Lunch had been booked at a French restaurant.

One of the color printers wasn't working and the other one had never been properly hooked up, so two of the samples had to be finished by hand. She was due to leave the office by ten.

At five minutes to ten, Clara buzzed Fanny. "It's Caroline. She's crying. You'd better talk to her. Oh, and the Sprain Parkway is closed. You'd better leave as soon as you're done with her."

Fanny pressed the button on the phone. "Caroline, what's wrong?"

"I'm cramping like mad. Feels like the curse. I don't know what to do. You've got to come home."

"Relax. Lie down. I can be home about four."

"You don't understand. You need to come here now. It's an emergency. I feel so funny. I think the baby's coming."

"Have you called Dr. Metra?"

"Yes. She says she wants to see me. You have to come, Mum. I'm frightened."

Fanny thought fast. There was no one else who could make the presentation for her. Caroline's voice sounded mangled and desperate. Fanny slumped back in the chair. "O.K. I'll be there."

"Come quickly."

Fanny speed-dialed Neil & Greer. Damien Herald had taken a chance when he'd given the account to Fanny. Several of his bosses had come in especially to be at the presentation today. She apologetically told him that she had a personal emergency and she would call to reschedule later in the afternoon. She could hear the annoyance in his voice, "That's the second time. How do you stay in business? We are going to have to revaluate the situation."

She told Clara to hold the fort and drove home. It was only mid-morning and almost dark. The side of the road had become a river. The wind had brought down tree limbs and power lines.

The house was dark. Fanny let herself in and called out to Caroline. She listened, but heard no reply. She tried to switch on a light, but the power was out. She ran up to the guest room, dripping water behind her. The room was disheveled, but empty. Caroline had been drawing. An open sketch book lay on the chair and colored pencils were scattered on the floor. She heard a noise from the bathroom in the hall.

Caroline, white-faced, sat on the edge of the bathtub clutching the sides. She pointed to a pool of liquid on the hallway floor. Fanny had thought it was rain she'd dripped, but there was too much.

Fanny said, "Your water broke. It's just the beginning of labor."

"It doesn't feel like the beginning. Isn't this a bloody cock-up. I hated being alone in the dark. I didn't want to bring you home from work. You're so busy and I'm in the way."

Fanny swept her hand over Caroline's forehead. "Come get your coat on, let's go see Dr. Metra."

That night during the rainstorm, Caroline birthed her baby boy. Fanny stayed with her during the labor, the epidural, the monitoring, the waiting, the intense labor, and the birth. Although she'd borne five children, and was conscious during the birth of two of them, she hadn't focused then on the wonder of it all. The making of a new life. The renewal. This was her grandchild and a new generation. He was such a skinny, beautiful, pink creature, scrawny as a featherless bird, but not helpless. He screamed and shook his little fists at the insult of the delivery. She fell in love with him instantly, something she'd never done with her own children.

She had forgotten to call Damien Herald in her excitement. She'd thought of him several times when Caroline was in early labor, but she'd thought there would be more time later and never got around to it.

Using Caroline's instructions, she dialed Tony from a pay phone at the hospital. A Chinese voice answered. Fanny asked for Tony Wong. There was a great deal of discussion on the other end in Cantonese, which Fanny didn't understand, before a female voice answered. "Yes. Can I help you?"

"I'm calling for Tony Wong."

"Tony is away. Who is this?"

"Mrs. Rider, his mother-in-law."

There was a long pause. "I don't know you. I am Cecilia Wong, Tony's mother."

Fanny said, "Then I have good news for you. An hour ago, your grandson was born. Actually our grandson was born. Congratulations."

Cecilia said, "A boy. That is very good news. And Caroline?"

Fanny said, "Tired, but fine."

Cecilia said, "My son will telephone you."

"Do you think he can come here? I would like to meet him. I think he should see his wife and son."

"He will telephone you. Perhaps you can make arrangements with him. He's very busy now. I think better if Caroline come home with baby."

Fanny didn't like the sound of the woman. Poor Caroline.

She returned to Caroline, who was almost asleep. She whispered, "Tony isn't home. I told his mother."

Caroline said, "I suppose, now that it's a boy, she'll want to take over completely. Mum, I hope you won't be offended. I've been thinking...."

Here it comes, thought Fanny.

"The baby, is going to have five grandmothers. More than he needs. Think about it. Cecilia, Ann, Jean and Gran. You, too. I don't want you to be a grandmother."

Fanny thought of the little fellow she had only just fallen in love with. Caroline was going to take him away from her, so soon.

"Will you be his godmother?"

"But, Caroline. I'm not religious. I am his real grandmother. I have more right to be than any of those people except Tony's mother. Ask Jean. She goes to church every week."

Caroline shook her head. "I'm not religious, either. What I mean is, you know the value of life and the importance of the spirit." She sighed. "I am so tired. Think about it."

Fanny sat with her until her breathing regulated, just as she had so many years ago.

Fanny thought that she ought to call Peter, but didn't really want to. She could thank Ann for the photographs. She looked at her watch. It would be two in the afternoon there. She rang Ann and Peter's number. A servant answered and fetched Ann.

"This is Fanny. Caroline's had her baby. A boy, the sweetest little thing!"

Ann cleared her throat. "You managed that quite nicely, didn't you? I expect that you think all will be forgiven now."

Fanny took a step backwards. It was as if she'd been punched in the stomach. She bumped into a nurse who was passing. She caught her breath before she replied. "I don't suppose it ever will be forgiven." She hung up the phone, stunned.

She woke Rider to give him the news. He wasn't happy to be called a grandfather, she could tell, nor was he in the mood to listen to her obsessing about Ann. When she told him about Caroline's godmother notion, he laughed and used his best Brando imitation. "I've always wanted to be a Godfather. Come home, get some sleep. Everything will look better in the morning. Godmother, grandmother, who cares? The baby will know who you are. You ought to know what children are like by now."

Fanny said, "You're right. I'm exhausted. I'm not thinking properly."

"Oh, and by the way, a very charming lady called. A Mrs. Julia Yau? She wants you to pick her up at Kennedy on Friday. Same flight you took, in fact. She's coming to stay for a while. I've written it all down. Oh, and Sarah is going home on the bus with Kelly tomorrow and needs a note which only you can write. My notes aren't good enough. You can write it when you get home."

Fanny walked back into Caroline's room. Windy rain blew onto the window by the bed. Caroline was sleeping with her back to the door. Fanny watched her for a few moments, then her attention was taken with some papers and a ballpoint pen that must have slipped from the bed. She bent over to pick them up. Even in the gloom, glancing at the top paper, Fanny could see it was a letter. A few words caught her eye: "…come meet my mother…." She didn't read further, but placed the papers carefully on the bedside table under a stuffed green crocodile that Sarah had given to the baby. She listened to the rain, the music that it made on the glass. The room was getting cooler. She pulled a blanket up from the foot of the bed and covered her sleeping daughter.

Acknowledgements

This book could not have been written without the life support of GROW: Renée Ashley, Neva Powell, Cynthia Webb and Margaret Williams. I will be grateful to these inspirational women for the rest of my life.

I thank my friends and teachers for their invaluable encouragement and support: Lindsey Abrams, Jerry Anderson, Sherry Cronk, Cynthia Cross, Muriel Fox, Dorothy Goren, Christine Hwalek, Christine Japely, Nancy Russell, Annette Stansfield, Jan Thompson and Meredith Trede.

Thank you to my agent, Regina Ryan for believing in the book.

Thanks for research assistance to Adam Hobson and Joan Hobson.

My family were especially patient on the occasions when I drifted away from them during this project and I thank them for their thoughtfulness and their unconditional love: Win Zibeon, Rebecca Nyx and Philip Kuperberg.

Fine literary fiction
from Avocet Press Inc:

The Long Crossing
Neva Powell

River Whispers
Glynn Marsh Alam

Resistance
Christine Japely